"In this riddled pageantric, insomniac, photographic, and university-infused world of eating disorders, triple suicides, astral projections, enigmatic bruises, and uncontrollable impulses, Candice Wuehle's poetic and narrative gaze on everything she Midas-touches is eyelinered, eyeshadowed, polished, Norwegian-lip-penciled, and loose-powdered with her devilishly inventive, singularly imaginative beauty and a devastatingly wry sense of humor. Her brilliance in *MONARCH* will lacquer, enamel, and wax you and turn your mind inside out like a monarch butterfly macerated in emulsion." —Vi Khi Nao, author of *The Vegas Dilemma* and *Swimming with Dead Stars*

"A wise, unsettling, and multifaceted masterpiece, *MONARCH* succeeds on all levels—as a portrait of an endearingly dysfunctional family, as a shadow history of Y2K and the hidden power structure underlying and undermining contemporary life, and as a profound exploration of the extremely dicey prospect of being a self in a body in the world. Unless you're hiding in an underground city or frozen in a kryokammer in the desert, you'll want to run out and get this one right away!"
—David Leo Rice, author of the *Room in Dodge City* trilogy, *Angel House*, and *Drifter: Stories*

MONARCH

MONARCH

a novel

CANDICE WUEHLE

SOFT SKULL
NEW YORK

First Soft Skull edition: 2022

Grateful acknowledgment for reprinting materials is made to the following:

Epigraph from "Blue Hour" in *Blue Hour* by Carolyn Forché. Copyright © 2003 by Carolyn Forché. Used by permission of HarperCollins Publishers.

Carolyn Forché *Blue Hour* (Bloodaxe Books, 2003). Reproduced with permission of Bloodaxe Books. www.bloodaxebooks.com

Library of Congress Cataloging-in-Publication Data
Names: Wuehle, Candice, author.
Title: Monarch : a novel / Candice Wuehle.
Description: First Soft Skull edition. | New York : Soft Skull, 2022.
Identifiers: LCCN 2021027558 | ISBN 9781593767075 (hardcover) | ISBN 9781593767082 (ebook)
Subjects: LCGFT: Thrillers (Fiction)
Classification: LCC PS3623.U35 M66 2022 | DDC 813/.6—dc23
LC record available at https://lccn.loc.gov/2021027558

Jacket design by www.houseofthought.io
Book design by Wah-Ming Chang

Published by Soft Skull Press
New York, NY
www.softskull.com

Printed in the United States of America
1 3 5 7 9 10 8 6 4 2

One can live without having survived.

—CAROLYN FORCHÉ

I wrote this book for women who survived and women who didn't, but mostly I wrote it for those still somewhere in between.

Part 1

THERE IS NO WAY TO TELL THE STORY OF A GREAT VIOLENCE.

To tell this story, the narrator became a child beauty queen. She enrolled in evening elocution courses. She trained herself to paint a second face atop her own face. (Masks are subtext read aloud, the private wish made public.) She performed the talent of the baton twirler, the musician, the tap dancer, the actress, and this proved that the truest talent is mime. (You know, it was the parrot, not the child, who first suggested the difference between the human and the animal is ability to self-reflect, to see oneself in a mirror and say: *That is myself.* Our narrator developed late. She will tell you this story soon, after she explains how she learned the language of the pageant.) At the age of nineteen, she learned to answer the questions of adults. Of course, she was already an adult, but she had not yet been asked any questions. She had not yet become interested in anything enough to ask a question.

She learned that a story is only the shape of a story. If anything about the story could act as a mirror, there was little left for her to do. That is, I suppose, what allows this to be a story about the dead.

Our narrator is now tapping. She is about to tell us.

CHAPTER ONE

WHEN I TRY TO REMEMBER THE LATE NINETIES, I MOSTLY remember climbing into a tanning bed with a rabbit's head sticker pressed to my hip. The same spot, every time, for the entire summer of '99. In Pompeii, the third cause of death was instant dehydration triggered by extreme heat. I learned this in school, but never thought of it as I pulled the plastic goggles over my head and lowered the lid. It felt wonderful; it was an actual bed of light. The goggles had tiny pinpricks in the middle covered with black lenses to protect the thinner skin of the eyelids. I felt a chill of success whenever I surveyed the augmented pigment of my skin.

Once, only laborers spent enough time in the sun to tan. If you perform a slight dissection on the word parasol, you get *para*=to shield and *sol*=sun. (The events I am telling you about take place after I graduated from a high school that sat in the middle of the country—the oeil de taureau of America, stoic and dry. Now I am seriously committed to the German, but as a student I took one year of each Romance language. *Je m'appelle Jessica. Mi nombre es Jessica. Mi chiamo Jessica.* I can recognize a root, determine what lexical waters a word has been washed in. Now, *Mein Name ist Jessica.* I am so much closer to the present.) Protection, of course, has always been the prerogative of the rich.

Gloves, wide-brimmed hats, mineral creams, smart glass, umbrellas, and veils protect the skin from signs of use. Tans now exist

5

because a French fashion designer spent too long on a yacht in the Mediterranean—she went sailing and it showed. But all she had to do was say she meant to do it. She was born in an orphanage and inverted basic economy with a dress that suggested less was actually more. At one point, she was a Nazi intelligence officer. She knew how essential intent is when it comes to assigning culpability. So the tan became fashionable. Another economic subversion: what was once a sign for poverty became a sign of wealth. Probably because I love deception, it impresses me when a person who traffics in images is adept at rhetoric. The designer's name was a diminutive of a diminutive; an abbreviation of the French *coquette*. My own name means "rich. God beholds."

I have always felt more the beholder than the beholden, which is why it is very hard to believe in God at all. If this story is about anything, it is about being somewhere in between; the importance of the aurea mediocritas. The opulent wedding ring twisted inward in public, the right balance of visibility and existence.

I spent all my time in that sun bed because I didn't have a job. When I finally got one, my skin had the glow of a ham under a heat lamp; the sacré-cœur of a country club Father's Day brunch. My own father didn't eat ham, didn't belong to a country club, and did not worship the sun. Before my disappearance, he was a professor of boredom, and, in fact, the founder and chair of the Boredom Studies department at the Midwestern University I dropped out of. My taking time out from the world to meditate on my dermis was rare, hard for him to understand. I believe it made me the primary subject in one of my father's case studies on boredom. Maybe even the inspiration for it.

There was something almost spiritual to his theories; he taught a course on Chaucer entitled "The Devil's Workshop," in which students considered Proverbs 16:27, the professed origin of St. Jerome's declaration, "fac et aliquid operis, ut semper te diabolus inveniat occupatum." Anyway, the final exam for The Devil's Workshop involved a staring contest. Grades were not curved.

Dr. Clink—that's my father's name—and I have not talked for a long time. I'd like to ask him if he ever thought, inversely, that boredom could be *harnessed*. Held in the same way that a poltergeist harnesses the body of its host. If this were possible, then it follows that intentional, controlled idleness could become a means by which the devil could be tricked into doing one's bidding. I doubt this idea occurred to him. His students occasionally went insane during the final exam. The insanity was temporary. That seemed to be more Dr. Clink's treatise on boredom—its impermanence.

His doctoral dissertation concerned juridical ethics and the sentencing of crimes passionnel.

A crime of passion is simply defense by excuse. Dr. Clink explained to me that this is a sort of perversion of mens rea that depends on proving the defendant holds no malicious aforethought. Literally, your mind isn't guilty. Your very *mind*. In essence, a crime of passion is an act of violence that wasn't planned on. It's best if you don't have the rope or the knife, etc., on your person when you walk into the room. It's best if you call the police yourself and remain at the scene.

Dr. Clink's research centered on the manner in which a jury of one's peers accepts or does not accept an excuse. Determination of guilt or innocence is just, like, the jury's opinion.

My father would, at this point, explain that there are a variety of tests used to determine culpability. My favorite is the Irresistible Impulse Test, also known as the "policeman at the elbow" test. If you can't resist committing what you intellectually know to be a crime with an officer of the law only one arm's length away from you, you have fulfilled the criteria of the Irresistible Impulse Test. I like to remember this as the "well, fuck it" rule, but that's incorrect. To say *fuck it* is a sort of negative existential exercise; a proof of the concept of agency via the action which removes the agency.

That's how the last half of the nineties was, though. While mostly I remember tanning and hair extensions and groups of syncopated pop stars dancing with the unity of a military drill, the other part of me remembers a love of trash. In the year 2000, a very pale, very insane actress once appeared on the red carpet of an awards show wearing a shredded garbage bag and the magnificent wedding ring given to her by her suicided husband. There was willing distortion, music was meant to sound like fuzz. If I listen to her albums now, they possess the polyphony of a whipped dessert, too sweet for teeth, too sugar for earth. Curated decay. I still can't decide if the sticky double G and guttural vowel of grunge was euphonious or cacophonous. Both.

I suppose that's why I now hold the idea of agency in my hand like the token for a carnival ride. I'll suffer if I lose it, although not mortally. In reality, the Irresistible Impulse Test is intended to determine whether or not the defendant is capable of self-control. It asks if the defendant was their own victim; prey to their own impulse. Dr. Clink liked this idea because it suggests that there is a spirit under the body that can emerge at any moment. But he never made enough of the word *victim*. I suspect that The Devil's Workshop was his way of testing the assumption that extreme boredom is the portal used to access the spirit body. He *wanted* those students to go insane, to commit crimes at the elbow of an officer.

His research began in the early eighties and reached the peak of its popularity among scholars in 1994 as the result of the trial of Lorena Bobbitt. This was a very good time in my life for me to meet Christine.

Christine possessed an unfettered sense of revenge accessible only to people with a supreme, nearly supernatural, sense of self-worth. She was the relation of a relation of a friend of my mother and was, supposedly, the granddaughter of a second wife of deposed Norwegian royalty. Who cares, right? Well, my mother, Grethe Clink (née Strindberg) did. Normally a woman with a vibrant melancholy (a rich misery that won't commandeer this story until it must), my mother became incandescent at the idea of royalty and the opportunity to speak her native language. She was, in fact, so taken by Christine's remedial Norwegian that, through the closed doors of Dr. Clink's office, I heard her raise her voice above its usual tone—a C major with a retained sixth, the mathematic inversion of what some scholars call the Devil's Chord—for the first time in my life. Like a flute overflooded with air she told my father that she would not "turn her back on her country" for him "a second time."

I thought that seemed a little overwrought. I sincerely doubted my mother, whose favorite show was *Good Morning America*, had ever sacrificed much at all.

Perhaps this is exactly what Dr. Clink said in response, because Grethe began to sob. The next words that floated through the door were "She has nowhere else to go." Several days later I was introduced to Christine.

Christine was a tonique possessing the defiance and dejectedness of a Victorian ghost. Her anger manifested itself in strange and seemingly inconsequential ways. She was very fond of a type of benign torture she called "dial and dash." The procedure involved calling people who had wronged her and then channeling her malice into the telephone. She told me once that she envisioned the rage she breathed into the phone to be the cloudy-clear shade of a G&T. Christine was my babysitter.

Christine especially liked it when I dialed the number and held the phone. "It's like how a tarot card reader can't let anyone else use their deck," she explained, "because they don't want to, you know, junk up the energy."

I nodded as if I had ever seen a tarot deck in real life. I gathered that energy was something personal to Christine.

"You don't want the phone to lose any of its power," she added heavily. She wore her lipstick liner slightly outside the ridge of her natural lip.

I regarded the phone. It was a gray-and-black plastic box that spent most of the day unmoored, separated from its charging station. Quite actually, energy-less.

My memory of Christine's face as she tilted her head and listened to it ring is too private. I was transfixed by the revolution her features underwent as she waited. All I will tell you is that, often, I knew her target had answered by the dull metallic scrape of the Fresca can crushed in Christine's grip.

You might be wondering why I had a babysitter at the age of thirteen. I have two theories. My parents didn't know the true timbre of my voice. I always spoke an octave higher and a decibel softer when I was with them. Did you know that the exceptionally traumatized often retain their childhood voice, frozen at the moment of trauma?

Let's step away from that, though. I'll tell you what I know about freezing at the start of the next chapter.

Anyway, my first theory as to why I was still being minded like a child at the age of thirteen had nothing to do with me.

My mother often offered Christine extra money to perform unnecessary tasks. She would ask her to vacuum the basement carpet, which still bore the tracks of the last grooming. She paid her overtime to sit around and talk about Norway (a place, I learned, Christine had never even been) in her terrible Norwegian. "Ya, været ved sjøen er veldig fint," Christine replied, no matter the question posed. Possibly, my father was studying the reactions she had to feeling useless. It was a waste of time, though, because Christine mostly did not live in her corporeal body. She regarded it as the basic technology needed to implement her will in the world. I doubt she even knew she was vacuuming.

It became clear that my mother felt more than a certain noblesse oblige toward her thrice-removed countrywoman. She actually truly liked Christine. Over the years, I would hear them on the phone occasionally when my father was out of town and Grethe felt especially low. Also, I think she wanted to offer the girl some money because she seemed like she needed it. For instance, even though my parents always left us a frozen pizza, Christine ate the jelly and honey out of all our jars. One January, she ate my leftover Halloween candy and puffed the jack-o'-lantern face of the orange bag back up as if were grinning and full. She was quite thin, tall, and heavy-boned and, for reasons at the time incomprehensible to me, she had my mother's full devotion.

My second theory was that my father had made too much progress in his research and had become a threat to the entertainment industry. Maybe in The Devil's Workshop he had discovered the cure for boredom and now film directors and writers and magazine editors and videogame designers and puzzle makers everywhere were desperate to silence him. What, after all, would contented people spend their dollars on? I imagined the people who were hunting my father as an America with the volume turned down, a perceptible dimming like when the lights of a flight are lowered to simulate night, promote sleep. I imagined they planned to kidnap and ransom me to keep him quiet, to keep the states loud.

A subtle panic undergirded the atmosphere of our home. My parents rarely allowed anyone inside the house (except of course, for the two people my father deemed *essential personnel*; his TA, Jeffrey LaPlant, and, of course, Christine). If my father was away on conference, my mother turned on every light in the house, double-locked all our doors and triply secured them by wedging a dining chair under the handles. Then, in a macabre before-bed ritual, walked around with the largest knife from the butcher's block.

My mother opened even the cabinet under the sink while remarking that Charles Manson was a very small man. Like Barbie, Abe Lincoln, and Frankenstein, I don't ever remember not knowing who Charles Manson was.

(Is this enough to explain to you why I believed there was some serious and maybe immediate violence always near me? Who are you, by the way? I've been imaging you as a sort of panel of judges sitting at a long, faux wood table in the front row of a convention center, craning your necks back to look at the talent, whispering amongst yourselves, never disapproving, sometimes amused, often confused. I imagine you as if I am a little girl at a beauty pageant reciting *Les Chants de Maldoror* while painting a self-portrait; I imagine you must be judging my French, my brushstrokes. I imagine that you are indulgent, as anyone must be who submits to listen so dedicatedly, at such length, as a thirty-year-old woman talks about the tragedy of being a teenager. I imagine you possess an above-average tolerance for trifles and trauma, but that you'd like me to get to some sort of point. I imagine you imagine this performance might end with me levitating. I see you scan the beams of the convention center for a glint of light off the fishing wire that will betray my trick. They always say an honest person doesn't have to convince you that they aren't lying, but, sincerely, I'm not lying to you. When I float at the end of this, it will really happen.)

After my mother finished her patrol and I went to bed, a heavily synthesized melody would drift from the speakers concealed in the floorboards. The sounds of a digital drum kit and xylophone thrummed the undersides of the wood and emitted a melodious roar, a subtle vibration. A glass of water placed too close to the edge of the nightstand would inevitably tip over. The floodlights surrounding the house flickered three times and reset themselves in a deep crimson. The yard looked like it had been scribbled over with a layer of red ChapStick. The same thing happened inside, but those lights were blue. It became more difficult to determine depth. At the time, I assumed Grethe had ordered our security system from her favorite television show, a true-life crime documentary series that considered alien abductions and actual kidnappings with equal regard. My mother had an uncharacteristic interest in secret history episodes.

Our elaborate system never deployed when Christine babysat, though. She was only five years older than I was, but she was essentially an adult. I sometimes marvel at the fact that, at eighteen, Christine was already more mature than I am even now.

Adulthood, in my mind, wasn't an age so much as a résumé of achievements. Christine had some vital accomplishments: she had a boyfriend, she had ex-boyfriends, she had been to Europe, she wore a huge black cross studded with amethysts and skulls around her neck, she lived in a studio apartment, she knew the name of the homeless man who sat in front of the Younkers department store downtown, and she had a job. This final detail was the highest expression of maturity. Christine was no longer a student. Her transactions resulted, unlike mine, in currency she converted to black lipstick, healing crystals, whatever.

Christine powdered her skin corpse-white, dyed her hair black as a wig, and made me her amanuensis for séances and other communications. I suspect we didn't need the *Unsolved Mysteries* music and lights when Christine visited simply because her presence rendered that particular mise-en-scène anachronistic. A ghost in the machine. No, I'm kidding, of course: Dr. Clink's students appeared on the first day of the semester with a digital understanding of this term; they thought it meant some unexplainable outside force had infiltrated and disrupted the institution. But soon they knew the phrase's actual meaning. The ghost in the machine is instead what animates the system. I mention this because Christine often illustrated this point to me: just as Descartes argued the spirit exists on an entirely separate plane than the body, so Christine existed on an entirely separate plane than the haunted house. Lace and lasers, united only by their liminality.

It's pedestrian to point out that angels and ghosts are both messengers from another world, so I am grateful Christine taught me that there are earthly messengers as well.

"In the East," she explained, "you don't have to die to be a saint." She spread a stack of tabloids and fashion magazines across my parent's dining room table. "In the West, we call our saints 'celebrities' or 'politicians.'" She looked me straight in the eye. "We call them *stars*." She removed a black marker and a pair of craft scissors from her backpack. "But that's all shit, Jessica. There's no such thing as saints, just people who have something you don't."

We defaced the magazines: the bare abdomens were removed, the smiles were blacked out and replaced with fangs, headlines were erasured and the cosmos subverted. It was an origin story.

A photo of Lorena Bobbitt and her husband at their wedding was published in one of the magazines. He wore a navy military uniform; she bloomed out of a wedding dress of antebellum proportions.

Christine took the tip of a scissor to John Wayne Bobbitt's face and, like a Christmas wrapper at a fancy department store, scraped the blade across the paper until it curled. She drew an ornate, oval frame around Lorena's face so she looked a little like the ivory silhouette on a cameo brooch. Christine was an artist. She told me she shellacked the defaced magazines onto canvas and sold them to galleries.

A few years ago, I tried to look up some of Christine's art on the Internet, but there was no record of her at all. It now occurs to me she could have been lying about the whole thing. But my parents trusted her to the point that in 1999 she was the one Dr. Clink called to see if she knew of any employer who might take me.

Christine and Dr. Clink had developed a sort of lopsided friendship by then. She said she and my father probably had known each other in another life.

"You mean like Buffy and Donald Sutherland?"

"Um," Christine hesitated, "yeah, sort of like Buffy."

"How did you know each other? Which century?"

She considered. "Sometime before Christ. I was probably an oracle."

This was an impressive answer.

Really, though, I think Christine won Dr. Clink's favor by simply asking a lot of questions about his work. If her initial presence in our home had been as my babysitter and my mother's confidant, she secured her place by becoming my father's spectator. The avenue that led to my father's heart was much brighter, straighter, and more boring than I had understood it to be as a child. He really just liked to talk about himself, and Christine listened. She even did her homework and showed up ready to brief him on pop culture that might pique his interest—Lorena Bobbitt, for example.

I stood in the hall outside my father's office door in 1999 and listened to him tell all about how pathetic I had turned out to be: lethargic, aimless, *bored*. I doubt these qualities troubled Christine. As his coup de grâce, he told her about the tanning beds.

(Did you know that Victorian socialites used to coat their skin in opium before bed and wash it off in the morning with ammonia to keep themselves translucent as a cadaver? Christine told me that.)

This was how I got a job managing the counter and working the darkroom at University Photography & Art Supply. Later, the conversation shifted to Christine and Dr. Clink's favorite mutual topic: the most famous defense of a crime passionnel in legal history. Information obtained through eavesdropping is not admissible in most courts. For this reason, I won't repeat what Dr. Clink relayed to Christine.

You are here to make a judgment.

My hope is that after you hear what I've done, you won't forgive it. My hope is you'll follow suit, with an officer at the elbow. For old times' sake—it's what Christine would do.

CHAPTER TWO

THIS CHAPTER STARTS WITH FREEZING AND ENDS WITH thawing. This is the chapter about my mother.

There are no photos from my birth. There are no photos of me as an infant at all.

Twice a year, my family made a trip to my father's alma mater. We drove eighteen hours overnight from the heart of the country until we arrived at the end of the highway and disappeared.

We passed through a series of increasingly smaller gates. For the last three, Dr. Clink had to stop the car and get out to open them with a key he kept around his neck. The final gate was at the end of a steep drop off on a dirt road. On the other side of it was a tunnel. I would guess we were in Arizona or New Mexico. Somewhere dry as the breath of a long snake.

Once we drove into the mountain, there was nothing to see except the headlights of the car melting into rock walls. My mother would recite a series of turns from memory until we emerged into a deep bowl of light with a campus in the middle of it. My mother leaned over my father to recite his university identification number to the campus security guard manning the chain-link gate. The university was made up of dozens of brick buildings from another century. Spires, iron angels, and the liquid outline of flowing fountains silhouetted against terracotta rock. It was incongruous, an ivy-less Oxford.

Before unpacking our things in the guest housing, my mother and father had to sign the Chancellor's guest book. I was not allowed access to the interior quarters of Chancellor Lethe's mansion, so I waited in the foyer, which was a long gallery of portraits commemorating his predecessors. The most interesting part of the display was 1857, the year in which the images shifted from illustrations to photographs. It reminded me of our own portrait wall at home, shifting from pictures of my mother before I was born to pictures of us when I was a toddler. She looks like two different women.

When she was younger, my mother was a beauty pageant champion. Her headshots lead in to our annual mother-daughter portraits on my father's desk. You could see me growing from her knees up to her exact height. There's an eerie quality to the final photos. We look less like mother and daughter and more like a woman and her doppelgänger. But genetics are uncanny.

Doppelgänger are evil in folklore. Christine once told me that all fairy tales are, in their paper hearts, nationalistic. According to her, the Grimm brothers were propaganda artists. I learned later on in a class that Jacob Grimm once stated: "Alle meine Arbeiten beziehen sich auf das Vaterland, von dessen Boden sie ihre Stärke beziehen."

Christine also believed fairy tales were a psychological programming device invented by the patriarchy. She said that only horror would bring us together and remove the fairy tale's patina of meaning, which served to confuse and disorient. She regarded any kind of narrative as a blinder; the tiny screens that convince the horse there is only one path.

But the doppelgänger can also be a manifestation of a utopic potential. Like, an angel. My mother had a rare sleep disorder. She would wake up and sense a benevolent presence sitting at her bedside. When she opened her eyes, she saw herself.

The angel was obviously me. Why did I do it? Because of a fairy tale.

Grethe Strindberg moved to the States in 1972. She was eighteen years old and unnaturally beautiful in the way of vampires, wives of plastic surgeons, and Prague in December. Dr. Clink paid for her ticket from Norway. She brought almost nothing from her home country and seemed not to miss the family she left there. I don't even know the first names of her parents, my grandmother and grandfather Strindberg. In a large Pierre Cardin purse, my mother packed her makeup, her jewelry and silk scarves, and a book of Norwegian folk tales. It was in this book that I learned that the Scandinavian version of a doppelgänger is one part ghost, one part yourself, and one part the future. It's called a vardøger and the Norwegians define it as a premonitory presence—the sight or sound or smell—of a woman before she arrives. Sometimes, the vardøger is corporeal and can be seen by its double performing future actions. Déjà vu in reverse.

If the doppelgänger is always a little sinister, the vardøger is always a little salvific.

That's why I did it. I just thought it would be nice.

You might be wondering how a woman who arrived in America in 1972 bore a daughter who could have been her twin in the late '90s. I didn't resemble my mother quite enough to play the vardøger trick until I was eighteen, the same age she was when she moved to the States. In 1997, Grethe Clink claimed to be forty-five years old, although she looked far younger. My mother wasn't healthy. She smoked Sobranie Cocktail cigarettes while she curled her hair and never applied sunscreen before driving her top-down, lime-green Camaro to the bakery or the liquor store or the pool or wherever. She loved American pop.

There was one weekly exception to Dr. Clink's no-guest rule: on Thursday evenings a group of my mother's beauty pageant friends would come over to our house and sit in the sunken living room and drink water with cucumbers in it. They reeked like a funeral. Shalimar. Diorella. Chantilly. Charlie. Arpége. I loved them like I love poodles: their faces were intelligent but unassuming.

They each embraced my mother at a slight distance, as if playing a game of Operation, and slipped a tightly rolled stack of bills into her hand. When she went to fetch their coffee or tea, she discretely placed the money in a jar labeled SUGAR. I once tried to count the bills but only got up to 180 dollars before getting caught. I would guess there was at least ten times that amount in the canister. The money was her own, kept secret from Dr. Clink. She had communicated this to me with a simple, "Your father doesn't need to know everything. Ja?"

She only evoked her native language when she was dead serious.

The beauty queens were there to buy Scandinavian Tupperware. My mother was their guru: a tall, tan, blonde woman who sat on the bench of a grand piano in the living room of a grand house and enlightened them on the benefits of freezing.

My mother didn't call it Tupperware, of course. "Gjentakelse Tvang," she told the women, "is engineered by a Norwegian bioarchitect who has perfected the science of freezing the genes which cause aging." My mother named those genes as she stepped from the piano bench into a clear plastic box. She lay down on the floor of the box with her hands crossed over her chest, mummy-style, and called me over.

My job was to slide the flexible plastic lid over the container and make sure it was securely in place and airtight.

"A uniquely engineered, highly oxygenated air is now being pumped into the kryokammer," my mother said to the women through the transparent plastic. "Every night, I set an alarm for eight hours and go to sleep while the Gjentakelse Tvang introduces therapeutic waves into my body." At this point, I would sit down at the piano and play a Norwegian lullaby while my mother continued to explain how the therapeutic waves located the aging genes and erased their memory of trauma from the previous day.

"You can drink, eat what you like, smoke, breathe in the chemicals at the hair dresser—anything you want!" my mother sang out. "Just go to sleep and the Gjentakelse Tvang will tell your body to forget about it!"

The women, of course, wanted their bodies to forget. They wanted to stay frozen. My mother made them sign a consent form that swore they would not stay in the box for more than eight hours. If they did so, neither my mother nor the manufacturers of Gjentakelse Tvang were responsible for damages inflicted by the gene reversal process. The side effects included irrepressible laughter, speaking in a child's voice, a numbing of the facial muscles, loss of memory, loss of voice, an urge to hula hoop or dance inappropriately, sexual amnesia, false awakenings or a dream within a dream, a compulsion to repeat one's name, emotional blunting, a compulsion to write one's name in odd places such as on the skin of a grocery store apple, and various heat-related phobias.

The beauty queens were not afraid of the side effects. (Later on I learned that if a body is disinterred, there is a mechanical sucking when the coffin lid opens. The lid of the kryokammer made the same noise when I let my mother out.) They told their friends, and by 1989, I estimate that nearly forty of that year's fifty Miss America contestants owned a Gjentakelse Tvang. So did all of my mother's friends in the neighborhood.

Also on Thursday nights, most of the fathers in the cul de sac met for a card game. Their children walked right out their front doors at midnight to meet each other for Night Games as the mothers fell into a deep therapeutic sleep. We took off our shoes and ran down the middle of the paved streets. We started cars we didn't know how to drive, our hearts beating as the engine thrummed. We poured shots of liquor into Dixie cups and made suicide punch in a rinsed-out pail from someone's sandbox. We developed a grammar of contempt for our parents. We did not want their shoes or cars or liquor. We hated the subdivision with roads that looped back into one another so that it was impossible to get lost.

You don't need to know the names of the kids I spent Thursday evenings with. They changed every year as different Jennifers or Brians or Stevens outgrew Night Games. I outgrew the games, too, eventually. But it was the first underworld I ever belonged to.

I mean *underworld* in the Greek sense, obviously.

There is a photo in my mother's book of Nordic fairy tales of the Yggdrasil, the Nordic Tree of Life that connects the heavens, earth, and the underworld. It looks like you would expect it to: the heavens are represented by the light on the tree's leaves, the earth is a flat, mountainous plane in the center of the trunk, and the underworld is a twisting mess of tree roots. The best part is that at the threshold of the roots sits a tiny house where the chthonic gods and goddesses live. It is black and shuttered. Night Games made this our house; Night Games made us chthonic children. We developed rituals and performed sacrifices.

It was Night Games that first made me consider my thesis that boredom could be controlled and used to rule the devil. It was very difficult to harness, though. Some kids drifted out of the neighborhood and into the yards of the surrounding country homes. I heard they did weird things: crept into farmhouses and watched couples sleeping, tied the tails of horses to one another, put a tape machine under the mattress of a crib so that mothers heard a child's voice say it saw a face in the window. Mostly innocent.

Academically speaking, the underworld is a passage, not a destination.

I'm sure it was because of Night Games that I was not at all surprised when photos from other underworlds developed in the darkroom of University Photography. Developing the photographs of strangers satisfied some ancient part of my brain. Dr. Clink kept several animals in cages and aquariums in his office to study boredom in different species. A box turtle I fed maraschino cherries, white mice he allowed me to make mazes for. He let me teach the mice the way out of the maze with a trail of Cheerios, then he taught them not to want to leave with tiny shocks. "Try," he said, pressing my small fingertip to steel rods on the floor of the shock box. It zapped me, less electric than the crackle of Grethe brushing my hair too fast. "See? It isn't so bad," he remarked as I giggled at the zap. My father was, once, a kindly presence. Occasionally, he even allowed me to pet the tentacles of his favorite subject—a small octopus I named Edith who learned to take the lid off her own cage. Dr. Clink said boredom cultivated the cephalopod's sense of deception; it was the only way to make the animal smarter. (The underworld is the same, isn't it? At a dinner party my parents once threw, I overheard a professor of literature explain that after the First World War, the only stories left were ones about a descent into the underworld. He said that to touch death and come back was inherently modern. He didn't mention what stories were left after the Second World War, but probably it was just stories about stories. What I mean to say is that if modernism is the story of the Creature's Keeper, then this is the story of the Creature's Creature. At some point, monsters learn to create their own art.) I felt like the octopus as I watched the photos develop: I felt like I was finally accessing a secret adult knowledge.

Our policy at University Photography was to process anything, "no questions asked." I saw some weird stuff. The images appeared out of nothing, frozen forever in a moment in time, absent the context that could stop them from floating around my mind like sarin gas in a subway tunnel. The things I saw—

I'm going to need to keep restarting this story until I've circled enough times to leave a gouge in the ground at the exact spot where my feet can't stop crossing. If I find it, I'll stand there in that sunken place and finish this.

For now, see if you can forget about the photos. Forget about the most awful thing you've ever seen.

I'll do the trick for you. The vardøger trick. I'll make a mask of your face and sit by your bedside, ready to ventriloquize you into telling yourself the story of your future. When you wake up, you'll have a compulsion to put your portrait up at the end of a long line of other portraits, a wonderful urge to self-memorialize.

Me, though—I never quite know whose portrait it is that I place *in memoriam*: my own or my mother's. Just when I think I am finally about to take a picture of myself, my mouth tilts and my tongue curls as if to pronounce one of the three extra letters of her native alphabet. The Norwegian *æ*, *ø*, and *å* are all it takes to transform the musculature of my face into a mirror of her. I can never quite get her extra language out of my mouth. (This manifests in the oddest ways. I'll find myself asking a server to seat me back to the wall, so I can see all the exits. I'll buy a mace that looks like lipstick and hold it for the whole train ride. Sometimes, I'll even open up a sugar canister and find I've hidden my own roll of cash and forgotten it. I'm always ready to get out of the situation, even when I don't know what the situation, exactly, is.) Even now that my mother has been dead for ten years, she emerges again and again on the walls of galleries where I hang my art, self-portraits that may not be me. I never tell the patrons this. People are more inclined to believe that proximity is complicity these days, and they aren't wrong, but they also don't need to know how close they are to a murdered woman.

Yes, Grethe dies.

When I need to feel close to her, I find a hot spot—a car in July, a patch of black asphalt at noon, a tanning bed—and I repeat what she told the beauty queens to do if they spent too long in the Gjentakelse Tvang: *Imagine yourself lying flat on your back in the middle of a wooden floor. Imagine you are in a dark room surrounded by candles. They form a perfect circle around your body. Now, imagine one candle melts too far. It catches the white linen sleeve of your nightgown. Imagine you have fallen so fast asleep you do not feel the flames until they consume your arm. You awaken when it feels as though a claw of heat is pushing out of your gullet. You scream the name of your father. At the door a figure appears. It rushes toward you. The figure has no cloth to dampen the flames that are now covering your body. You see the figure retreat. You can no longer scream. You think of nothing but heat. When you are fully engulfed, the figure appears before you holding a wet, black blanket. Just before the blanket embalms you, you see the face of the figure. It is not, as you had assumed, your father. It is yourself. You have now been thawed.*

CHAPTER THREE

Deep shame overcomes me at the memory of the mother-daughter beauty pageants.

Certainly, you have connected some of the knots of my life by now—my beautiful mother, my obsession with my own skin, my over-indulged vocabulary, my aloneness—enough to see that I was a child beauty queen.

In 1993, a few months after she began to visit our house, I decided I liked Christine enough to allow her to behold my Caboodles of industry-grade cosmetics, my closet of tulle and sequin, my tiaras.

Truly, I was a brat. I expected her to be enchanted.

Instead, she removed a green sucker from her mouth and remarked, "Gag me with a spoon."

Even if I wanted to, I assumed Grethe would never allow me to quit pageanting. It would be like a death to her. It would, in fact, be the double death of both of us; I had no memory of a time before the pageants. They were my life. They were our life.

As a four-year-old, I could sit motionless for over five hours in the backstage area of whatever high school auditorium or mall we were competing in. Grethe dressed me in one of my father's button-down shirts, a self-styled artist's smock, and then painted my face until I looked like a living doll. She brushed my hair back and shellacked my head in a thick cloud of hairspray before inserting a rat-sized bundle of pre-curled blonde wig atop my head. Earlier in the week, we both visited a spray tan booth at her fancy salon. Naked, we held our arms over our heads and spread our legs wide while a technician used an air gun to mist our bodies with a fine, cold spray of DHA. I could hold my breath for nearly three minutes. I don't know how long Grethe could go without air; a long time.

Right before we stepped on stage, I opened my mouth wide and my mother slipped a flipper over my baby teeth to match them to her immaculate dentata. It never felt wrong, to be masked over like this. It felt safe. My first memory is of a lipstick stain on a napkin.

We spent most of our time preparing for the pageants, including coaching from a woman named Crystal St. Marie. Crystal was the wife of one of my father's colleagues in Boredom Studies. Although she was not herself an excellent competitor, my mother said she was an excellent coach. She was squat and underdeveloped as a gymnast. Presciently, she consistently wore stretchy exercise pants and a sports bra. It would take another decade for the rest of the country's upper middle class to realize they could always look like they were arriving to or departing from the gym. Her breath reeked of strawberry SlimFast.

I had no feelings at all toward Crystal, who, like my father, regarded me with the neutral attention a trainer gives to a show dog. This was, to some degree, confusing; although they never said so, I knew I meant a great deal to both my coach and to Dr. Clink. Crystal included a photo of me in a lavender gown the size of a small cloud on the cover of the brochure she gave prospective clients. Beneath my photo, in a loopy font, the words: THE BEST IN THE MIDWEST! Dr. Clink's affection was displayed less directly. Instead of tucking me in for bedtime or—I don't know—keeping my photo in his wallet, he named his most beloved discovery after me. The Greenglass Method

(Greenglass is my middle name), published when I was four years old, combines hypnosis, cryotherapy, and proprietary Gjentakelse Tvang technology in order to erase short-term traumatic recollections. He had never gotten the funding to prove it worked on humans, but he did restore a number of shelter pets to absolute tranquility with the Greenglass Method. Occasionally, Dr. Clink would sneak up next to me and snap his fingers beside my ear as if to test my reaction to sudden noises, just as he did the dogs. It was his way, I guess, of checking on my health. Crystal's care was more practical. She discouraged my oleaginous nature and taught me that my life was to be performed in the service of the audience. She taught me to stop begging to be petted.

I suppose she was a cruel woman. She sometimes spent so many hours preparing me and my mother for the pageant's interview portion that my voice became as hoarse as a barmaid's. *Train under duress, conquer every stress.* This was the cornerstone of her philosophy.

Over the decade that we competed in pageants, I watched so many other children break that it would not be possible to account for them all here. Sometimes I dream that I am standing on a stage reciting their names. In the dream I have to urinate desperately, but I know the names will never stop and my act will never end. I've never dreamt the whole dream.

The little girls broke in different ways. A Tracy who couldn't stand the hot wax poured on her face to remove the baby hairs above her upper lip. A Lisa who limped off the stage, one ballet slipper ombréd pink silk and red blood, who found that her smallest toenail had fallen off entirely. A Lindsey who loved Dippin' Dots and didn't fit into her gowns the day of a pageant. A Kimberly who was so exhausted she wept her false lashes off. A Belinda who, standing naked in the service hallway of a conference center, could not stop shivering as her coach

repaired a tear in her leotard. A Samantha who hyperventilated after forgetting her prepared answers to the judge's interview. A Britney
who developed a bronchial infection from inhaling so much dust at the
manicurist. They would be swept off the stage like day-old confetti.

"Duress," Crystal said as she surveyed a backstage glittering with
girls who had not slept, eaten protein, or spoken to a normal child in
weeks, "is a contagion."

Her techniques were mostly built on duration and repetition.
They often involved a shiny object, a candle, or a mirror. In one exercise, I looked at myself in the mirror while Crystal stood by my side,
slightly outside the frame, and spoke to me about looking in the mirror.

"Jessica," she always said my name as if we were just meeting, "This
is the perfect moment.

"You are in the perfect time.

"You are in the perfect place.

"You are calm.

"My voice is the perfect voice.

"It is the only voice you can hear.

"Look into the blacks of your eyes until you can see yourself reflected. Breathe deeply.

"The air you take into your body is clear, the air you exhale is black.

"Feel the blackness of your own breath surrounding your body.

"It is the perfect blackness."

The pupils of my eyes began to shift and widen. My breath shal-
low, my eyes became empty pits.

"Now, be gold," Crystal instructed. My eyes filled as if champagne
poured into a flute. Her voice was the low pitch of a diminished piano
chord.

Over time, Crystal taught me to remove my entire face and replace it with another. Eventually, she removed the mirror itself. I stood in our darkened basement rec room next to the pool table and let various faces flow over me. Crystal told me in confidence that my mother could do this as well. In fact, when I could not see her, Grethe's face was permanently gone. She was so expert at focusing her mind that I did not even see the slippage in the moment that she assumed her Mother Face. By the age of eight, I could do this as well. It was then that I truly began to excel in pageant circles.

It was so easy to feel myself drain out of my feet and fill back up again with whatever I chose that at some point it no longer felt like I had a body. Even with my muscles and vocal cords aching from talent practice and my fingertips trembling slightly from exhaustion or hunger, I could sit pleasantly through hours and hours of hair brushing and pinning and waxing and waiting—mostly waiting—until it was my turn to walk on stage. I was not like the other girls; I could not be broken.

Sometimes we practiced by watching videos of the other girls competing to determine their weaknesses. Crystal adjusted the footage so that after a dropped baton or missed note or any other idiotic mistake, an image of my father weeping appeared for a split second. Sometimes the images changed and I didn't recognize the men spliced into the pageant. Sometimes they were in pain. In one, a man whose hands were my mother's hands appeared to be choking himself to death. There were often needles and electricity involved. Thumbs and teeth, I learned, were a great vulnerability.

Crystal advised me to be friends with the other girls. I had a Child's Face I could put on when I spoke to them. The Child's Face held eye contact for the right amount of time, became distracted at age-appropriate intervals, and moved as though she were wearing a pair of cashmere gloves; thin, but not so thin that I could use a crayon any better than anyone else.

Though my face was fake, some of my friendships were real. When I was thirteen, the year I quit pageants, the Child's Face fell in love with a Teen Queen named Veronica Marshall. She had long, dark hair that brushed my shoulder when she leaned over to whisper in my ear. Her voice was hushed and clean as a skate cutting ice.

"How do you do it?" These were the first words Veronica ever whispered to me. I was used to the question from desperate girls, girls whose parents had taken out mortgages to pay for coaches and gowns and beauticians. "How do you keep the glitter from getting every-where? I swear to god, I'm shitting glitter by the end of the day."

This was the first time another child had ever directed something so profane to me. And so casually, too. As if we were already intimate and did not need to vet one another through a series of conversations about what kind of television we approved of, what diets we had tried, what we knew about the secret lives of our parents.

The Child's Face did not have the vaguest idea how to react. It split. I heard Jessica laugh and then I was Jessica again.

"Your monologue was awesome," I said. For her talent, Veronica performed a famous soliloquy from *The Taming of the Shrew*. She got to use words like *fie* and *toil* and *bandy*. One line, *come, come, you froward and unable worms*, would play on a loop in my head as I fell asleep at night. I imagined using the word *froward* in a conversation with my fa-ther. It sounded incorrect—the ghost of *forward* cocooned inside it—but it wasn't. I imagined him correcting me and, in turn, triumphantly cor-recting *him*. This was the greatest revenge I could imagine on Dr. Clink.

Veronica snorted in reply. "My monologue is *terrible*. My coach thinks I need to do something smart because I'm tall." She held the *r* on *terrible* so the emphasis was in the middle of the word. "And because I don't really have any other talents."

We both laughed. It was hilarious to not take the pageant seriously. Hysterical.

"So why do you do it?" I asked.

Her eyes widened. "Pageants?"

I hesitated. Maybe I had crossed a line. "Yeah," I quickly dithered into a compliment, "I mean, you're so beautiful. I get it."

"Oh, fuck that. I do it because of Ronny." She rolled her eyes in the direction of her mother sitting at the other end of the bleachers. "She needs me so she can keep competing. She's an addict."

I gasped. I thought she meant drugs.

"I mean, like, addicted to pageants. She's been doing it since she was a kid. She was Miss Sweet Pea of 1975 or something. My dad wouldn't let her do it anymore after they got married because he thinks the judges are—" she pantomimed a crude gesture as proxy for her father's thoughts about the judges. "But she convinced him the mother-daughter pageants are, you know, wholesome."

"Totally," I confirmed.

Mirroring is an art and a science. Chancellor Lethe once told me that before a human is even born, she mimics the beat of the mother's heart in utero. An alumnus of the Desert University had just conducted a study at the University of Parma and discovered that the brain of a macaque looks the same whether it is eating a banana or watching another monkey eat a banana. It's called *limbic synchrony*. When he told me the name, I imagined a movie I had seen on the old films channel where a camera looked down on an ultra-blue pool to capture a group of women wearing little white caps and gigantic swimsuits. They twirled their limbs in unison.

Chancellor Lethe said that some people have more neurons in their brain that help them mirror other people's facial tics, breathing patterns, and vocal habits. Those people are natural artists. People born with an average or subpar number of neurons to assist their limbic synchrony must learn to adapt. They are scientists. There is a third type of person as well; the person born an artist who dedicates themselves like a scientist. He took my hand in his like an old courtier and leaned over to look me in the eye before he said, "You, Jessica, are that third type of person."

I guess it shouldn't have been a surprise that I built rapport with Veronica so quickly.

Up until that point, I had been able to convince myself I had crushes on an assortment of boys. A doctoral student of my father's who wore a stupid hat and carried a briefcase. He was nineteen years old. A boy at my school who shared the name of my favorite singer. None of my crushes liked me back. The truth is, the art and science of limbic symmetry don't work when held in standard to authenticity. And there is no one more authentic than a teenage girl with a crush. Next to my classmates, whose own hearts beat erratically, who made awkward eye contact, who could barely speak to their crushes, I was an electronic doll.

Veronica was often alone. Her father had an unglamorous job as the owner of a local chain of grocery stores. He was quiet and tired, like all fathers. His single claim to my memory was the time he asked me if my mother "had religion" because she was "a Scandy." Veronica had one brother, Matt, who was five years older and still lived at home. He spent most of his time managing the grocery warehouse or lifting weights in their basement, which was also where me and Veronica watched TV on an old orange couch. Matt never talked to us.

I asked Veronica once if he was depressed. "No," she said. "Just really religious."

Veronica wore a gold ring with two tiny disembodied hands reaching across her finger to hold a heart. Inscrutably, the heart wore a crown. She said it was called a Claddagh ring. That the hands stood for friendship, the heart stood for love, and the crown stood for loyalty. She said that when the tip of the heart was pointed outward, it meant the person wearing the ring was still a virgin and open to the world. In an Irish ceremony, the ring would be removed and replaced with the tip pointed inward, toward the wearer's heart, to indicate she was married. In Veronica's Catholic schoolgirl lore, though, the gesture doubled as definitive signal that one had consummated a serious relationship, nuptials or not. If a girl at her school flipped her ring, she had to walk around with her hands in her pockets for fear of corporal punishment from the nuns. The Claddagh was solemn business in Veronica's world—in fact, she said the ring was the only religious thing about her, and that she wore it because it was Irish and weird and pretty. She said that when she was supposed to pray in church, she just looked at all the stained glass. She said the things they wanted her to repent for were not sins and so she sat silently in the confessional on Sundays. The priest was bound not to tell, no matter what happened.

Her full name was Veronica Dearbháil Marshall. She told me in a hushed tone that Lorena Bobbitt was "devout." When I asked Christine what Veronica meant, she concurred with a "Fuck, yeah!" Me and Veronica spent days sitting in front of the television and eating store brand chips from Mr. Marshall's grocery. The chain was named Ronny's, after Veronica's mother. I suppose technically it was named after Veronica as well. But that's what I'm trying to say about etymology: Veronica was the inverse of a derivative of a derivative. She was like finding an original so odd, so unimaginable, it had never even been named. If I think of that part of my life now, the two months where I was falling in love with Veronica, it seems like it was years and years. We listened to an Irish band named after a sour fruit that sounded like ethereal yodeling. We watched a show about two beautiful FBI agents who investigated paranormal activity. Sometimes we whispered the show's tagline to one another before walking onstage at a pageant to try to make the other laugh: *trust no one.*

The texture of my memory of Veronica is neon. I was synesthetic only for her. It felt like spray-painting graffiti on my own life. A creative destruction.

My pageant performances began to suffer.

First, the waists of my expensive dresses had to be let out because I was eating so many of Ronny's generic Cheetos and frozen pizzas at Veronica's. Second, I lost the dull sheen of exhaustion that had prevented me from questioning my rigid training schedule. I began to rebel against Crystal. Third, I stopped practicing the mirror technique. Crystal and Grethe assumed when I sat in a dimmed room by myself for several hours, I was training. Instead, I slept or made Veronica mixtapes or drew pictures of her Claddagh ring on the squared lines of my geometry textbook. Recently, Veronica had turned the point of her ring in the direction of her heart.

(I can't tell you the story of the day Veronica turned her ring inward yet. Just a few weeks prior, the president told people like her to, basically, mind their manners in his *don't ask, don't tell* policy. Me and Veronica already knew that, though. We hadn't been bothering to *ask* or *tell* anybody anything in a long time anyway. I don't know if you know what it's like to be fluent in code. I do, literally. My happiest memory of Dr. Clink is of sitting in the car parked in our driveway one autumn night and drinking shakes while he clicked the headlights of the car on and off and slowly taught me the syntax of dots and dashes that constitute the letters of Morse code. When I started elementary school, I was expected to do homework from a workbook called *International Cipher*. At the end of every section, I wrote a short essay in code that my father graded. I learned to use the Bible as my ciphertext because it could be found in any hotel in America. Obviously, I won't be using the Bible to decode Veronica, of all people and all books. I wouldn't profane her. What I'm saying is that I don't know where you and I meet yet; I don't know the common book to decode our common language with.

I mean I can't explain it.)

Lastly, my memory began to fail. I couldn't recall the thousands of answers Crystal had drilled into me for the judge's questions. I missed a step in a dance routine. I forgot to smile as I walked on stage. This disturbed her, Crystal said, because it indicated corrosion at the point of connection between my long-term and working memory functions. Crystal believed memory was a concealed weapon and it was vital to keep your weapon sharp.

"Long-term memory," Crystal said, "is what you keep in your body. The body keeps the score."

Working memory, she said, is a series of structures and processes used for storing, analyzing, framing, and manipulating information. It's just like short-term memory, but requires attention. If I were to tell you the recipe for a cocktail, first your inner ear would hear me say *one part whiskey, one part vermouth, one dash bitters, add ice and stir, top with a cherry*. On your way to the bar, your inner voice would repeat those words in a loop, each loop tracing slightly deeper in your memory. If it took you thirty seconds to get to the bar, you would make the drink and be done with it. If it took you thirty minutes, you might remember the recipe for the rest of the week.

Some people's loops run deeper than others, obviously.

But, as Crystal pointed out, once you understand the loop, you can also disrupt it; you can learn to sow doubt. It's simple to do. Imagine instead I said: *top with a cherry, one part whiskey, one part vermouth, add ice and stir after adding one dash bitters.* You would rearrange the information in the order that you planned to activate it; essentially, you would modify your memory.

This is what worried Crystal. She wanted my long-term memory and my working memory to be exactly the same. Her function was to make sure I paid attention and remembered everything. She wanted every loop in my record to run so deep they left swift divots.

I don't know how she found out about Veronica. Maybe it was no secret.

I realize now that in any other family, my mother would have simply forbidden me from seeing her. This kind of thing happened all the time. This is the reason they teach *Romeo and Juliet* in high school; because children understand, more than anything else, what it means to be separated.

If they had told me I couldn't see Veronica anymore, I would have been furious for a while, but I would have understood. In fact, I might have forgotten about Veronica entirely. A face in the pageant photos from 1994.

Instead, what they did changed the shape of my brain. It put Veronica in my body forever.

What *they* did. But it was me. Crystal told me to eliminate Veronica from the pageants and I did it.

There were no directions, no explanation, no acknowledgment that Veronica was, at the least, my friend.

We were on the couch and it was late. After midnight, the television was probably tuned to the amaranthine coil of music videos shown on MTV, an intravenous drip of art.

Veronica was asleep. The edge of her head rested on my thigh, her legs thrown over the arm of the couch so that her body was arranged almost as if cradled; a pietà in teenage girl. She wore a long T-shirt that she had cut the neck out of, *Flashdance*-style. It was gray and emblazoned with the green crest of her summer camp: a Jesus fish jumping into a lake. Her head tilted back a little so I could see the curve of her trachea, the perfect cartilaginous tunnel of it underneath her skin. Veronica was an expanse of softness. She bruised so easily that for pageants she used full body makeup to cover bruises from gym class. She was a rough competitor, when she wanted to be.

I put the tips of my fingers on her collarbone and traced them up to the torn edge of her shirt. She didn't stir. I was surprised by how easy it was to nearly encircle her entire throat in one hand. She was sleeping so heavily. I waited, my hand resting on Veronica's bare skin while one video passed and then a second and then a third and finally I heard the metal scrape of the garage door opening and Matt's soft tread as he walked through the laundry room that connected the garage to the basement. He came home from his Friday night shift at 1:00 a.m. without exception.

"Veronica," I whispered as I pushed the edge of her T-shirt, letting it slide off her shoulder so that in the dark room her ultra-white flesh reflected the flashing neon of the television screen.

"Veronica, wake up," I said quietly. Her eyes still closed, she lifted her mouth to mine as I took her breast in my hand. Matt opened the door so softly that Veronica did not even hear.

His eyes met mine for a full breath before he walked up the basement steps, closed the door, and disappeared to shower off the stink of spilt groceries.

By the next afternoon, Mr. Marshall had removed Veronica from the pageants and was on the phone with a Catholic school in Chicago that agreed to enroll his daughter even though the semester was nearly over. I stood on the other side of the wall as Grethe gossiped with the pageant mothers about Ronny and Veronica Marshall's sudden departure. When I heard Grethe repeat, "Josephinum Academy of the Sacred Heart? Yes, certainly, Catholic. But just for girls?" I felt a vile black laugh, an inverse gag reflex.

It was five months after I gave up Veronica—the day before my birthday—that Christine convinced me to quit the pageants.

When I told my mother she shrugged. "Your life is your own, now," she said in the sleepy way she spoke when I was her only audience. She was so distracted I wondered if she was having her *own* affair—she kept a tiny key Dr. Clink didn't know about taped to the inside of a pastel box of Summer's Eve. The douche had never even been opened, but the key belonged to an unassuming diary she kept in her bedside drawer beside a silk scarf she'd brought with her from Norway. I was disappointed to find there was nothing inside except the number for the bank account where she deposited her sugar jar cash when it began to overflow (I recognized the number already because she'd told me to memorize it) and few phone numbers, all of them beginning with +47 or +49, which I knew to be the country codes for Norway and Germany, respectively.

So the pageants ended and my mother receded far from me, into her own private life. I was at the very start of the long corridor between my job at University Photography and that moment in 1994; the traceless space where I left no tracks.

CHAPTER FOUR

My mother did not have religion. She worshipped herself.

Once, I went to Mass with Veronica and the priest explained that until the spirit enters, the body is *a mere shack*.

Me and Veronica peeked at each other with lowered eyes and smirked. After service was over, we profaned the lyrics to a song Veronica's mom had on cassette, *Love shack, baby, it's a little old place where we can get—with—Je-sus*. We wiggled our hips like pop stars while making the sign of the cross. This gesture was performed so quickly at Veronica's church that I didn't understand at first that it was the shape of the crucifix. I thought the congregants were waving the spirit toward them, like how when Dr. Clink parallel parked our long blue Chrysler, Grethe got out of the car and beckoned him in the right direction with tiny, polite movements

I also did not grasp the meaning of Corinthians 6:19–20 in the pews that day. I found the priest eerie, exactly like the old priests I saw in movies about exorcisms. He sang atonally at odd intervals as if he were trying to frighten us; the modulations of his voice did not sync with the expressions on his face. He was like a poorly ventriloquized dummy, his dummy-ness always pointing toward the invisible hand that controlled him.

I, too, believed my mask was my face. Only later would I be able to identify the feeling that arose when Father John read, "Do you not know that your bodies are temples of the Holy Spirit, who is in you, whom you have received from God? You are not your own; you were bought at a price. Therefore honor God with your bodies." I thought, at the time, that I felt incredulous when I heard those words. Later, I would think of that odd beginning, the direct address from the apostle Paul. I conflated it in my dreams of Veronica's Shakespearian monologues; she spoke from a crucifix, her face beatific and her palms bleeding, the symbolism blatant and unlayered.

Mostly, I returned to the words *You are not your own; you were bought at a price.* How much? And by whom? The memory became intrusive. I would find myself at odd moments standing in the photo lab alone staring into the darkness and running my fingers up the fine hairs on my arms or squeezing my wrists. Rituals to make sure I was still there, even though I wasn't.

(There was only one other employee at University Photography, an art student named Kevin, who occasionally walked in to the darkroom while I was developing photos to "make sure I was still alive." There was a light like the beacon of a police car affixed to the wall outside the photo lab that glowed red when a switch inside the studio was flipped. If the light was on, everyone—all three of us: the owner, me, and Kevin—knew not to enter because we could disrupt the photo process and ruin a customer's film. This was the only rule at University Photography: mind the red light.

Kevin always carried a camera on a strap around his neck when he wasn't working. He photographed everything. This was, of course, before the era of auto-documentation. It was pre-truth. Archivism was an act of devotion. He told me a professor once excused him from a college exam to go photograph a vulture roosting on a statue of the campus mascot. He was a serious boy and his concern for me was serious, too. He wasn't kidding when he said he wanted to make sure I wasn't dead.)

That day, when the priest ended the homily by telling us that once we accepted the spirit, our bodies would be not shacks but thrones for the Kingdom of Heaven, I thought of Grethe, who already seemed to me as austere and ancient as the most stunning cathedral. People stopped her on the street to tell her she looked like Geena Davis or Sharon Stone or Michelle Pfeiffer or Claudia Schiffer. They didn't mean she really resembled any of those women; they meant she looked like a star, a light in the act of burning. If religion meant believing Grethe's body was a shack, religion was cancelled for me.

I thought about that as the congregation lined up to take the Eucharist. There was a lulling quality to their unison chant, memorized without emotion. They were the opposite of actors in a play; instead of emoting and elocuting, they turned inward. A somnambulistic ballet. When it came our pew's turn to stand, I kept my seat, just as Ronny had told me to.

"Honey, only people who have been baptized into the Catholic Church can take the body and blood," she'd explained lightly on the drive to the church. She spoke so fast it sounded like she said Buddy'n'Bud.

"Only the *pure* shall partake," Veronica had added in a high British accent. It was her Princess Diana voice; she reserved it for mocking authority. I thought Ronny might turn around in her seat and slap Veronica, but the slight seemed to go over her head. I mean, Ronny really *believed*—it didn't even occur to her that her daughter was kidding.

At the church, I could see the devotion in her eyes that day as she approached the altar for the wafer, which was pressed onto her exposed tongue by the priest himself. Her head was titled back and the tips of her top teeth shone.

I imagine Father John might have gotten a smear of Ronny's Revlon lipstick on his thumb. I wasn't baptized, but I knew Stormy Pink was too bright for church. She left a roseate smudge on the lip of the golden chalice.

I asked Christine about it and she said that it was all basically just a spell to worship the Pope, a real man in Rome that they thought of as their direct line to God. Christine herself must have been raised in the Catholic Church, because she gave me an effortless tutorial on the rite of the Eucharist: "That wafer is 'the body of Christ' and the wine—it's really grape juice—" she rolled her eyes, "is 'the blood of Christ.' They do it because at the Last Supper—" she paused and looked at me to see if I knew what she was talking about.

I nodded. I had learned about *The Last Supper* in Art History.

"Yeah," she continued, "at the Last Supper, Jesus told the apostles to 'do this in memory of me,' so Catholics, like, bring him back every week so he's still with them."

"You mean it symbolizes his body and blood?" I asked.

"The priest performs the act of transubstantiation to turn the bread and juice into flesh and blood."

Normally I nodded when taught new information even if I didn't quite understand it. It was my nature to store things I didn't know in a corner of my mind.

My face stayed blank, though, so Christine continued, "So it *really is* the body and blood of Christ and they eat it so they can carry him around with them and be a vessel of God. It keeps Christ alive, like, literally."

"Wait," I said, "so they were drinking blood?"

"Yeah, that's what I'm saying."

It was a relief that I had been forbidden from taking the Eucharist; I felt the same keen sense of reprieve I felt when the principal's voice crackled over the school intercom and summoned someone else to his office.

"But why couldn't I do it, too?" I asked.

"Because you aren't a holy vessel. You have to confess your sins to God." I knew about confession from Veronica. She had disappeared into something that looked like a palatial photo booth for a few minutes before Mass. "You aren't pure enough for God," Christine concluded.

I once used *The Divine Comedy* as a ciphertext, so I knew from the second book, *Purgatorio*, that the sins included gula, avaritia, acedia, ira, invidia, superbia, and luxuria. Lust.

This illuminated a much larger mystery I hadn't even mentioned to Christine. Veronica did not stand with the rest of her family to take the sacrament. Ronnie squeezed her daughter's knee so hard that her acrylic fingernails (also Stormy Pink) left little crescent shapes on Veronica's knee. She finally got in line without Veronica, seething.

Veronica slipped her foot out of her kitten heel and pulled down the edge of my sock with her big toe. She seemed pleased to have rejected the sacrament.

And now we're here, at the point of sacrifice, just as I promised.

First, though, let me say that I thought the church was fantastic. When I find myself alone and listless in strange cities, I still walk into the biggest Catholic church I can find. I take a quiet seat and pretend I am a plant in a beautiful terrarium, the air around me thick from the flowers arranged around the altar: calla, rose, lily of the valley. *Eau de Christ*. I count the gold and silver and opal and lapis lazuli saints. I look into the eyes of the Virgin Marys scattered like coasters at a cocktail party. I especially love to inspect Veronica's patron, St. Francis, who is usually depicted with a golden tree adorned with golden birds. Veronica told me that he was the patron saint of animals. In the pictures, the birds have come to listen to him preach about the glory of feathers and flight. I sit in a beam of light sifted through red stained glass and find the exact spot where the sun is filtered by the incarnadine heart of Christ, an offering. The most glamorous oblation.

Obviously, I don't pray. Instead, I recite to myself a story from Grethe's fairy tale book about the twin sisters who decided to create the universe. One sister is named Twin and the other is named Queen and they have an enormous pet, Wolf, who does their bidding. Wolf is so massive he can till the fields with one sweep of his giant paw and change the weather by breathing a cloud of hot air into a blizzard. To make the world, Queen has to kill both Wolf and herself. She does Wolf first, whose body she rests in a clearing of open grass. His colossal corpse transforms into the volcanoes, his blood into the rivers, his hair the forest, and from his skull come the heavens. To die, Queen lays down on a sort of altar created by lava. She points her feet to the south so that mankind will be rooted in the earth. She points her head to the north so that mankind will ascend to the heavens. She opens her arms to accept the blade Twin plunges through her heart, and as she feels each part of herself die, she assigns that part to a place in the cosmos: *and so my eyelashes shall be love, and so my fingernails shall be faith, and so my skin shall be warmth,* and so on until the world is finished. The story ends with Twin, alone, beholding the lake in which her reflection will always be that of Queen.

✦

Chancellor Lethe taught me that there were five reasons to perform a sacrifice. He had a presentation on the subject that included slides and a blackboard. On the blackboard, he wrote in red chalk:

1. *To maintain the cosmic order.*
He then projected a diagram of the cosmos, which looked like layers of stars palimpsested upon blueprints of a city palimpsested upon cartography. The word SEWER was next to JUPITER; MILKY WAY was beside CEMETERY, and so on.

"Sanitation and creation are equal on the spiritual plane," Chancellor Lethe opined. "All are interconnected in a synchronous tessellation. Often, there is overabundance, but there is never lack. In order to uphold order, we must sometimes perform a subtraction. Jessica, how do you make 2+2=5?"

"Subtract 1 from 5 so it equals 4."

"Correct." He then added to the blackboard in blue chalk:

2. *Ghosti
"Next slide," he said to the secretary controlling the projector.

An image of a sleeping servant girl was projected on-screen. A white vapor blushed from her body into the space around her, a glow wrapped in a fog.

"You should never forget that the word *host* is housed within the word *ghost*. Sacrifice is performed by one so that the other may survive, and so on, into perpetuity. *Do ut des*, and so forth." Chancellor Lethe turned to me and again asked, "Jessica, how do you make 2+2=5?"

"You collect the excess energy of the *equal to* symbol."

"And how do you know you've done it?"

"You don't."

"Very good. The asterisk indicates the word must never be spoken, but the math can still be done." Next, he wrote in yellow chalk:

3. *Evocatio*

He nodded his head to the back of the room and the image flipped to a grave blossoming with mushrooms, a hummingbird drinking from an open-mouthed flower engraved on the tomb.

"Although a less celebrated survival relationship than predation or parasitism, mutualism constitutes for forty-eight percent of life strategies amongst the terrestrial ecosystem. The grave provides the mushroom with carbohydrates and in return the mushroom provides the grave with nitrogen, phosphates. Jessica, how do you make 2+2=5?"

"You collect the extra energy from the plus symbol."

"And how do you know you've done it?"

"Prosperity endures."

"Something like that." He wrote:

4. *Ban of the Wolf*

The projector clicked to a hand-drawn image of three concentric circles. The first circle was made of golden bricks, the second circle was constructed of thick green leaves, and the third circle was a deep trace, a harsh lead etching in the paper.

Chancellor Lethe pointed to the golden circle. "This is what you know. Laws, rules, society."

He then pointed to the green circle. "This is what you know you do not know; the dark forest you can see but do not enter."

Lastly, he pointed to the trace. "And this is what you do not even know enough to imagine." He pressed his finger to the outside circle. I could see the tip of his finger go white from the pressure. "Everything that is now outside was once inside. I am saying that only what was once sacred can be sacrificed. Precisely because you are encircled, you have the power to live but you do not have the power to die.

"Jessica, how do you make 2+2=5?"

"Add a silent one."

He finally lifted his finger from the outer trace. A silver smudge of ink transferred from the transparency to his thumb and then on to the blue chalk he used to write the fifth reason:

5. Willow in the Wind

I sucked my breath in as the final image was projected on to the screen. It was the Yggdrasil, the Nordic Tree of Life from Grethe's book of folk tales. It must have been copied directly from Grethe's book because I recognized the smudge of my own thumb on the lower right corner. In this copy, the gatehouse, which led from the Upperworld to the Underworld, was on fire.

"Modern sacrifice takes new forms." Chancellor Lethe's voice softened. "Dreams, limbo competitions, Ambien, the storm that deprives an entire island of a species, but drops it off on the beach of a nearby continent. Your permanent condition is liminality. What you touch and feel and call the world is only a threshold. You accept this.

"You accept that sacrifice is not a *removal* from this world, but an *addition* to another. In this way, you dwell in bounty. Jessica, how do you make 2+2=5?"

"I believe in the proof."

The projector flipped off and its low hum sighed into silence. The crooked beam of the desert sun setting through stained glass cosseted us in a heavy light. The catechism was over, for now. It had happened so many times already.

Vaguely, I was aware that my family made its semiannual pilgrimage to Dr. Clink's alma mater so that my father could present his research to fellow scholars and my mother could sit in the alumni clubhouse and gossip with the other wives.

I don't know why Chancellor Lethe decided to mentor me. It was November of 1991 and I was eleven years old when I was first invited to his chambers. It looked a bit like the math classrooms at the university where my father taught, but instead of small plastic desks, there were leather and velvet couches. Instead of a clock affixed to the wall and kept secure behind a metal cage, there was a grandfather clock that had to be wound twice a day. The floors were a rich cherry oak and the walls were lined with bookshelves. There were thousands and thousands of books sectioned off by subject: COSMOLOGY, THE ANIMAL, DIVINATION, AFFECT, DISTANCE, HAGIOGRAPHY, THE MOON, EPISTEMOLOGY, ETHICS, MEMORY, ALIENATION, BEAUTY, BOREDOM. There was a single stained-glass window of an image Christine eventually told me depicted a tarot card called the Tower. Two people, a man and a woman, are shown suspended in mid-air outside a burning building. It is impossible to know if they have been thrown or if they jumped.

(Christine said that while the card seemed like an evil portent, a lot of the cards that you would guess were bad omens—the Death card, the Hermit—actually only indicated that change was coming. "Death is only another transition."

I nodded. "Sure."

"Drawing the Tower means you're about to break free of the patriarchy's fucked-up normative values. You get to be your own creator.")

Chancellor Lethe rarely left the underground campus. The wives speculated that he kept a cave of gold in a snake-infested part of the desert. Some people said he owned an island. Some said he had a ship big enough to live on for years without docking. Others claimed he was poaching experts from ROSCOSMOS, the Russian space program. Grethe said I should never tell Dr. Clink about the rumors.

Chancellor Lethe's lesson on sacrifice was repeated at odd intervals, but the first instance was right before Crystal suggested I should eliminate Veronica.

He sat across from me in the darkened room at the end of the lecture and took both my wrists in his hands, his thumbs on my pulse points, and looked me straight in the eye as he explained the etymology of the word *sacrifice*. "From the Latin, *sacrificus*. *Sacer* as in 'sacred' and *facere* as in 'to make, to do.' A sacrifice makes sacred the sacrificed. It is the permanent gift of *homo sacer*."

About a year after Veronica was sent away to Josephinum Academy of the Sacred Heart, a rumor traveled all the way back to her old high school and then to mine. People said she ran away and was living in a commune outside Portland. It was called the Fellowship for Utopic Being. The website said they only ate what they grew or found. I could see why it appealed to her, the grocer's daughter. The people in the photos looked thin and happy.

So what I'm saying is that if you still need to know why I did what I did to Veronica or if you want some communication of remorse, then your lens is too small. What I am telling you is an expression of a much larger vengeance.

I, too, thought it was about Veronica once.

Something in me glitched when my mother shrugged and agreed to let me quit the pageants.

What was Veronica sacrificed for, if not the pageants?

I walked into the basement and sat down in the wooden chair where I practiced mirroring.

I realized I didn't have to do it anymore.

Crystal would never again make me answer questions until I was trembling from hunger. I had already ripped off the last bathing suit glued to my ass with Elmer's.

I gathered up all my dresses and sashes and makeup. It took five trips to the trash. I stared at the now empty half of my bedroom and then walked over and lay down in it. I made a carpet angel and stared at the popcorn ceiling.

I looked at the space in my mind where all the monologues and answers and routines were stored. I emptied it out.

I thought of St. Francis surrounded by birds. Once I held a parakeet in my hand at the pet store that was so light it felt like there was nothing there at all. All heartbeat and no heart.

CHAPTER FIVE

I BECAME A PERV FOR OBLIVION AFTER THAT.

From 1994 to 1999, I remember little. A five-year dream in which I am certain of a few images: a neon orange paper bracelet hand-stamped with the words Club X that I had to cut off with a steak knife, the interior of a limousine, the oil smudge from my forehead lingering on an airplane window, a leather punching bag, a navy blue guestbook with a silver ribbon placeholder, the chime of a clock.

Memories require belief. There is nothing indirect or dreamy about what I am claiming. This is personal, between you and me. Identity is fundamentally unstable. Or maybe I mean that to believe in the idea of identity at all is to be unstable.

I mean a stain can be washed out, but those will always be the panties you bled through during assembly.

I have recall of all sorts of events: the bombing in Oklahoma City, the death of Princess Diana, the cloned sheep, the adulterous president, the two boys who massacred twelve classmates and a teacher before shooting themselves.

Those five years are like a strand of popcorn, each kernel distinct in itself. It's the string in between, the invisible ligature, which gives me chills.

The blank spaces began about a month after I quit the pageants.

First it was just a bad taste in my mouth. Bitter like the apple cider elixir Grethe served at her Tupperware parties. I wondered if I had been sleep-drinking the cloudy gold water. My mouth smelled strange, a sort of bad-good like a puppy's breath. I sniffed my toothbrush to confirm the stench, but I only smelled mint.

The first time I noticed the taste was November 9, 1994. Christine and me were standing in the living room, the television remote suspended in her hand. On the screen the long, white-tiled walkway of a Hollywood mansion surrounded by overgrown palmettos was flooded with blood. The walkway led to a gated threshold at the foot of which was strewn a twisted body covered in a digital fog.

The jury had just been sworn in for a murder trial that would not start for another three months. In lieu of actual news, the station replayed the violence.

"You shouldn't be watching this," Christine mumbled, but she didn't take her eyes from the screen. Obviously, though, I had seen it before. They were projecting pictures of the woman in life—blonde, tan, healthy—as the newswoman repeated that the body of Nicole Brown Simpson had been found slashed to death in her Brentwood home in June. The newswoman looked just like the murdered woman and the murdered woman looked just like Grethe and Grethe looked just like me. A photo appeared of the woman with one eye filled with blood, a purple and black bruise surrounding it, her eyebrow split like the seam of a peach.

"Jesus Christ," Christine said and we both sat down on the floor of the living room, a return to our automatic vigil.

Time passed, but the loop of the news, the figure eight that gave the illusion of forward progression—the body, the body of the blonde woman—made it impossible to know how long we watched what we already knew. The taste in my mouth was so strong it made me think of the stink of the *Ginkgo biloba* trees on the campus where Dr. Clink taught. They were ancient trees, he said, so old that dinosaurs once ate the buds and redistributed the seeds all over creation. "Six," he said, "survived the bombing of Hiroshima." He knew everything about catastrophe.

At some point I turned to Christine and leaned forward.

"Smell my breath," I said and exhaled like I was fogging a window.

"That's nasty," she remarked. "I'll bring you a yellow jasper. You can soak it in sunlight to solarize the stone and then gargle with it."

The next time I saw her, she brought me a smooth, goldenrod stone resting in the bottom of a bottle of Evian. I swished the water in my mouth, but nothing changed. I still woke up randomly with the sour taste on my tongue.

The next year, the day before my birthday, Nicole Brown Simpson's murderer was acquitted. I woke up with strange bruises.

The thing about being a teenager is that everything seems normal because nothing is normal. Over the course of the year, I often was jerked out of sleep by spasms in my calves that made my feet so rigid I couldn't walk. Grethe fed me a banana and a glass of water spiked with salt before bed because the doctor said the problem was potassium deficiency. My limbs grew so quickly that my dermis tore into perse lesions and left little scars that covered my upper thighs and the space between my bicep and armpit. I fainted if I stood for too long during choir practice. I sometimes cried at things I did not find very sad. Grethe said it was normal to feel like growing was dying. She said that when I was eighteen, I could start to sleep in the Gjentakelse Tvang. If the growing pains were still happening, the kryokammer would certainly stop them.

I became a little obsessed with sleeping in the Gjentakelse Tvang. I begged Grethe to let me nap in it to alleviate the pain for just a few hours, but she refused. She said she could lose her license as a

Gjentakelse Tvang therapist. I could remain frozen in the moment of trauma if I used the kryokammer prematurely.

"The literature states that the wound must be fully realized before it can heal," she said as she batted my hand away from a zit on my nose. "You aren't ready to recover."

My mother's response would have baffled me if I didn't believe I knew her so well. My natural aging depressed her in the way that only the mother in a mother-daughter pageant duo can be depressed by her daughter growing older. It seemed to me that with every growing pain I had, Grethe felt her own ache at moving away from her final pageant glory. She coped by, alternately, spending too long in the kryokammer—numbing out, forgetting—or moving more funds to the secret account.

By the time the bruises started appearing, I was so used to my body's revolt and so weary of my mother's odd behavior that I didn't even bother to tell anyone. They were usually oval shaped, the size of a very rich woman's wedding ring or a small rabbit's tail, and they appeared most often on the backs of my upper arms or the sides of my thighs. A few times, I woke up with hangnails. I read in a fashion magazine that this kind of thing could happen if you took too many anticoagulants and didn't drink enough water. I did take a lot of Advil—I was always sore—and I swallowed it with Orange Crush, never water. The disorder had a sort of cheerful name, Easy Aspirin Bruising, which made the idea of blood refusing to clot less alarming.

Sometimes the bruises looked familiar, like the marks the girls on the soccer team got. Ink-black and twilight-blue landscapes, the suburbs at sunset, spread across the expanse of my thigh.

I began a fumbling investigation to find out if I had been sleepwalking to the more brutal Night Games. I had never seen them, but I knew some of the other kids in my neighborhood gathered at a gazebo in the children's park to watch each other fight in a competition that had elaborate rules. This subset of Night Games called themselves the Dead Ringers because they put on white ski masks before entering the ring. It was important that you not know who you were fighting. It was an equalizing measure to prevent older kids from pulling punches on littler kids. I think it was also a way to equalize the sexes, erase gender. As much for the boys as for the girls.

Dead Ringers was repulsive to me. I was terrified of disfiguring myself—Crystal said a beautiful woman with a crooked nose is no longer beautiful—so it was impossible to believe that I would sleepwalk to that part of the neighborhood. There were all sorts of other bizarre things I might have done during Night Games: stolen lingerie from the drawers of sleeping mothers, eaten tubes of cookie dough until I vomited, gambled with Grethe's jewelry. After seeing the body of the blonde woman crumpled at the threshold of her own home, my reaction to violence on television had become severe. I memorized the times shows like *Homicide* and *Picket Fences* aired, and I flipped quickly over those channels on my way to MTV. If I saw a corpse, my mouth filled up with saliva and I curled my fingers inward until my nails left little crescents in the crease between my wrist and palm.

I had, I suppose, become as terrified as Grethe. Compulsively, I retraced her steps and checked cabinets and corners before bed. It was no more a choice than sneezing.

The first time I visited the Dead Ringers, it was October of '96. Heather Rich had been murdered in Oklahoma a week prior. If she had lived one day longer, we would both have been sixteen. In the portrait they showed of her on the news, she wore a loose red cheerleader's uniform.

The air that night was already supersaturated with cold crystals. Gritty and moist and hard on the blood. Kids were blowing tubes of steam into the air and into each other's faces, the harbinger of an early winter.

I stood at the edge of a group of about ten kids, far enough away from the gazebo that the splatter wouldn't reach me. I heard there would be blood.

I was the only one there without a mask on, but I had a vague sense of who a lot of the others were. A lock of red hair slipping from the back of her ski mask betrayed Gabbi Thompson. Mark Westfield's sheer height stood out. The butt of Angela Ricco was distinguishable even in sweatpants.

Mark passed our house every day when he walked his family's elderly Lhasa Apso, Sprinkles. Sprinkles was slow and shaped like a mop's head, so Mark was slow, too, and carefully guided her away from puddles. He was seventeen and way over six feet tall, so watching him bend over to pick up after Sprinkles made him seem kind. I was pretty surprised to see him at Dead Ringers.

"Hey," I said, my arms crossed tightly over my chest and my teeth chattering.

If he was surprised to see me, too, I couldn't tell.

"What's up, Jessica? You here to play? You gotta wear a mask."

"No, no. Just here to watch."

"Cool. Cool. Not a lot of 'watchers.' I've got an extra mask if you want to join."

Two kids were walking into the gazebo. Someone I couldn't identify stood in the middle holding a buzzer from the board game Taboo.

"What's with the buzzer?" I asked Mark.

"We buzz to start and stop the fight. If you start before or end after, you're banned."

"Are you fighting tonight?"

"Already did." He held out his hands so that I could see his bloody knuckles. "Didn't win. That guy did."

He gestured to the gazebo, where a broad-shouldered figure was stretching his shoulders.

"Is that Devon Clark?" Devon was a football player who had already gotten his early acceptance to a Big Ten school on a full scholarship. I had Sociology with him. His backpack rustled with the empty husks of Snickers wrappers as he walked down the hall.

"Don't know, don't ask," Mark said. People said this now, instead of *I don't care.* "All I know is he beat me and gets to keep playing."

The buzzer trilled and Devon lurched toward a much smaller boy. He was wiry and under six feet, his posture slightly crumpled.

Devon's feet dragged a little. He was clearly exhausted.

"How many fights has he been in tonight?" I asked.

"This is his fourth. I've never seen anybody make it past four."

The other kid in the gazebo made a sort of duck's bill shape with his hand and jabbed Devon in the space between his jaw and neck. As Devon stumbled back, curled in on himself, the kid swung his leg back and swiveled with enough velocity to knock Devon off his feet. The boy had to be Joe Keller. He was a grade below me, but it was common knowledge that his favorite movie of all time was *Road House.*

"Is that fair?"

"Everything is fair." Mark shrugged. "Oh, except, like, weapons," he amended.

Joe moved in on Devon, who was curled like an embryo on the gazebo floor. The buzzer sounded. The other kids howled and clapped. Angela walked into the ring to help Devon up.

"Closing time," the kid with the buzzer yelled. A few people booed.

"We stop at midnight on school nights," Mark explained. "Think you'll get in it next time?"

I realized I had been howling with everyone else. I could see the blood on Devon's gums.

"Actually," I paused. No one at all knew about the sleepwalking, not even Christine. I was aware somnambulistic activity was a known sign of insanity. I was afraid that if Chancellor Lethe found out, he would cancel our sessions. I saw no other choice, though, and so I simply asked, "Do you think you've ever seen me here before?"

We were walking out of the park now, careful to stay outside the circlets of light that spilled from the streetlamps. Mark pulled off his mask and looked me up and down. I was wearing a khaki miniskirt from the Gap with thick wool tights and a black puffy coat. My hair was curled.

"In a mask," I clarified, "Like, have you ever seen me . . . fight?"

He shrugged again. "Dude, if you were wearing a mask, how would I know?"

"Have you seen anyone you might guess could be me?" I persisted.

"Sure. The drill team and the cheerleaders both come to haze the new girls every fall. A lot of them coulda been you."

I nodded. He was right.

"Most of those girls are afraid of getting hurt or getting their face messed up. It's easier to tell a bad fighter apart from another bad fighter, because the technique is usually pretty weird. Everybody punches the right way about the same, but most people punch the wrong way different."

"I don't know how to punch at all," I said.

"Well, if I saw you try, I could probably tell you if you've been here before." We had arrived at the turn off to his cul de sac. "See you," he said. I watched as he jogged lightly over his lawn and used one hand to jump the fence.

I ran my tongue over my teeth and thought about what it would feel like if they met a fist. I thought of snapping a wishbone.

I couldn't fight, obviously.

I lay in bed that night trying to think of ways I could find out if I had been to Dead Ringers, but came up with nothing. Mark was right—no one could tell me from the drill team girls.

The sky outside my window was the color of wet paper, moonless and plump with clouds. I listened to the house hum softly, the syncopated drones of the air vents and refrigerator at odds with the arrhythmic gurgle of the pipes.

If a midwestern night sky is saturated with enough ice, the atmosphere will perform a sort of inverse reflection. The suburb lamps and city lights will reflect back from the crystals in the clouds. They burn and melt as the sun rises. The blackest moment of the night is right before the sun rises.

Downstairs, the Gjentakelse Tvang clicked open like a can of beer. It must have been 5:00 a.m. Grethe's slippered feet made no noise as she moved around the house.

She would be up to wake me in two hours. Experimentally, I punched my pillow. It was unsatisfying. I lay my head down in the divot. I must have fallen asleep, because when Grethe woke me a few hours later, I felt new bruises forming on my neck. They were getting worse.

That night I found a jump rope in the garage, attached it to a post on my bed, and tied it to my ankle. For several weeks, this seemed to work. I stopped waking up to disarranged drawers or bruises or odd tastes. Sometime near Halloween, I began to sleep through the night. On the night Bill Clinton was reelected to the presidency, I was well rested.

Of course, I did not give a shit about politics—I remember the exact day because it was the rare instance in which strangers were permitted entrance into our home for Dr. Clink's election party. I spent my after-school time that Tuesday helping Grethe decorate the house with red, white, and blue confetti and blowing up balloons that would drift around the house until they shriveled and were thrown out in preparation for Thanksgiving dinner. Dr. Clink was confident Clinton would win; we hung a victory banner before the polls even closed.

Around midnight, I was still sitting on the bench of our grand piano, drinking cider and reciting the Bill of Rights for rotating groups of drunk professors. Grethe told me it was time for bed and for the first time in a long time, I thought, *But I'm not tired.*

Thanksgiving came and went. We threw out the balloons and ate lingonberry jam instead of cranberry sauce.

I got better.

An entire year passed.

And then in December of '97, I woke up on top of my covers, the jump rope gone. There were gashes on my knees and palms like I had been crawling through gravel.

The problem with the aphorism *It's always darkest before the dawn* is that it presumes one knows how dark it can get. It assumes survival.

At the bottom of my closet was a ski mask from a trip to Colorado.

I took it out and placed it on my vanity, right where a white satin sash used to hang. That weekend I would go to Dead Ringers.

It was the first Friday night of winter break.

Forecasters were frenzied about the snowiest winter on record. The city had already run out of salt for the roads. A ban was placed on parking on the left side of the street that would not be lifted until March 1.

This is all to say that the children's park had not been plowed. A narrow path had been dug out with a stolen snow shovel. The gazebo was entrenched in a hollow of frozen snow, lit with beams of bouncing artificial light.

The snow muffled the sound of the gathering crowd. There were at least three times as many kids there as the last time. I didn't recognize a lot of them. It was possible they were prep school kids, home for break. Some of them wore the industrial Carhartt jackets I had seen on truckers and farmers. I wondered if the rumors about Dead Ringers had traveled all the way to the farm towns outside the city.

The snow packed edge of the circle of people was splattered with blood. I thought of the famous painting at the entrance of the Art Institute I visited with Dr. Clink and Grethe every year. The blood patterns looked like the Pollock that Pollock would have painted if he were demented instead of drunk. I thought, for a hovering second, of Lorena Bobbitt and the attendant blood spatter analyst. Perhaps he regarded her as a sort of abstract miniaturist.

I found Mark towering over the disguised crowd. He had run away from home the spring before and was now repeating senior year.

Chancellor Lethe once lectured me on masks. It was common, he said, to fear a person in a mask. In fact, maskaphobia is a normal stage in childhood development. "To be deprived of basic knowledge about a person's facial musculature, to be uncertain of the origins of a human voice; this is to experience horror," he explained.

He proceeded to extol the virtues of wearing a veil myself. "If you are ever kidnapped, your attacker will place a hood over your head. In all likelihood, he will use a sensory deprivation kit—an eye mask, duct tape, and noise-diminishing headphones—even before he places the hood over your head. This does not place you at a disadvantage, necessarily. It grants you access to your alien nature. Remember that the great anthropologist Claude Lévi-Strauss once said, 'The mask serves as the medium for men to enter into relations with the supernatural world.'"

Regardless, I felt uneasy in the crowd. "Hey, it's me!" I said.

Mark looked at me blankly.

"Jessica!" I threw my hands open like I imagined I might if I ever had a blind date. My generation was obsessed with blind dates.

"Dude, shut up," Mark said, "You're wearing a mask so people *don't* know it's—" he paused and recalculated, "You know, *you*."

He meant I was an easy target. I had gelled my hair with a tub of L.A. Looks and pinned it carefully, the way I did before putting on a wig in the pageants, so that it would be impossible for my opponent to use my hair to pull me down. I also wore my dance leotard, Danskin tights, and leg warmers underneath a thin snowsuit. Room at the joints to maneuver, but enough layers to pad a punch.

I made eye contact with half a dozen people—I had blacked out my own eyes with a tube of Wet n Wild MegaLiner so that in the white mask I looked like an insane panda—and saw no click of recognition. I was, I realized, actually anonymous. I felt the tiny muscles around my rib cage relaxing. The extra oxygen in my lungs billowed out of me as I exhaled into the arctic air. My arms swung a little more than usual as I walked over to a girl who was obviously Brenda McCarthy from my gym class. The eyebrows she had shaved off and penciled back on to look like Drew Barrymore peeked out of her eyeholes.

Like many girls at school, Brenda hated me. Grethe said they were all jealous, but it seemed to me to be something deeper. Brenda actually once spent her time scratching her complaints against me into a bathroom door. It struck me as a particularly deranged crime—to bring a tool sharp enough to scratch iron to perform an act of slander all alone, witnessless. I knew she had done it because she told me so. She said she used her protractor. If anyone would recognize me here, it would be her.

"Hey." I heard a voice come out of my mouth, but I did not recognize it. It was lower and slower, a bit fried at the edges like burnt toast dipped in honey. I sounded a little like Christine.

"Hey," Brenda responded.

She had no idea it was me. I felt my teeth unclench and my tongue fall into the basin of my mouth.

Yells echoed in the hollowed snow and I felt a sense of tranquility befall me. The sensation took the same route as a sip of stolen cognac, through my throat and stomach straight into the blood, hot.

"Next," the kid with the buzzer yelled from the gazebo.

I watched as my hand reached out and wrapped itself around Brenda's. She wore no gloves and her nails were arsenic green.

We were walking into the gazebo. A velvet curtain of human noise surrounded us.

The boy with the buzzer spoke at us and Brenda and me removed our snow boots. We stood about four feet apart; Brenda tilted slightly back, her weight on the heels of her feet and her arms in tight fists in front of her.

This is the part of the story where I levitate.

From the rafters of the gazebo, I watched as Jessica dropped to the ground and swung one leg out to catch Brenda's heel. *Charlie Chaplin*, I thought, as I watched Brenda fall flatly on her back, her head banging against the wood, her feet slung momentarily into the air.

Jessica advanced, lifted her foot above Brenda's fingers, and the buzzer trilled.

Brenda rolled out of the ring and staggered to the sidelines.

Jessica stood in the center of the ring, rolling her neck from side to side and lightly shifting weight from one foot to the other. She spat. She was at ease, breathing lightly, her brow dry.

Scott Ricci was getting into the gazebo. He was one of those sullen boys who got to school an hour early to use the gym's weight room and listen to bizarre mix CD compilations of Marilyn Manson, Ozzy Osborne, and Savage Garden on a boom box. At the age of sixteen, thick black hairs blanketed his entire body.

Jessica took a few steps closer to the edge of the gazebo. Her forearms were at a tight vertical from the elbow in parallel to her chest, her right fist slightly above the left and her body hunched forward just a bit.

Scott walked toward her, his arms held loosely at his sides. She danced into the ring at an angle.

He lifted his arms to fight and as he tried to pivot on one heavy heel, Jessica jetéd forward and slapped him, open handed, on the ear. He recoiled, and in this moment of hesitation, Jessica threw a closed punch to his nose. It streamed like a drinking fountain as Scott lunged at her. He pulled back his left arm, keeping it low to land on her exposed solar plexus. Mid-punch, she curled her body back and threw all her weight into a blow to Scott's right temple. Her body hung for a second in the air like an apostrophe, a hinge between worlds.

Scott crumpled.

The buzzer sounded.

And it kept sounding for another hour, kids climbing into the gazebo and then crawling back out. Jessica was loose on her feet, calm, even laughing. She declined a shot of Everclear. She lifted a foot over her head to stretch her hamstring. She joined in with the crowd between fights to sing a spontaneous chorus of a Backstreet Boys song. She won six fights before she decided to stop.

As I hovered behind her as she walked out of the park, I thought of the moment in *Peter Pan* when Pan has to sew his shadow back to his own feet and I wondered if I would have to wait until Jessica was asleep to paste my soles to hers.

"Hey! Hey." It was Mark. "Wait up!"

Jessica turned to face him and they both pulled their masks off. "Hey."

"Dude, that was fucking crazy." He was out of breath, eyes wild. "You know no one has ever done that, right?"

She shook her head. "Which part?"

"I mean, all of it. You beat the record. Jesus, dude, how did you do that?"

How do you do it? I heard Veronica whisper in my left ear. The levitation ceased; I dropped back in.

I shook my head. "I don't know."

I felt empty, like I was nothing but opening. Why was I here? I looked at the crusted blood on my knuckles.

"Mark, was it me?" I remembered. I was here to find out about the bruises.

Mark looked confused, "Yeah, duh."

"No, I mean—have you seen me here before?" I was clutching his upper arm.

He backed away and held his hands up, palms facing me. "No way. I've never seen that here before." He retreated quickly. "I've never seen that *anywhere*."

On my way home, I slipped between the chain-link fence and gate to the high school stadium and sat up high in the snow-covered bleachers above the field. It was a perfect oval of uncracked snow, oblivion made manifest. Dr. Clink believed oblivion and boredom were sister affects. He devoted an entire lecture to his critique of Plutchik's Wheel of Emotions, which he claimed did not accurately understand boredom. The Wheel looked a bit like a mandala, petals overlapping other petals and blooming out into the universe.

Boredom unfurled from the branch of loathing, while pensiveness unfurled from the branch of grief, which were connected by an intermediary emotion: sadness. Dr. Clink said this was the critical error—it was not sadness that linked the two, but shock. The freezing that occurs in the moment of unrecorded melancholy. I considered etching the Wheel in the snow, but I didn't want to leave a trace.

I stared vacantly at the high school and mentally walked down the corridors to the east wing bathroom's last stall and stood there looking at what Brenda, in her own boredom, had written about me: JESSICA CLINK IS A PSYCHO LESBIAN.

My hands were numb. I reached up to touch my numb cheek. I didn't feel anything.

CHAPTER SIX

I MUST HAVE GRADUATED FROM HIGH SCHOOL SIX MONTHS after that. I have seen the certificate of completion in Dr. Clink's files, so surely it happened.

A letter came in the mail telling me *congratulations*; I was accepted to the Midwestern University. I don't remember applying and I don't remember choosing the batch of courses I had to buy books for at the college store in August of 1998. They seemed to be courses selected by someone else, Christine maybe: Gender Studies 101, World Systems Analysis, Eastern Philosophy and the Female Body, Introduction to Clinical Psychology.

But I do remember a dream I had again and again.

I am standing on a dark stage looking at an auditorium full of girls in tulle and silk and sequined dresses. They stand on the theater's Victorian red seats, their pumps pushing into the fake velvet. Each girl has her own spotlight. There are hundreds and hundreds of spotlights. On stage, I am singing as if I am performing, but no sound is coming out of my mouth. The girls, in unison, begin to rise to their tiptoes. They hover en pointe, faces wan beneath their blusher.

And then they keep rising, hovering in their spotlights. A door opens in the back of the house and a beam of light from the white lobby glints across the thousand thin threads suspending the girls: fishing wire, garroted around their necks.

The hems of their dresses droop like black, wet tulips as they twist in the auditorium.

The silence of my singing intensifies as a silhouette in the opened doorway steps into the light. It's Grethe. She looks past the hanging girls, straight into the blackened stage where I stand.

Through the darkness, we make eye contact and she lifts one finger, touches it to her lips.

Shhhhh.

CHAPTER SEVEN

IN THE SUMMER OF '98, I REMEMBER DR. CLINK SITTING AT his desk, vigorously speaking into his old black rotary phone, saying things like *request a revise and resubmit* or *find out who put it into production* or *organize an emergency colloquium at Camp Oublier* or *make sure that doesn't get to press*. The cord of his telephone was specially ordered from an office supply shop. It was a thirty-foot-long rubber spiral, a black Möbius from his mouth to the world. He had his own line installed, so that his calls went directly to him without interception from Grethe, or, I suppose, me.

He was finishing an important issue of the academic journal he had recently founded, *Boredom and Behavior in the New Millennium*.

The wood-paneled walls of his office were papered over with mockups of the articles various scholars around the world had submitted. They all had long, tedious titles like "Cognitive Saturation and Boredom: A Study on Life Quality in the Information Age" or "*Pater Peccavi*: Tedium as Penance in Modern Religious Societies." The essays ranged widely in scope, but from what I could gather during my walk from the office doorway to the desk (a journey I made once a day to kiss Dr. Clink goodnight), they all addressed new possibilities for harnessing boredom in response to the modern condition.

The modern condition, put simply, was the Internet.

My favorite thing about the Internet in the late '90s was the silver

CD-ROM discs AOL littered all over America. Christine hoarded them to use as postmodern coasters, but eventually her project expanded into a collection of sharp, metallic ball gowns made of polycarbonate plastic dipped in aluminum. She rented a gallery space in a dark warehouse downtown and held a fashion show titled Viral//Sick of Fashion. Girls from her art school floated around the gallery wearing surgical facemasks with a red X taped over the mouth. They handed visitors a printed-out email from an AOL account that was basically a bunch of copy-pasted text from online encyclopedias about labor practices in the haute couture fashion world spliced with newspaper articles about worker exploitation at overseas software manufacturing companies. There were lines like:

THIS SEASON, PRET-A-PORTER ASBESTOSIS IS ON THE RISE

I was allowed to go to the show even though cans of PBR were served. The first time I would ever enter University Photography & Art Supply would be to pass through the shop after hours on my way to the flight of steps that led to the gallery above it, which was basically just an empty room. Christine had invited me to "walk" as a model in the show she was holding there. She instructed me and the other girls to cough like we had consumption as we maneuvered the runway.

The next day, I went to the public library and looked consumption up in the encyclopedia. There was a wonderful photo in Bartleby's of about thirty schoolboys wearing stocking hats and scarves and lounging in lawn chairs on the green of a hospital. *Boys in recovery*, the caption read.

While Grethe ran errands, I retreated to the basement to practice my cough, which I had read should be "wet and racking."

We loved models in the '90s; in general, I think we loved things that seemed like they were about to vanish: Kate Moss's body, morality, the century itself. So that summer, I subscribed to a magazine called *Top Model*. It was a simple accrual of the excess of every other women's magazine: stuff about numerology, eating like a famous person, buying everything. In short, it was aspirational, not informational. There was no craft to it.

Even Christine had never heard of the magazine. And it's true, it wasn't popular—I had to lean over to the very bottom shelf at Barnes & Noble to pick out my copy. They stocked it between issues of French and Italian *Vogue*.

Claudia and Cindy and Linda and Kate looked like European museums shut down for the night: vacant and highly structured. When I attempted to mimic their slack jaw and drooping bottom lip in a family photo, Dr. Clink told me I looked "like a gormless infant."

"This looks like the official literature of the Joy Division," Christine remarked when I spread the magazines out across my bedroom floor for her to peruse.

I picked up an issue with Karen Mulder on the cover and held it to my chest. Karen was my favorite; I considered her under-sung.

"What do you mean?" I asked Christine for perhaps the millionth time in our relationship.

"*Freudenabteilungen.* Nazi stuff," she said. "I know your dad made you take AP Euro."

I nodded, he had. But, of course, I knew what a Nazi was aside from that. We had read *The Diary of Anne Frank* in junior high. Obviously, I was obsessed with Anne. In one of our dearest father-daughter exchanges, Dr. Clink pulled a stack of books on the Holocaust from his own library, leaving a gap like a lost tooth in the otherwise over-stuffed mouth of shelves, and gave it to me.

"The Holocaust," he explained, "is extremely important to Boredom Studies."

So certain was I that I had already intuited his meaning that I did not bother to ask him why. (Or, perhaps, I didn't want to know what he meant. Dr. Clink omitted many details, but when asked about a subject directly he did not lie. He was, in his old-world way, honorable.)

"I know about the methods of the Third Reich," I responded to Christine, importantly.

She raised her eyebrows. "That woman on your magazine looks like Hitler's mistress."

My eyes widened—I apologize ahead of myself here—in indignation.

"Karen Mulder is much more beautiful than Eva Braun!"

"Chill out," she said, her voice calm as she explained. "The Joy Division was a group of beautiful blonde German women that Hitler picked out specially to promulgate the Aryan race because they had, like, perfect genes."

"Promulgate?"

Christine taught me lots of words: hegemony, objectification, abjectification, aporia, subaltern, alterity, mimicry, androcentrism, homonormativity, and so on. Her speech had the same effect as, say, seeing a Degas crumpled in a trashcan: it was a beautiful thing framed by filth, articulation surrounded by slang. It has taken me my life to understand this was a choice.

"'Perfect' German men had sex with the women in the Joy Division and they were supposed to have a bunch of kids. The women raised the babies in a special facility."

"What happened to the men?"

She shrugged. "Who cares?"

I was quiet for the rest of the afternoon. I could not have told you why what Christine said disturbed me so much. It was no worse than anything else I had read about the Holocaust, and in some ways, I thought, it was more innocent. It was an act of creation, at least.

The next time Christine came over, she waited until my parents were gone and then pulled an immaculate white CD case out of her purse. The word CLOSER hovered above a black-and-white photograph of a tomb composed of layers and layers of cement drapery and stone hydrangeas. At first, all I saw were the waves of white stone. The composition of this image impressed me so much that over a year later, developing photographs at University Photography, I continued to think about the light in this picture; the way it perverted the image so that the eye couldn't adjust at first, like a puzzle on the back of a cereal box. Maybe I was five years old, or even younger, when Dr. Clink caught me looking at a box of Cinnamon Toast Crunch and explained that optical illusions work because the brain wants, more than anything, to make sense of oblivion.

So when I first saw the cover of *Closer*, I thought it was a statue of drapes and flowers; Grethe's parlor. Then my eyes adjusted to the chiaroscuro silhouettes and I realized there was also a man, kneeling in front of a slab of concrete. And finally the body, so saturated in light it was almost erasured from the photo, of the dead woman the man was mourning.

Christine handed me the CD solemnly, "This," she said, "is *also* Joy Division."

She explained that they were a band from Manchester and that most people thought they were Nazi sympathizers because of their name, but that was only because most people are dull and incurious. "Pedestrian," Christine said. In reality, they had named themselves Joy Division because all of their fathers had fought in the Second World War.

"It's not a *tribute*," Christine said, rolling her eyes, "to their dads or anything. It's, just, like, an acknowledgment of the way the past is connected to the present. I mean, their point is that experience is hereditary. They're post-punk."

I was in awe; I yearned to be "post-" anything.

Silently, Christine put the disc in my boom box. We sat next to each other on my bedroom floor, our backs against my bed, and listened. Sometimes, I thought it sounded like the instruments were committing suicide, and sometimes I thought it sounded like they were deciding to live. Some of them shrieked and burned, but there was always at least one sound like a heartbeat underlying it all; discordant and efficient as a mob. The lead singer's voice was flat, his mouth so close to the microphone and then suddenly so far away.

This is the way, step inside, he repeated again and again. A broadcast from a radio at the bottom of the ocean. I thought of Dr. Clink blinking his headlights in series of dots and dashes against the house, his way of saying *Goodnight, I love you*.

"Listen," Christine said, "it's bullshit if anyone tries to tell you that you have to suffer to create art, and that isn't what I'm trying to tell you right now. But you should know suffering can sometimes— not much of the time—become great art." She turned and looked me in the eye.

I had seen many emotions cross her face, but never this one, never tenderness.

"You don't have to understand who you are or why you are that way to be an artist, Jessica. You don't even have to tell people how it feels. What you have to do is make them feel the feeling."

She glanced at my stack of magazines. "My point is, don't push your self away from yourself."

We talked about the lead singer of Joy Division, about how he had seizures he couldn't control and how instead of quitting, he made the part of himself he wasn't even there for a part of his art. Christine told me I didn't have to control everything to understand everything. She said the context was always larger than the content. She said when new beauty arrives, it is always ugly because it is alien and that if I found out I was alien, my art would be teaching people how to see me.

Later that night, we made brownies from a Duncan Hines mix and she asked me to walk in her fashion show.

Telling you this now, I realize that was the best night. That was the best night I can remember from '94 through '99.

I practiced very hard for the show. Since quitting the pageants, my mind had become an empty ballroom.

The competitions were gone, yet I was still compelled to exert the energy of the child beauty queen. It was as if I had once grown an arm out of the middle of my back, useless and aberrant, and now that it was removed I could feel it grasping; a phantom limb, vestige of a vestige.

I devoted my freakish energy to modeling in Christine's show, and when the night finally arrived, I walked so perfectly, I so embodied the grace and pathos of Christine's project, that I did not even need to ask anyone if I had done a good job. As I walked down the runway, I felt the heavy aluminum dress sway in perfect meter. For the first time in my life I experienced the deep satisfaction of realizing a vision.

It was a private gratification, like kissing yourself in a dream.

After the show I walked around the gallery and ate Brie served with Ritz crackers from a little paper plate and let people ask me how it felt to wear the dress. Was it heavy? *Yes.* Did it hurt? *A little.*

They also wanted to know what it was like to know Christine, which surprised me. Girls just a little older than me—undergraduates at the art school with pale skin and black hair and piercings and fish-netted stockings—asked reverential questions about her. Is it true she never sleeps? *I doubt it.* Does she really only eat flowers and blood? *No. She likes Twix.*

I didn't have the language to tell them what Christine was really like, and so I circled around the room listening to different conversations and receiving compliments until 11:00 p.m., the time I had promised Grethe I would return home.

I couldn't find Christine anywhere to help remove my dress, so I went into the dressing room (really just a sheet nailed to the corner of the room next to the exit to the balcony) and carefully tried to wriggle myself out of the silver cascade of software.

It was dark and smelled of cigarettes drifting in from the balcony door, which had been propped opened with a phonebook. From behind the sheet, I heard Christine's laugh fill the room as she walked back into the gallery.

I was about to call for assistance—I was stuck in the dress—when I heard her say, "Yeah, teen beauty queen."

I froze with my mouth open.

"She's basically like what would happen if Barbie and Dr. Strangelove had a lovechild." The girls with Christine laughed.

"Her dad teaches at the University, right? That creepy course UISHR keeps trying to ban?" asked one of the girls.

She pronounced the acronym like "you sure," and I knew from overhearing some of Dr. Clink's phone calls that she meant the college's student-run human rights organization.

"Oh my *god.* I went on a date," I could tell from the way the girl speaking paused before and after the word *date* that she had held her hands up and stiffened her fingers to create a sort of bony punctuation, "with his teaching assistant and he told me some crazy shit about these, you know, unauthorized experiments her dad does. On *humans.*"

"For real?" a third voice asked, as though astonished. I assumed she was scandalized by the idea of unauthorized experiments on humans, but she clarified, "You went out with that guy?"

"Well, we had drinks. Have you ever tried Fernet-Branca?"

This tiny detail confirmed that this girl had indeed gone out with my father's pervy TA, Jeffrey. His breath was often rank with the medicinal Italian liquor, which he once told me was "so much more refined than absinthe." I tried a sip of it from the rattan bar cart my parents kept fully stocked for their occasional social events. The Fernet-Branca was vile, herbal, and earthly. Grethe smelled it on my breath the next morning, and in a rare fit of motherly instinct, she forbade me from being alone with Jeffrey or wearing my pajamas without a robe when he was over. I had, many times, walked around the house in a hideous pair of size XXS Joe Boxer men's briefs and a Mandy Moore concert tee in his presence.

"Ew, no," Christine replied.

"I can't believe you went out with him," said the third voice, still scandalized.

"Why? He's smart. He got a Fulbright to Norway when he was only, like, twenty-two."

"I just think his vibes are a little . . . you know, Polanski."

"Well, I didn't go out with him again. Anyway, I was just trying to say that he told me that girl's dad gets university funds for these fucked-up experiments. Supposedly he has this chamber that he locks his subjects in until they go crazy. The Greenblatt Method or something."

"Greenglass. Yeah, I've heard he's like, a *fascist*." The friend was ready to let the date with Jeffrey drop, apparently.

"You don't even know what a fascist is, Lenore," Christine cut in quickly. "Anyway, he isn't one. He's just . . . certifiable."

The other girls laughed and their voices melded into the crowd.

Certifiable. I had always thought Christine respected Dr. Clink, and although I myself often found him eccentric and a little absurd, it embarrassed me that Christine thought so, too.

It was true that Dr. Clink's comportment had become increasingly bombastic as the summer of '98 wore on. He installed an intercom in the house so that he could speak to Grethe and me without getting up from his desk. He became mistrustful of his octopus, who he had come to believe was *too* intelligent. He frequently had Jeffrey LaPlant over to check the house for wiretaps because he was paranoid that the articles he was publishing in *Boredom Studies* would be poached by a better university. In particular, he was suspicious of an Ivy League institution that I knew Chancellor Lethe had been expelled from in the 1960s. Dr. Clink said they were desperate to discredit the Chancellor's intellectual contributions.

"The Chancellor is becoming too powerful for them," I heard him hiss into the telephone in late July.

We had only one television and it was in the den that Dr. Clink's office adjoined, so I frequently heard oddments of conversation as the door opened and closed. As I've mentioned, I was in the liminal space between high school and college that summer and I could imagine nothing to do aside from preparing for Christine's show and watching TV, so I was often outside my father's office.

Mostly, I watched MTV. Britney and Christina and Jessica videos aired again and again until they became soothing ritual chants. Often, though, in the summer of '98, even the white noise of MTV was interrupted by Kurt Loder or Matt Pinfield talking about the president's scandal or the sentencing of the Oklahoma City bombers. I heard the words "Catholic Sex Abuse Scandal" and "al-Qaeda" for the first time and was astonished. This feeling would dull over time from a sharp electric current to a numb thumb pressed to the fat of the thigh.

Spliced in between news reports of fresh catastrophe was the voice of my father. By the day I was set to move into the campus dorms, Dr. Clink's frenzy neared hysteria. I recall sitting on the couch in between my packed suitcases, watching as the president announced Operation Infinite Reach and declared his intention to send cruise missiles to embassies in Sudan and Afghanistan, and hearing Dr. Clink's voice rise to a scream through the door of his office.

"Halt immediately," I heard him yell, "halt the publication!"

Grethe appeared before me holding the keys to the car and a plastic bucket filled with things I would use in the dorm shower: flip-flops, body gel, shampoo, a loofah.

"Your father won't be able to drop you off at the dorms as we planned," she explained. "So we should leave now."

I felt oddly saddened. I nodded and did not ask if I could say goodbye.

I hope you never have to live in a small space with other girls.

My dormitory was called Mayflower. It was famous on campus because in the 1970s three freshmen jumped off the roof.

The RAs insisted on calling it a Residence Hall because it was partially owned by a private law firm. They had erected the thirteen-story brick box in the 1960s and put a pool in the basement and a piano in the lobby. It was, I realize now, the college's luxury dorm.

Mayflower was set slightly off campus, and we had our own dining room and shuttle service to the quadrangle, the skyline of which we could see across the river. At any given moment between the hours of 6:00 a.m. and 10:00 p.m., a group of girls huddled at the foot of Mayflower's wedding cake steps in their L.L.Bean or J.Crew catalogue-ordered coats and waited to get a three-quarter mile ride to the heart of campus.

Usually, I walked. Riding the bus made me feel like I was in one of those truckfuls of nurses you see get dropped off on an army base for a wartime dance. There was a certain musk on the girls from Mayflower. The smell of expensive shampoo, perfect hygiene, and a hormonal compound that had never been exposed to stress, that did not over-emit the sour-baby scent of cortisol-drenched sweat on cheap fabric. Mayflower girls were pure privilege.

Mostly, though, I avoided the bus and its Mayflower stop because its particular vantage point forced me to look across the river and down at the very top of the Performing Arts Building, where I knew watt upon watt of light shone into the black box theater below. It always made me think of how I was looking at the same sight those girls had seen before they jumped. It was hard to reconcile the college's tidy sublimity with an act so reckless and uninspired.

I hope you've noticed by now that this is a story, at worst, about preservation and, at best, about creation. What I have to tell you is as anti-death as any ghost.

The idea of suicide repulsed me physically. Capillaries burst in my chest into peony-shaped blooms when my Clinical Psych professor discussed abnormality and suicidal ideation. I itched until the teaching assistant pulled me out of class and sent me to the University Health Center, where they told me I had hives, gave me a hot pink Benadryl, and instructed me to take a nap.

The other girls at Mayflower were infatuated with the triple suicide. They were like red roses with white worms rotting inside of them. As Halloween neared, they put on expensive sweats from a lingerie store in the mall—words like PINK or JUICY were written on the ass of each of their outfits in a glitter crust—and sat in the common area to discuss their plans for the dorm's haunted house. Between mouthfuls of salt-less popcorn, they speculated whether or not the girls had been holding hands when they jumped. The apparitions they had seen on their way to the bathroom at night were always alone, headed to the roof. It was passé to deny the existence of ghosts at Mayflower. I couldn't tolerate their trips to secondhand stores to buy Halloween costume supplies: the bellbottoms and flower crowns they hoped the girls were wearing when they jumped. They even made arrangements to drive to the mall in the next town and buy a Ouija board.

By midterm, my favorite thing to do on Friday after my last class was sneak into the dorm through the service entrance, pick the lock of the laundry room specially used for washing our towels and sheets, and spend the whole night lying on top of piles of flatly folded bedding. I would bring my Walkman so I could listen to the mix CDs Christine gave me before I left for school.

I wasn't the only depressed girl in Mayflower. There were so many of us it seemed normal. This was something I learned from Intro to Clinical Psych: abnormal versus normal behavior is mostly defined by context. Other girls did much stranger things. They would sleep on the floor of their closets or hoard perishable food under their beds. Sometimes they were sent for a psych screening at the Health Center, where a nurse inspected their bodies for self-harm and made them answer questions about their sexual history.

Comparatively, I was highly functioning.

Also, I had a patch at the base of my skull that I compulsively rubbed. The skin was raw, a thumb-sized blood crater. I knew I should hide it, especially from a college nurse.

But this was my only injury! The sleepwalking had stopped entirely and I was well rested, healthy even. Holistically, my life had improved a great deal since moving out of my parents' house. One of my most distinct memories of college is of the Sunday afternoon my roommate, Jane, looked up from a biology textbook, watched me flip the pages of a magazine and said, "Jessie, you're just so *lucky.*"

Jane was fantastically capable. She had taken courses at something she called a "lab school" in Chicago, where her parents owned a failing French restaurant. She had been accepted to Northwestern and the University of Chicago, but hadn't received scholarships. Instead, Jane plotted to excel for a year at our lesser institute and reapply for aid from Northwestern. She called it the *Crown of the Midwest* and claimed that she needn't spend time making friends at Mayflower as she would soon have her pick of better company in Evanston. I gritted my teeth as she said this and held my breath as she flat ironed her hair until it singed. She frequently offered me SnackWell's or dry handfuls of Special K. She tried, many times, to watch films made in the 1980s with me. She worshiped a director named John Hughes, a man I had once heard Christine refer to as a purveyor of nostalgia smut and key figure in the normalization of date rape culture. I didn't tell Jane this. Jane was the most boring person I had ever met.

Her worst quality was her compulsion to compliment me via threat. Daily, she would remark something like, "You're so skinny. I hate you." Her most violent comments related to how little I studied in correlation to my 4.0 GPA. "I would kill to be as smart as you, Jessie." The way she looked at me when she said it made me think perhaps it was me she would kill.

In reality, Jane was remarkably intelligent. At first it was hard to tell, because she spent so much of her time lying on the linoleum floor of our dorm room doing leg lifts and clamshells and donkey kicks with a pair of five-pound sandbags around her ankles. She usually had a textbook open in front of her as she pulsed her quads eighteen inches above the earth, but she never seemed to be reading it. Also, there was always a half-eaten carton of ninety-calorie strawberry-banana Dannon Light opened somewhere near her. Eventually, I learned that Jane consumed food in forty-five calorie allotments.

"You want the rest of this?" she asked at least once a day, holding her tiny plastic cup of yogurt out to me. I never wanted her remaining three tablespoons of chemically enhanced goo. I had known a lot of girls with eating disorders from the pageants and so I knew Jane wasn't one of them. She wasn't trying to hurt herself and she didn't think she was fundamentally flawed or anything like that. No, Jane was always in total control; she was always acting in what she had determined to be her own best interest. I started to admire her ability to set goals and stick to them. She told herself she would get a 4.25 GPA, and she did. She told herself she would learn Chinese so she could speak with her great-grandmother when she visited Guizhou over summer break, and she did. About once a month, she would make a long-distance call from the communal phone on our floor and everyone could hear her speaking in what seemed like fluent Chinese to her grandmother. Most impressively, she told herself she would get an internship with the government, and she did. She sat at her PC filing paperwork for hours every night and she met with some guy in a black suit every Tuesday afternoon.

Jane was, in the parlance of a high school counselor, *driven*.

On Thursday afternoons, someone in Mayflower would rent a new release from Blockbuster. While the rest of the University observed Thursday night as the official start to the weekend by patronizing the sports bars that ringed the edge of campus, the studious girls of Mayflower met in the dorm lounge at 9:00 p.m. to drink diet Snapple and eat air-popped popcorn and watch a movie featuring Sandra Bullock or Ashley Judd or Sarah Michelle Gellar or some other allegedly relatable star. Jane and me always skipped the viewings. No one cared much that I didn't go—I'd gone out of my way to be unapproachable. Weird, even. Each of these girls was a self-styled Natalie Portman, a soi-disant Julia Stiles, a counterfeit Claire Danes. They were college-pretty. But once I had been gorgeous, and so now I just didn't give a fuck. They weren't good enough competition to warrant a warm-up lap.

Jane, though—they wanted her in their coven. It was harder for her to skip their viewings of *Cruel Intentions* or whatever. The way she declined the invitation one night in late September stayed with me.

"When I make a promise to myself, I keep it," she said. She looked exhausted, the flesh under her eyes older-looking than it should have been. "No one else is going to do it for me."

This was the closest she ever came to admitting that she was there on scholarship. Jane's family was poor, though I doubted they had always been that way. Grethe would call her "a lady who has fallen on hard times." Her clothes were old but well preserved, carefully washed and impeccably mended. She never mentioned money, either by way of spending it or complaining about not having it. Just the same, I could tell she knew the value of a dollar from the way she used her makeup until she hit pan. I didn't care, but I had noticed she fished my discarded tubes of lipstick out of the trash. I never saw her wearing them, but I suppose she must have been saving them to dig the remaining quarter inch out with a hairpin.

I started leaving almost-full tubes on top of a clean paper towel after that. I guess I wasn't all bad. Or, maybe I actually liked Jane a little.

After that declaration to the dorm, Jane turned on her heel and left. I followed her, but not fast enough. Before I retreated I saw some eyes roll in contempt and others glance at each other knowingly, as if they had placed a bet on who the Schol Hall Scrub was (this is how they regarded kids who got in on merit at Mayflower—as losers, leeches on the udder of the University). I watched as Janet Bothell pulled a fifty-dollar thong out of the wedge created by her hundred-dollar sweat-pants and I knew Jane's brief popularity was over. Her own underwear looked like it was government issued.

The dubious elastic waistband of Jane's underpants was pretty much all the explanation I needed as to why she was such a psycho about her schoolwork. In the pageants there were twelve-year-olds who knew their ten-thousand-dollar win was the only thing that was going to keep the lights on for their whole family. These girls would rather let an unsnapped safety pin stab them until they bled than lose points for adjusting their costume. They practiced their tap routines until their feet changed shape. Like me, they learned to compete as if they had no body at all. Unlike me, they did it because they had no other choice. If they couldn't make it in the pageants, they'd probably have to try to make it in the foster care system, or worse.

I knew I could and should be nicer to Jane, but she was just so fucking annoying. She never left the room, and so I had to step over her interminably clamshelling legs dozens of times a day. When she wasn't doing calisthenics in the middle of the floor, she was picking at the disgusting cold sores that circled her mouth.

So, yeah, I could see why Jane was jealous of me.

There were times, especially on a weekend night after the lights went out and Jane and me were nearly alone on the floor, harnessed like oxen by our loneliness, that I would look at the ceiling and imagine telling her about Chancellor Lethe and the Desert University.

I could turn to her in the darkness and not have to see her face as I explained that it was possible to hypnotize yourself using a regular pencil and the mirror from a compact and that in the hypnotic state, she would have total recall of everything she learned. I could tell her there were special pockets of skin in her hands that she could pinch very hard when she felt upset that would make her face slacken and allow her to keep her thoughts private. I could tell her that she should never listen to the noise of a crowd or look at a PowerPoint presentation, but instead choose one focal point or sound—the blipping light of a fire alarm, her own breath—and concentrate on that and nothing else. I could tell her how to avoid mediocrity, the way to appear as if in the middle while actually levitating slightly above it. Hell, I could tell her how to levitate.

"Levitation," Chancellor Lethe once told me, "can be much more than a crude autoscopic drift. When performed correctly, one can hover above the psychical plane not just to observe it, but to control the body left in it. Not astral projection, but astral action."

It had been over a month since I'd last seen the Chancellor. Our final session had been held a few weeks before college started. He began by telling me it might be the last time we ever met, but also, that it would be the most important of all of our meetings.

As usual, he stood behind his lectern and regarded me, a seventeen-year-old girl with a sunburnt nose and my chipped lavender Hard Candy nail polish, as if I were a full lecture hall.

His overhead projector displayed a black-and-white image of the ocean consumed with smoke. At first it looked like a fireworks display, but then the grainy ships materialized and I knew it was a photograph of the bombing of Pearl Harbor.

"Define *esprit de corps*, Jessica," he began.

"C-O-E-U-R or C-O-R-P-S?" The Chancellor had a thick New England accent that sometimes made it sound like he was yawning.

"C-O-R-P-S."

"The body's spirit?"

He continued to stare.

"The spirit of the body? No—the group," I corrected, "The spirit of a group."

"Denotation and connotation?"

"Denotation: a collective of like-minded individuals. For example, a military unit. Connotation: a shared enthusiasm or belief system?"

"Example?"

I faltered. I couldn't quite see the difference between the actual and the symbolic, so I guessed, "Also a military unit?"

"Good." He stepped toward the image of Pearl Harbor and for a moment he was cast in the dark. Then he raised his thin willow wood cane and tapped the sinking ship three times. "Collectives are intensely stupid, Jessica."

The room was quieter than usual and it occurred to me suddenly that his secretary was not running the projector today. We were alone.

"Nearly everyone on earth values harmony over dissonance. People want to speak at the same volume, in the same voice, don't they?"

I nodded. I agreed.

"Is your voice the voice of all other voices, Jessica?" he asked and stepped into the light.

Veronica, I thought, but I said nothing.

"By its very nature, the group is inarticulate. It makes space for even the dullest, most corrosive ideas because it fears destruction. It adores consensus. Above all, the group cares about staying in the same shape as the group."

I suppose I may have gasped. It was as if there was a bell in my head that only I had ever heard ring and now here it was in his hand. I knew he was right from the pageants, from the beauty queens, from the shape I myself was curled into.

"Soon, you will be tempted more than ever to speak in the voice of the collective. You will live and bathe and eat with them, but you must never sound like them. You must, instead, maintain a spiritual sovereignty that resists the frailty and cowardice of the crowd." He stepped toward me and, in an unprecedented gesture, sat beside me on the leather divan. "You must think your own thoughts." He took my hands in his. "You must remember what you've learned here, from me."

His face was very close to mine for a moment. The thick band of his gold ring dug into my hand. I stared at the insignia engraved on it: a crown surrounding the earth. It reminded me of the Claddagh.

He stood up again and returned to the lectern. He quoted Solomon Asch, Søren Kierkegaard, and Irving Janis as if they were his friends. At some point, his secretary returned and the overhead flashed quickly through projections of slumber parties, communist rallies, sorority hazings, lynchings, church choirs, herds of animals, nuns walking the streets of Vatican City, a congressional hearing, Girl Scouts, and finally an image of a class sitting in a lecture hall. Three weeks later, I would recognize it as Seashore Hall, where my Intro to Clinical Psych lecture was held.

"Curtains," Chancellor Lethe said to the back of the room, and via an invisible pulley system, the navy velvet drapes that covered his office windows opened. The silver eyes of the woman jumping from the stained-glass tower looked down upon me. I could see a vast garden of cacti, aloe, desert marigold, brittlebush, ghost plant, and yucca filtered by the windowpane, curling in on itself as the sun set.

Chancellor Lethe walked over to a globe, which opened on a hinge and contained a small set of crystal tumblers and various amber-hued liquors. He poured two glasses and handed the glass of cognac to me—it smelled of fuel, wax, and sweet pear—and by way of a toast said, "Well, then, synthesize the lesson."

This meant I was supposed to determine a thesis for the day's lecture and rephrase it in the form of a quote or fable.

"Ummm . . ." I thought for a moment. "When at times the mob is swayed / To carry praise or blame too far, / We may choose something like a star / to stay our minds on and be staid."

The Chancellor clinked his glass to mine. "Frost. The poet's poet. Excellent."

He lifted his glass to his lips and I did the same.

That night, I fell asleep and didn't wake up for two days.

I didn't tell Jane about any of that. Instead, I retreated to the dormitory basement. Sometimes I slept there. Sometimes, if I felt really bad, I put my back to the boiler and let its vibrations radiate through me as I practiced mirroring. It helped me to slide into the body of a student in my classes.

It was all just so fantastically boring at the Midwestern University, which, I suppose, was exactly as Chancellor Lethe had intimated it would be. There were dull crowds and numbing PowerPoints and lifeless lectures. I felt the tedium of my class schedule, of responding to bells, of listening to the interminable low-slung hum of the campus as if it were factory work or gambling, something mindless performed out of necessity or compulsion.

The summer burned out fast, and by the end of October, the girls in Mayflower rarely left. It was too cold and they were too serious about their schoolwork. The trees surrounding our dorm turned quickly; black leaves swirled around us, revealing the small mansions set higher up on the hill. From me and Jane's tenth-floor room, I could look out at night and see the dozens of jack-o'-lanterns glimmering expensively from Victorian porches. The air blown in off the river smelled clean, ultra-ionized, laced with the char of autumn bonfires in the city park. It made me think of Chancellor Lethe's cognac.

So I suppose I shouldn't have been so surprised that I lost control; the irritants had been in the air, the intolerable dander of a state university. But as I sat on the floor of our dorm room and listened to Jane quietly explain to me what had happened, I was as fascinated and estranged from the story as if it were a campfire legend. Something that had happened to someone else, a long time ago.

On Halloween morning, Jane explained to me that the night before I had been sleeping badly, itching my neck and waking up intermittently to ask her if she knew how to get to the roof. She said she thought I was kidding at first, trying to freak her out.

"You kept doing it, though," she said, "and I kind of realized you weren't kidding because you were really sleeping. Like, Janet and the Halloween committee were making a lot of noise outside our door around eleven and you didn't even notice. And, you know, usually you'd tell them to shut up."

I probably would have told them to shut the fuck up, but I nodded and Jane continued.

"So when you got out of bed at one—sorry if this is weird, I was worried!—I followed you to make sure you were okay. It seemed like you were sleepwalking? Like, you walked around the room in circles for a minute before you walked out the door." She indicated the tiny space—about the size of a hula hoop—that I had circled. "You were walking weird, low to the ground—like an animal? You walked straight past the bathroom to the staircase and so I asked you what you were doing, but it was like you couldn't hear me." She paused. "Could you hear me, Jessie?"

Only Jane called me Jessie. I shook my head: *No, I couldn't hear you.*

"I didn't think so. So I followed you up the stairs to make sure you were okay and you went straight to the door to the roof, which is usually locked, but Janet Bothell and those girls had propped it open somehow. It was like you knew they were up there, doing that séance to contact the dead girls. Why didn't you ask me to come with?"

I shook my head again. "They didn't invite me."

"Well, you walked straight to them. They had a bunch of candles set in a circle and they had, like, a Milton Bradley Ouija board, but instead of a planchette, they were using a shot glass over the letters. Anyway, you walked over like you couldn't see them either and you stood right on the center of the board and you started to recite a poem or something. In another language? The wind blew really hard and your nightgown flew up, but you didn't do anything about it." She paused, embarrassed. "You were naked underneath."

"Jane, who cares? What was I saying?"

"I don't know. I think you were speaking Swedish?"

"Try to repeat some of what I said. Just mimic it, as best you can."

Jane, in a surprisingly perfect accent, said, "Vi hoppet ikke."

Not Swedish. Norwegian. I knew enough of it from Grethe and Christine's conversations to plug the phrase into Babel Fish. A chill went up my spine when the digital translation box posited its result: *We didn't jump.*

"Then what happened?" I asked.

"You were clawing at your neck like crazy. I saw blood on your fingertips. The other girls were freaked. And then you just sort of crumpled and we carried you back to your bed." She gestured at my bed, where there was a bloodstain on the pillowcase. "You've been asleep since then. Do you think you should call your mom?"

Jane was constantly suggesting I call my mom. It was the kind of thing a girl with a mom who cared about her would suggest.

"Or maybe just . . . shower?"

I looked down at myself. She was right, my hands were bloody and clenched.

After that, I walked slowly to the bathroom and stood, staring into the mirror for a long time. Eventually, I curled open my hand. In it sat a tiny chip, green as a Japanese beetle and electronic as the motherboard of Dr. Clink's PC.

It was, I realized, what I been itching at. I had pulled it out of my own skin.

As I walked to the phone in the dorm's common area to call Grethe, the whispers around me were like their own weather system. The other girls stared openly. I could already imagine the graffiti in the bathroom, the face of the RA who would walk me to the mental health center.

Grethe picked up in two rings.

"Come get me," I said. "I'm done with college."

I dropped the bug I had pulled out of my skin in a recycling container. It sank into a half-empty yogurt and I felt myself relax.

CHAPTER EIGHT

Returned to my childhood bed after only two months of college, I began to have a series of dreams about Chancellor Lethe's secretary.

I did not know her name, what she looked like, or even if she was one or multiple women. I had only heard the click of her heels against the oaken floor of the Chancellor's office and occasionally seen her silhouette outlined by the light of his projector. She was the same to me as the Mountain Spectres in Grethe's book of Nordic Myth: shadow creatures who loomed at the peak of a mountain when a traveler was lost, their god-like heads haloed by rainbow rings. Always, the lost heroes in the myths followed these apparitions—through flowing lava fields, black sand beaches, and up glassy shale cliff-sides—until they reached their homes, nearly dead, only to discover that the apparition was merely the backscatter of the lamplight the hero held in his own hands, reflected in droplets of mist on the mountain.

Sometimes, though, the shadow creatures were real and they led travelers further and further into the mountains until they died by their own faith in the light, in their certainty that the glow was leading them somewhere glorious.

In the dreams, the Chancellor's Secretary appeared as a woman-shaped shadow.

Sometimes, the Chancellor's Secretary made a noose from the

cord of Grethe's ironing board and hung it from Dr. Clink's office door. Through the loop I could see Grethe sitting at the desk, writing a history of my body in a leather-bound volume.

Sometimes the Chancellor's Secretary sat at the desk herself and invited me into the office to *play the yes-yes board*, but instead of any kind of game board, there was a catalogue of the body parts of Christine, Veronica, Jane. Next to their names, prices. Knees: $30,000. Eyes: $10,000. Heart: $1,000,000.

Sometimes she held the Chancellor's guest book and in it I saw my name written again and again, the only name in the book, but when I pointed to it she would shake her head: *That's not you.* I would look past her to the Chancellor's quarters to see the room filled with Dr. Clink and his colleagues sitting at a table that was also a map of the world covered in dozens of red *X*s. Grethe would then materialize at the head of the table and I would wave, relieved.

I had the sense in the dream that I had been lost for a long time. That I had been in hiding. There was dirt under my fingernails.

Grethe looked at me and shook her head: *No. I don't know her.*

As Chancellor Lethe's secretary closed the doors to the chambers, the walls around me began to move, to slither and writhe, to refract like too much light through a lens. As if I were in an over-exposed photo, I saw myself burned into whiteness.

CHAPTER NINE

SO FAR THIS STORY HAS BEEN A STUDY IN CIRCLES, BUT BY the end of this chapter we will finally be ready to start talking about spirals. We will become more confident, more violent, safer than ever before. Our story will start to curl outward into time; I'm saying we will be an anti-pearl, I'm saying we will stop being slugs and start being snails; I'm saying we will finally leave the '90s with a corkscrew in one hand.

But first, the year before the end of the millennium.

I returned home on Halloween day of 1998. The University was only twenty minutes away from my parents' house, but I had not been back since starting college. For my birthday in early October, Grethe and Dr. Clink had driven into the college town, parallel parked on the narrow streets of campus, and taken me to a steak house with linen tablecloths, a dress code, and *maccheroni e formaggio* on the menu. It is impossible, in the Midwest, to disabuse a menu of macaroni and cheese. Grethe ordered one glass of red wine and a rare steak and by the end of the night her teeth looked tinted with blood. Dr. Clink left the table several times to make calls from the payphone in the dive bar across the street.

I think that night was the first time it occurred to me my mother and father were profoundly strange. Grethe wore an opalescent silk gown that was the exact color of her hair, so she looked like a milky spill, a column of salt from another century. Her clothes were rich, curated by a buyer in Europe, and always too extravagant for any occasion.

Dr. Clink's clothes were much worse. I knew, vaguely, that he had been born in a colonial state—Massachusetts or Maryland or Delaware or somewhere like that—and for that reason he had never stopped dressing like he was about to board a ship. I did not know Grandfather or Grandmother Clink, but I was aware from photos and miscellaneous trinkets—cufflinks, silver framed photos, a money clip engraved with a family crest and the letters CWC for Clark William Clink—that my father's family was wealthy in a way that didn't exist west of the Mississippi or east of the Rocky Mountains. We didn't talk about why my father was estranged from the rest of the Clinks, but I knew from an RA that I had been admitted to Mayflower on the basis of some sort of familial connection.

Anyway, it struck me for the first time that night that my parents looked like characters in the board game Clue. They both spoke with accents that caused great anxiety in waiters. That night, in particular, they managed to behave even more oddly than usual. I recall Dr. Clink lifted a silver spoon to his crystal glass, clanged thrice, and said my full name in what I assumed would be the commencement of a birthday toast, but instead was simply an intense monologue about clarity. By that point in our relationship, I made a point not to commit much of what my father said to memory and even now that I would like to remember, I cannot tell you exactly what he said that evening—although I do know I believed it had nothing to do with my birthday.

Perhaps their most idiosyncratic habit was the way they coordinated their conversation so that if Dr. Clink said something he thought was interesting or important, Grethe would instinctually remove a small blue notebook with a spiral flip top from her handbag and transcribe everything he was saying. Sometimes he spoke in coordinates and she would spin to a section of her notebook lined in graphing paper, the kind I used in geometry class, and quickly chart out whatever he was talking about so that her book was covered in twists, in the curled old fingernail of the Fibonacci sequence.

That night, I watched Grethe hold the little golf pencil she kept in her evening clutch for impromptu dictations. Her handwriting was tiny, precise as a font. The beds of her fingernails had taken on a slightly blue cast from so many years in the kryokammer. Maybe I was staring, because she actually asked me how I was feeling, although even that she could not manage to do like a normal mom. "Any . . . intrusive thoughts?" she inquired.

I shrugged. I had been thinking about how her pageant-style hair and makeup, which I'd always found beautiful, actually looked like a wig and mask.

Eventually, Dr. Clink came back after his third phone call at the bar across the street and announced to Grethe one of the nonsense phrases that always conveyed great significance between them—that day it was something about a lepidopterist and a meadow. Then he summoned the waiter by snapping (this was something else he did that had begun to humiliate me), and requested the check be "delivered promptly."

We hadn't had birthday cake yet.

In the car on the way back to Mayflower, Grethe handed me a package. Since the year I had learned to read, I had received a new ciphertext from them on my birthday: *The Velveteen Rabbit, Peter and Wendy, Through the Looking-Glass, and What Alice Found There, The Wonderful Wizard of Oz,* The Holy Bible, *Grimms' Complete Fairy Tales,* Edith Hamilton's *Mythology, Romeo and Juliet, Paradise Lost, The Divine*

Comedy, and, for my seventeenth birthday, *Catcher in the Rye*. I could tell from the package that this year's book was probably a volume of poetry or a short religious text; I was hoping for a collection of Zen koans.

(The only lecture I'd retained so far that semester had been in my course on Eastern Philosophy and the Female Body. My professor, a lithe woman in her fifties who originally fascinated me because even though she was silver-haired and wrinkled, her skin damaged by the sun and even sagging, she was also somehow still beautiful. Ultimately, though, I became fascinated with the class not because of the professor's chaturanga-ed biceps or youthful posture, but because of a series of lectures on something called the "Original Face," which she explained using a koan that asked, "What did you look like before your parents were born?" She then projected an image so technical in its execution of a mystic concept that it could have easily fit into the Chancellor's own lectures. An illustration of bodies contained within other bodies, like Russian nesting dolls bisected, but the bodies didn't represent dolls—or even bodies. They were rather, the professor explained, the spiritual sheaths through which one entered into relation with the universe.

"This is the secret of spiritual life," she said, reading aloud a projected quote from a swami whose name I did not write down, "to think I am the Ātman and not the body, and that the whole of the universe with all its relations, with all its good and all its evil, is but a painting . . . scenes on a canvas . . . of which I am the witness." I'll admit, I was riveted by this radical take on what I immediately recognized to be very similar to Crystal St. Marie's mirroring technique.

I'd sequestered myself in the Mayflower basement that evening and tried to imagine expanding out of my body and into the universe, but I couldn't get past the first sheath. A long, lacquered nail kept appearing to snag me back into my body.)

I ripped open the baby pink paper of my birthday gift, but it wasn't a book. It was a pair of kidskin leather gloves.

"To wear while you wait for the bus," Grethe explained.

I said thank you and watched as they drove away, the orange tip of Grethe's cigarette burning in the dark car as Dr. Clink sped out of town, back to the suburbs.

I was eighteen years old.

In the nine weeks that I had been away, my parents' house had devolved into chaos.

The *Boredom Studies* articles had begun to creep over the windows of Dr. Clink's office so that the room was cast in darkness, lit only by the emerald green tint of a banker's lamp perched on my father's desk. To read his papers, Dr. Clink walked around the room with a flashlight in one hand and a neon yellow highlighter in the other. There were so many books on the floor that a small walkway was carved out so Dr. Clink could circle his office while he talked on his rotary phone. It looked like the track a dog who spends his life on a leash makes in the dirt.

The rest of the house appeared as if it had been robbed. The lid of the grand piano had been detached entirely; all of the glass lamps covering the ceiling lights removed so that naked bulbs glared throughout the once-dim house; the pull-down stairs to the attic remained permanently distended, the attic lit at all times so that a column of artificial light shone into the upstairs hallway like a beam from another world.

Dr. Clink was convinced that the house was bugged.

As we approached '99, he became as paranoid as Grethe about security. In the nook under his desk, mere inches from his feet, he kept a lightweight, military-grade khaki haversack. The bag contained a first aid kit, a ham radio, a knife, three days' worth of bottled water and a canteen, a pack of matches and a flint, an oilcloth tarpaulin, a multivitamin, maps of locations known and unknown (to me, anyway), a directory of encrypted phone numbers, duct tape, a signal mirror, his birth certificate and passport, a fake birth certificate and passport, and a small gun. It might have been a flare gun; I wasn't sure.

I knew better than to tell anyone. Truly, there was no one I would have told. I rarely left the house, and when I did, it was to walk around the mall alone, get my nails painted at the Korean salon where no one spoke English, or check out DVDs from the public library.

Christine didn't babysit me anymore. As Grethe's fingertips grew bluer and Dr. Clink's rants went longer, Christine had actually begun to seem a bit freaked out by my parents. Last July, about a month after the fashion show, Christine had a long conversation with Grethe and then she came up to my bedroom to give me a few mixtapes and tell me she wasn't going to be my sitter anymore.

"But if you ever need me," she said seriously, "just call. You can call me anytime." She looked like a ghost haunted by an even spookier ghost. Grethe could do that, though—she had taken to holding on to people's hands for too long when she shook hello or goodbye as a way of getting some warmth into her frigid limbs. I had seen her clasping both of Christine's hands when I peeked over the banister. "I mean it. *Anytime.* Even in the middle of the night."

I shrugged. This was my response to everything.

After that, my parents stayed close to home and then I was off to college. The first time Grethe and Dr. Clink left the house with me alone in it, I almost asked for Christine before remembering she was gone. I also realized that I was eighteen, I could drive, I had lived away from home; even they couldn't argue I needed a babysitter.

I had never been in the house completely unaccompanied. I was surprised by how afraid I was. I turned off the constant news coverage of the president's impeachment charges and popped in a DVD of *A League of Their Own* with the volume turned up loud so that I could hear Rosie O'Donnell and Madonna shouting at each other in bad accents from anywhere in the house. Then I walked around and looked at my parents' things. That was when I found the bug out bag hidden under Dr. Clink's desk. I'll admit—my first thought was that Dr. Clink had discovered the world really was going to end with the new millennium.

He often referenced the "instability of clock time." In fact, this was one issue he raised with anyone: his TA Jeffrey, the grocery store clerk, Christine. As an eschatologist, Dr. Clink was an amateur, but that did not deter him from lecturing about the nature of time as a continuous narrative moving in the shape of a spiral. It reminded me of the Dragon, a rollercoaster at a nearby amusement park that became famous at my high school because it completed four 360-degree loops that caused a boy in our class named Bryce Thursten to vomit upside down. It seemed that Dr. Clink believed that time moved from one discrete point to a second discrete point, but that on its way, the angle and velocity of time convened at irregular intervals to end ordinary perceptions and force an encounter with the divine—to turn everything upside down. This usually manifested as a form of violence—Bryce puking—but after it was completed, the world could be experienced again.

However, Dr. Clink was certain that this first discrete point—the part of the Dragon where a tired teenager in a waterproof plastic vest clicked passengers into their harnesses—couldn't be determined with any empirical accuracy at all. In short, it was impossible to know when the world began.

I had been listening to Dr. Clink discuss this problem my entire life. Apocalypse and boredom were framed by the telluric certainty of a consciousness outlined by Before, Now, After. Later, I learned that Dr. Clink got into some trouble for using university research funds to support an offshoot of the Greenglass Method—a study that involved sensory deprivation tanks and solitary confinement in order to prove that there was a correlation between individual and communal perception of time itself. He thought that if he could determine the average length of time it took for a person suspended in Now to break down and lose their sense of identity, he could correlate that to larger historical movements and begin to develop a theory on the Space-Time-Identity continuum.

The last I heard of him, Dr. Clink was forced into hiding after allegations surfaced that he had in some way been connected to enhanced interrogation techniques during the previous president's regime. A vague insight into his possible work was outlined in a scholarly article written by his protégé, Jeffrey, detailing the results of sensory deprivation experiments. Boredom, Jeffrey argued, could be channeled. However, when combined with the absence of stimuli, subjects suffered brain damage after only fifteen days. They became highly suggestible to implications of paranormal phenomena. It was rumored that my father fled to a secret city twenty-five miles west of Knoxville, Tennessee. One of the recovery sites built by the Manhattan Project, I suppose. Jeffrey, however, managed to secure a position at the University of Michigan.

I guess I might have had a premonitory instinct that this would happen—that my father would unhinge completely—because if my first thought upon discovering the escape bag was that the rollercoaster of time was about to flip and Dr. Clink knew it, my second thought was that there *was no rollercoaster*. Dr. Clink had lost his mind.

Even after overhearing Christine call Dr. Clink insane at the fashion show, I hadn't really considered it anything but a value judgment, a character assessment. But sitting on the floor of the study, surrounded by an assorted mix of books on history, religion, psychology, late capitalism, and pseudoscience, I wondered for the first time if there was something wrong with the chemical makeup of my father's brain.

I recalled an essay from my Intro to Clinical Psych class on the brain structure and function of a sociopath overlaid with the lecture on Ātman from my Eastern Philosophy and the Female Body course overlaid along with a diagram of Hierarchical Structure from my World Systems Analysis survey overlaid with my own in-class essay in Gender Studies 101. I saw myself write the words *childhood memory is inherently mediated by the patriarchal language structures from which it is processed, recalled, and integrated; in this sense, our relation to power is permanently determined by our childhood experiences* in a bluebook. I hadn't known what I meant—neither had my professor, I received a C—but as these fragments from the Midwestern University palimpsested themselves atop one another, I saw a larger constellation of points between them. When connected, the dots made me wonder if I had been raised by a madman.

Momentarily, I lost the sense that I was looking at myself from above and instead actually felt my fingers tremble—felt that I was in my own body—as I pulled open more desk drawers. One of them contained an over-stuffed accordion envelope titled "Alternative Currency." Inside of it were a variety of seed packets, several bottles of different medication and antibiotics, tampons, and paper money from countries all over the world. Another file was titled "Collateral" with pages and pages of fingerprints and encrypted names. One of the desk drawers contained nothing but Polaroid photographs from parties at the elite East Coast university Dr. Clink had graduated from in the '60s. Weirdly, I noticed, there were photos taken in the same wood-paneled room of his fraternity house from the '70s, '80s, and '90s as well. The last was dated from September of that very year. In one drawer there were dozens and dozens of CDs with coded titles and a brown envelope marked "I.C.E./ Blackmail" that I opened and quickly shut—it was full of photos of partially naked people. They seemed unaware of the camera.

The final drawer revealed Dr. Clink's college yearbooks. It was odd that they weren't on the shelves. I opened the topmost book, which fell naturally to the page devoted to the Senior Society my father belonged to. There was a description of the society from Mathers Witherspoon (a classmate of Dr. Clink's I met at the Desert University more than once) at the top of the page: *If the society had a good year, this is what the "model" group will consist of: a football captain; an editor in chief of the* Daily News; *a prominent radical; a swimming captain; an infamous drunk with a 93 average; a photo journalist; a politician's son; a future YDS luminary; an editor in chief of the* Lit; *a foreigner; a playboy with no fewer than two motorcycles; an ex-military man; an oriental, if there are any to be had; a guy nobody else in the group had heard of, ever . . .* There were signatures from the society members under each description. Clark William Clink was written in my father's handwriting under the last type of group member: *a guy nobody else had heard of, ever . . .*

I replaced the yearbook carefully and made my way to the shelves of the office, which contained mostly books, but also a few tanks for lab animals: betta fish, mice, occasionally frogs. Because it was so dark in the office, I hadn't noticed that there were no animals in the tanks anymore. I shone the flashlight we kept in the kitchen sink into the cages and saw clean bowls, pristine newspapers. I flashed my light to the bottom shelf to check the rabbits and gasped.

There were a dozen tiny kryokammers arranged in three rows of four. They were each about the size of a deck of cards. I looked at the unused cages again and realized that Dr. Clink was keeping the mice in a state of suspended animation; permanent cryosleep. I knew from Grethe's presentations that this—more than anything else—was forbidden by the Gjentakelse Tvang Association. Other than the obvious fact that a body deprived of water and nutrients would soon die, the bioarchitects who had engineered the Gjentakelse Tvang simply didn't know what would happen if a body was exposed to the therapy for more than twenty-four hours; my mother didn't tell people this, but they theorized it could lead to a severe psychic regression, to a return to the state before being; an erasure not just of daily trauma, but of days in utero and out.

I don't know where this scene starts or ends; I left the office and sat down in front of the television, the volume still up all the way. Over the next several months, I began to fear the kryokammer. It had taken on a different presence in the house: there were no more Scandinavian Tupperware parties because no one but Jeffrey LaPlant was allowed to visit. Each morning Grethe appeared further from reality when she emerged from the tank. She was cold all of the time and so was I.

I never asked her to fulfill her promise to get me my own Gjentakelse Tvang when I turned eighteen. In fact, in the months after I moved back in with the Clinks, I took a longer route around the house to avoid the room the device lived in.

Instead, I bought a monthly subscription to a tanning salon in the mall where everything was orange, oily, and obvious. The fake sun made me feel the boundaries of my body as my skin crisped and tightened. I liked the feeling that my chemical composition was advancing, that I was wrinkling, that I wasn't frozen in the pageants or in

Chancellor Lethe's chambers. A part of my mind started to believe the next day would happen.

And that's where I started this story: in the tanning booth at the end of the century.

So you already know that next I get the job at University Photography. Dr. Clink allowed me to idle around for a gestation period—nine months—before he decided at the end of July 1999 that I needed to get out of the house. I guess he decided my boredom wasn't going to produce any notable results. All he had was an orange daughter with pink nails and broken blue capillaries under her eyes.

It had been a July full of crashes. In the middle of the month, the heir apparent of a political dynasty died in a plane he himself had been piloting. The bodies of the politician, his wife, and his sister-in-law were recovered from the Atlantic Ocean, only seven miles away from the coast of Martha's Vineyard. Jeffrey appeared at the house just as the story broke. It was unusually late for him to arrive—Grethe was already in the Gjentakelse Tvang—and he was wearing jogging shorts and a T-shirt emblazoned with a NASA logo. His father had been an actual astronaut. A trail of sweat darkened the gray across the expanse of his spine as he stepped into Dr. Clink's office. As the door closed, I heard him ask my father if he thought it was a suicide.

About one week later, a flight departing from Tokyo International Airport was hijacked by a man with an eight-inch knife. Although the plane didn't crash, its 503 passengers dropped to a mere three hundred meters above the earth; three football fields above Japan. Only the pilot died, but Dr. Clink was interested nonetheless because the hijacker was found to be of unsound mind; guilty but not very responsible. For a minute, it seemed like Dr. Clink might have a new Bobbitt for his studies, but his excitement was quickly darkened by the intentional crash of the Lunar Prospector on the last day of July. I knew the Lunar Prospector had discovered water on the moon and that meant something significant to Chancellor Lethe, who summoned my parents to the Desert University on August 1.

That morning, I drove them to the tiny airport forty-five minutes from our house and then went directly to my new job at University Photography.

I didn't know anything at all about living in the world, and it had not occurred to me that I would need to pay for parking throughout the duration of my eight-hour shift—parking at the mall and the nail salon was free. University Photography, though, was located in the oldest part of the city, where the streets cracked open and revealed the red bricks of roads that had been there for hundreds of years. They called it historic and were proud as hell of it, so they metered for the parking.

This is how Kevin became my friend. He had a pocketful of quarters and he lent me one at two-hour intervals to avoid getting a ticket the very first time I was allowed to keep the car while Dr. Clink and Grethe were out of town. It was a critical favor.

I thought Kevin was much older than me because he played Herbie Hancock and Charlie Parker all day long on the store's old speaker system. I mean, the songs he listened to didn't even have any vocals. He also wore clothes from thrift shops. I didn't know if it was for fashion or for economy, but it made him look mature and eccentric.

Most of all, he was quiet and patient. In retrospect, he was probably only twenty-three—an art student, like Christine—but I was a college dropout, I lived with my parents, and I didn't know about parking meters. I still wore underwear purchased by my mother and I had no idea how much money I was making an hour. In my purse, there was a checkbook filled with blanks signed by Dr. Clink. I had no training in anything except for answering questions, wearing dresses, and putting on makeup.

I knew enough for Kevin, though, who said I reminded him of Yutte Stensgaard. I had learned by this point (from Christine) that if an art school kid told you that you resembled someone, then that someone was probably obscure beyond reason. Yutte Stensgaard was no exception. She was an old Danish actress famous for appearing in gaudy vampire movies. Kevin said I was phantasmal yet apparent; unearthly earth, desacralized ground. He meant I had a loud way of being invisible.

If Kevin hadn't decided to like me, I would have been fired within the week. He had to show me how to do everything from using the cash register to developing film.

Most of the time, me and Kevin were the only people in the shop. Shifts were divided between the two of us and the owner, Mr. Brewbaker, who spent the other half of the week running the store alone. It was obvious even to me that University Photography wasn't a thriving business. Most people got their film developed at the Walgreens three blocks over, so our customers were professional photographers and old people. After a month of sitting behind the glass counter with Kevin and listening to *Bird Is Free* on repeat, I realized the store had made less than a thousand dollars from our sales of replacement parts for rare cameras, a bottle of Stop Bath, and a few cartridges of Polaroid film.

"How does this place stay open?" I asked Kevin. It was a football Saturday in September and the air was already coated with frost, the scummy halitosis of winter.

University Photography's storefront was an old-fashioned

department store display window with nothing in it but a few expensive cameras Kevin or I had to secure under the desk before close every night. I had a clear view of the city outside. Herds of inebriated college students passed by intermittently as though they were each a private parade. I was vaguely afraid of them in the way I had been afraid of all crowds since stepping into the gazebo at Dead Ringers almost two years before.

"Contracts," Kevin said and reached for a key on the ring he kept attached to his belt. I knew one of the keys was for the darkroom, one for the shop itself, one for the display case, and one for the cash register, but there was a tiny fifth key that I had never seen Kevin use.

I myself would not be allowed access to the keys for another month. I had to prove I could show up regularly, not ruin any photographs or steal—and that was about it.

Kevin slid the little key into a filing cabinet under the counter. It had never occurred to me to even try to open the door to the big metal container under the desk. I assumed it contained discarded holes from a paper punch.

I was wrong. The filing cabinet opened up with a satisfying shuffling noise to reveal rows and rows of tabs labeled professionally with titles like "ICPD Case File 30017," "CRPD Case File 30103," and so on. Kevin pulled out a file at random, peeked in it, and handed it to me.

"Mug shots," he said.

Inside there were three strips of negatives; in each frame, a drunken-looking white man with a black eye and unwashed hair faced the camera at different angles. His name, birthday, and arrest date were handwritten with a silver marker in the lower right corner.

"Are these all mug shots?" I asked.

"About half of them." Kevin was replacing *Bird Is Free* with *Bird on 52nd St.*, so his back was to me as he said, "The rest are crime scene photos." The shop filled with a screaming trumpet and the foam-thick white noise of a live recording.

"Crime scenes?" I said stupidly. I remembered the pictures I had seen on the news with Christine. The blood of the blonde woman splattered across the steps of her own home.

"Yeah, mostly pictures of blood spatter or real close-ups of fibers. Mr. Brewbaker has a contract with the surrounding police departments to develop their crime scene photographs."

"They don't have their own lab?"

"Apparently not. Mr. Brewbaker does all the developing on those himself."

"Is that what he's doing when he's here alone?"

Kevin reached up and pinged an old-fashioned bell that was rigged by an ancient string to ring when the front door opened. "Yep. If he hears the bell, he comes out. Otherwise he's in there doing detective work."

"Really?" I was as naïve as ever.

"No, not really. I'm just kidding—he does speculate on the crimes, though. If you ask—which I don't recommend." It occurs to me now that Kevin must have liked me precisely because I was so disaffected; because I didn't know a stupid question from a smart one and so I just asked everything.

Once I asked Kevin if his backpack had gotten sprayed by a skunk. Once I asked him why a particular couple—regulars at the store—bought so much Polaroid film in addition to their high-grade Kodak. Once I asked him if the guy who brought him his lunch on the weekends was his brother.

For the most part, I found every man I had ever met terrifically dull until I met Kevin. He took himself seriously and he took me seriously, too. We spent twenty hours a week together, most of it side-by-side, during which Kevin showed me his own photographs and asked me what I thought.

It took months of him asking me what I thought about things—the news, art, articles in the *New Yorkers* we stocked but never sold—before I started to figure out how to develop an opinion.

It was the opposite of mirroring or my studies with Chancellor Lethe. Instead of projecting inward until all I could see was a tunnel focused to a blinding circular spotlight on what I already knew, I had to project outward until I found some sort of illumination that included the outside and the inside. I could feel myself changing. It occurred to me that I was aging and I wasn't afraid.

Every time I gave Kevin my opinion, I felt reptilian, like I had just wriggled out of a layer of old skin and needed to drag myself to a quiet place, a hot rock, to rest. We fell into a routine: we talked in the mornings while we did inventory and listened to jazz, ate lunch in silence, and then I retreated to the darkroom to develop photos if there were any. If there weren't, I would just sit quietly in the lab's red light.

Kevin never questioned it, although I know he knew something wasn't right. Probably, Kevin thought I was dangerously depressed. As the winter set on, I stopped getting manicures and my nail polish chipped off entirely, I began to arrive at work wearing the same thing I had worn the day before, I forgot my lunch periodically. Kevin took to bringing an extra sandwich for me every day and at some point, he brought a comb and left it wordlessly in the cup where we kept the pens. I guess I had stopped brushing my own hair.

Christine would have said Kevin and me were on oppositional karmic trajectories and that we had entered a symbiotic state of energy transference. It was natural for people who spent time in close proximity to feed off the other; she would have given us each an amethyst to absorb our own energy.

The situation was less mystic to me.

Kevin's boyfriend, Nathaniel (never Nate), had started to stay and eat lunch with us sometime around Thanksgiving. He was attending the local culinary school a few blocks away and so he brought us elaborate gourmet meals: tiny pink lamb chops drizzled with glittery mint sauce, scarlet lettuces shiny with exotic oils, oranges charred until they smelled like perfume. We ate parts of animals I didn't know were edible: pork belly, tongue, something spongy Nathaniel called sweetmeats. By the end of '99, the entirety of my diet was strawberry Nutri-Grain Bars (Grethe had stopped cooking because Dr. Clink seemed to have stopped eating), so I gained a little bit of weight from Nathaniel's lunches and my skin gradually began to appear less parched and dead.

I also started laughing. Left alone with me, Kevin was mostly solemn, earnest about his work and his art, but with Nathaniel he became a lighter version of himself—he was funny. The first time I laughed at something he said, it felt like an involuntary reaction, like sneezing or weeping; muscles I had forgotten were in my body twitched, the curve of my spine changed, and I almost cried as the palate of my mouth relaxed. I realized my teeth had been clenched for . . . years.

The last time I had felt like there was a body within my body was over a year ago, the night I woke up to Jane telling me what I had done on the roof of Mayflower. And before that, with Veronica.

"The nuns in health class say it's like a sneeze," Veronica had said, and then she laughed, huge and symphonic. Her laugh was utterly unlike her voice. It was as if the sounds she made operated on a hydraulic system: for every ten words she whispered, she had to laugh wildly to balance her internal pressure. Or, maybe she just loved being alive.

(We've almost arrived at the point where I complete the circle; I'm about to tell you what I wouldn't several chapters ago.

I love how close together are the words vulgarity and vagary. It's a sonic trick, to yoke two sentiments by sound that are in fact inverse. Vulgar; from the Late Latin *vulgaritas*: "of the common people." And vagary; from the Latin *vagari*: "to stroll, wander, or spread about." One word a collective of sentiments, the other word its dispersal. I mean that if I've been vague about my relationship to Veronica up to this moment, now I will be vulgar: I will bring us together.)

"Wait," I responded. "How do the nuns know?"

We were talking, of course, about the abstinence class Veronica was required to take at St. Catherine's, the Catholic High School she attended. The minute the door to my bedroom closed behind her that day, Veronica announced that the nuns had taught them how to masturbate at school. I was shocked: at my school, our sex education unit consisted of memorizing the symptoms of social diseases, watching a sad documentary about AIDS, and accepting a condom from a basket that was quietly passed around the room. Most kids blew their condoms up like balloons and played volleyball with them in the cafeteria. At any rate, we had certainly never been told how to do anything. Everything I knew about sex came from MTV. The very idea of it seemed as real as being on television: distant and framed by commercials.

The first time I touched Veronica she felt more real than I had imagined, her mouth much hotter, her body more solid than my own. I mostly remember being with her in short reels of time. I remember standing in the middle of my bedroom, an inch or so apart, and sliding my hands under her skirt to place them on her hips. I remember that her underwear was scratchy, old lace, and her skin was soft underneath it. I remember bowing my head down to meet her lips and realizing for the first time that I was taller than her. I remember her hair kept catching in my lip gloss. I remember watching her Claddagh ring rub rhythmically against my pubic bone until my body uncrumpled and smoothed itself out into her hand, alien to me as a letter written in a trance. I remember she tasted like spices from another century: anachronistic and overwhelming.

This is why people care so much about bodies, I remember realizing. Chancellor Lethe had explained to me that the body was a great commodity, and that this was apparent to everyone because anything of great value is under constant attack.

"Every force on earth," he told me, "conspires to separate you from your body and keep you for itself. This is as true of the sun, who will burn you, as it is of the average human predator, who will rob you."

It wasn't until I was with Veronica that I realized my own fortune.

So the truth is that Kevin and Nathaniel made me understand I was impoverished, that my body had no home in itself. After years spent controlling my uncontrollable impulses, I could barely tolerate stimuli that let me know I was alive and embodied in a form I was not allowed to inhabit. Watching my friends was a brand-new kind of pain—realizing what I'd been taught to believe impossible . . . wasn't. But it was already too late for me to return to my true self. Like one of Dr. Clink's maze mice, I was conditioned to stay in the labyrinth even now that I knew the way out. To soothe myself, I tried to use a technique taught to me by Crystal in which I imagined Kevin and Nathaniel touching each other's faces softly or kissing hello. I would freeze the image in my mind and then I would let it slide off the screen of my imagination. I did this again and again, but it never worked. I never managed to cordon their love for one another from my psyche.

I stopped looking in the mirror after that. My mind was broken. By December of 1999, I could walk down a crowded street and no one would see me. If I tried to enter the mall through its automatic doors, nothing happened. The motion-triggered lights surrounding my parents' home stopped turning on when I pulled into the driveway at night.

Dr. Clink was almost never home, and when he was, he didn't look at me. Grethe seemed to have entered some sort of partially defrosted state that prevented her from making eye contact or composing first-person statements. The blues of her eyes had started to whiten as if they had a thin layer of freezer burn, and her hair had begun to grow out—not gray, but a moon-ish silver. In only a year's time, she had become a specter of herself. I had become the specter's daughter. Anyway, there was no one to notice me disappearing.

Except Kevin, though there wasn't very much he could do about it except to make feeble half-jokes, half-commands throughout the twenty hours a week we spent together. "Eat, eat, little vampire," he would say during lunch. Sometimes he suggested I take a walk in the sun or a nap in the break room (there was an old plaid couch against one wall). Once, he even realized that I might like to listen to my own music and so we put on a New Order album. It felt wrong, though. I was embarrassed as soon as the music started playing. I felt like I had asked for ketchup at a nice restaurant.

I started spending almost my entire shift in the darkroom. By Christmas, I just couldn't talk to Kevin and Nathaniel anymore. It wasn't that I didn't want to, I just couldn't think of anything to say.

I had erased myself.

To track my progress, I borrowed a Yashica 2¼ x 2¼ from Mr. Brewbaker and started taking self-portraits in my bedroom every morning. I developed them privately, secretly, in the darkroom at University Photography so that I could see how much of myself was evaporating from the frame. I acquired a technique in which I set the camera to long exposure and walked around my room in a circle. Over time, the space my body was supposed to occupy in the photo became a blur, a gaping white hole.

The odd thing about the photos isn't that I was tracking my own disappearance: it's that the photos were good. They reminded me there was still a border between myself and the rest of the world—and that I was skilled at controlling it. I read about the art of photography in books Mr. Brewbaker kept behind the counter, and I learned how to control light and dark, how to manipulate the developing process to create different impressions, and how to choose which film and paper to create my photos from. If Christine had seen my self-portraits, I think she would have said they looked like a hybrid of a fashion magazine and funeral photography. This is to say, I think she would have fucking loved them.

She had always adored the documentation of demise.

We find ourselves at the end of the circle. There's nothing left except for me to tell you how I began to spiral outward to Now.

There's nothing left except the awful part.

It was December 30, the eve of the eve of the end of the century. The already deep snow had developed a finger-thick layer of ice overnight, and Kevin's shitty old Honda didn't have four-wheel drive, so I was at work alone for the first time.

On Christmas Day and for four days after, the shop had been closed. In my time off I had taken hundreds of self-portraits that I was desperate to develop, but there was also a backlog of holiday photos that needed to be taken care of. I estimated that if I got the first batch of the customers' film in the baths before 8:00 a.m., I would have at least an hour to work on my own pictures before Kevin got into the store.

He had developed an irritating habit of checking on me while I was in the darkroom. He claimed to be worried the chemicals were making me ill. "Still alive, Jessica?" he would call through the wall as he flicked the red lights on and off.

To save time, I broke protocol and skipped over dusting the counters and counting the cash in the register and instead picked up the envelopes of film that had been pushed through the store's overnight drop-slot while we were closed. There were about thirty rolls. Half of them were from the same customer: D. Dave Harris.

I flipped the red light to indicate to Kevin that I was developing film if he happened to come in and step through the cylinder that connected the shop to the darkroom—I loved stepping into the round black room and sliding the circular door shut behind me; for a moment, there was complete, untouchable darkness, a gate between the white and red worlds—and started mixing the developer in the big plastic tubs we used.

Once the chemicals began to mix, I pulled out the old beer bottle opener Mr. Brewbaker used to unhinge canisters of film, removed the lids from the canisters, carefully cut off the plastic spindles affixed to the negatives, and started loading them into reels. Next, I took the first reel through the agitation process. I enjoyed the procedure of taking the film through various chemical solutions, shaking it carefully as if it were an explosive martini, and then washing the tape in a rush of running water. By the time I hung the negatives to dry and harden on the old clothespins we kept permanently attached to wires crisscrossing the darkroom, I entered a kind of meditative state. I didn't arrive back in my body until I flipped on the negative viewer—a four-by-four table made of light—and checked the tiny images for imperfections.

At first, I thought there was something wrong with the Harris film. The negatives were too dark, as if they had been shot much too close. I leaned closer to the film.

I had never seen anything like these photos, except in my own self-portraits. They looked like multiple frames had been melded together—like the film had gotten too hot in the camera and melted—so that pieces of different bodies were overlaid in each frame.

A foot from one photo was next to the head in another; the arms were twisted at unnatural angles. The limbs were bare; there was no clothing to orient me.

As I continued through the negatives, I realized that in every picture there was a wig, a child's shoe, and a stain on the film. The stain was unlike any chemical discoloration I had ever seen; the shade was richer, less damaged by light, and it was always in the middle of the bodies, bleeding out onto the surrounding carpet.

Then I realized it was blood.

I told you earlier I don't believe in memory and here's why: there was no order that I saw the photo appear in. In one moment, it had been a collection of hands and hair and limbs, and in the next moment, those parts combined into the body of a small child. There was no discrete moment that I saw her face emerge or that I realized the wig was actually her hair. There was no order to the way the disordered body appeared before me.

The body of the little girl in the photo had been smashed, nude, into the floor of a small, filthy room. I had not seen her face at first because it wasn't where a face was supposed to be—her neck had been broken and she was turned to look over her own back. Her arms and legs had been spread open. To the edge of the frame there was a life-sized Barbie doll and a pile of clothing. The doll looked more real than the child.

I lifted my hand to my chest and began tapping my sternum with two fingers. This was a technique that Crystal taught me back when I was just starting to mirror. She said that if I ever felt like I was "stuck" in a life that wasn't my own, I should tap my chest hard enough to feel the reverberation through my entire body and repeat my name out loud to myself until I "came back." If that didn't work, she said I should grip my left wrist with my right hand as tightly as I could and repeat the name of my father.

"It will be like waking yourself up from a nightmare," she explained. "You'll know something is wrong, but you won't know what it is. You'll have the sense that you can go into another plane of existence—that you can wake up. When this happens, you need to shake yourself to consciousness. It will be very hard, but you have to do it." She didn't explain what would happen if I didn't.

I encircled my right wrist and squeezed.

"Clark William Clink," I whispered. "Clark William Clink. Clark William Clink."

But nothing happened.

Instead, I felt the pictures in front of me expanding outward into other images. I saw myself in a hotel room, my hands holding a menu written in Farsi. I could read the words although I didn't understand the language. I saw a bloody mattress in an expensive house. I saw my own nude reflection as I passed by an ornate mirror. I held a knife. I was sixteen years old.

I began to back away from the photos. There was a strange taste in my mouth. I blinked rapidly. My tongue was dry and I was choking. My hands, I realized, had moved to my throat.

As I backed toward the door, I passed by my own photos—images of myself I had developed and left to dry before Christmas. At first, I thought they were pictures of Grethe. Finally, I realized it was me. I was still inside myself. The body in the pictures existed.

I pushed through the cylinder, back into the brightly lit shop, and, like I had done after I fainted at the dorm, I called Grethe.

I could only make strange, animal keening noises into the phone.

"Jessica?" Grethe sounded tired. There was a sort of latency to her voice, as if she were across an ocean. "What's happened?"

"Photos," I managed.

"Are you at work?"

"I think I was—" I began. But I didn't know what to say. I didn't know how to explain I had seen images of myself in another country, images of myself with bloody hands.

"Are you ill again, Jessica?" She still sounded tranquilized.

"Yes. I think so." I sat on the floor of the studio now, my knees pulled up to my chest and my back to the corner of the shop. "I just developed some photos."

"Are you sick from the chemicals? Did you take an aspirin?"

"And they were of—" I now had my eyes closed, I was rocking back and forth with my fists clenched, "a dead girl."

There was a pause from Grethe. I thought that she had hung up on me, but then I heard the shuffle of her shifting the phone to her other ear. I knew she was stepping into the kitchen pantry and closing the door behind her so that Dr. Clink wouldn't hear her speak.

"Did you develop them all?" she asked. Her voice was suddenly firm.

"What?"

"Are the rest of the negatives still in the chemical bath?"

I didn't know she knew anything about the development of photos. But she was right, the other negatives were still in the bath; they would be destroyed if I didn't get them out immediately.

"Y-y-yes," I stuttered. I couldn't go back in and get them out. I couldn't go near the photos again.

"Listen to me," she said in a loud, articulate voice. "And repeat after me."

I nodded, although she couldn't see me.

"My name is Jessica Greenglass Clink."

"My name is Jessica Greenglass Clink," I repeated. My voice sounded distorted, the tongue thick and heavy.

"I was deactivated in 1998."

"I was deactivated in 1998," I mumbled.

"I am clear."

"I am clear." My voice grew stronger on the second half of the word *clear*, as if it were the bell that wakes one from a deep meditation.

"I am not monarch. My heart is in the air."

"I am not monarch. My heart is in the air."

"I am not monarch. I feel my feet on the ground."

"I am not monarch. I feel my feet on the ground."

My feet connected to the cold tile of the store, to the earth beneath. I looked at my hands and it occurred to me that only I could move them.

"You are going to hang up the phone," Grethe said, "and walk into the darkroom and finish developing those photos. Then you are going to come home and you will not speak to anyone on the way."

"Yes."

"Tell me the name of the customer."

"D. Dave Harris." As I said it, I understood that D. stood for Detective. Detective Harris of the police department just three blocks east of University Photography. I had accidentally developed crime scene photos.

I hung up the phone and moved toward the cylinder in a fugue state. I must have finished the photos, locked the shop, and begun to drive home in the snowstorm. I think it might have been around 9:00 a.m. when I left University Photography. Police reports show it was around 10:30 when I crested the bend of my parents' subdivision and saw that the house was lit. There were red and blue police lights reflecting off the unbroken snow, illuminating the yard in a surreal radiance. Three police cars were parked at the end of the drive.

I wasn't sure exactly why Grethe had called the police. I drove slowly past them and pulled into the garage. I clicked the button to pull down the remote-controlled door even though I could see an officer hurrying down the driveway toward me. He slipped on the ice and fell just before the door sealed shut.

When I stepped out of the car, there was Christine.

She was standing in the doorway, her black hair huge, her eyeliner smudged, and her skin paler than ever. I hadn't seen her in over a year.

"Don't get out." She was pushing something into my hands. Her eyes were red and I realized she had been crying.

"What happ—"

She was guiding me back into the car. The object she had pressed into my hands was rough and heavy—Dr. Clink's escape bag.

"Your mother is dead and your father is gone, Jessica."

She reached past me into the car and clicked the garage door opener. I saw the fallen officer right himself and begin toward us.

"Go and don't come back."

The officer lifted his hand and called my full name.

"Now!" Christine screamed.

I put the car in reverse and got the fuck out of the suburbs.

Part 2

CHAPTER ONE

THE SMELL OF THE MOURNERS AT KAYLA GAVIN'S FUNERAL wafted across the cemetery's gravel road, over the long front yard, and up to the second-story window from which I observed the service.

Grief smells like perfume. Latin: *per*=through; *fumus*=smoke.

I had nothing left except for etymology. Well, etymology and a bag of supplies for the end of the world. Anyway, in this part of the story there won't be any more dreams or meditations. This is the end of veils. We won't do anything but go straight to the origin until we find the very first word from which all other words sprang.

Obviously, we begin in the underworld. Here we are in the town where the little girl was murdered. I would have guessed that the entrance to hell looked just like this: hundreds of women and children weeping in front of a hole in the frozen ground. It was so cold that a small cloud of condensation hovered inches above the crowd. Inside the hole was a cheap, short coffin made of blonde wood and trimmed in painted gold. Inside the coffin was the body of the child.

The casket was, of course, closed. The mourners instead paid tribute to the school photo of Kayla taken a few months before her murder.

Kayla's sandy hair had been specially curled for the occasion. From her upper gums, two adult teeth were emerging.

I couldn't reconcile this portrait with the body I saw in the photographs. I suppose that was the murderer's point: utter effacement.

For New Year's Eve, I broke into the deserted Sheriff's Offices right at the rural-most edge of the county where I'd developed the photos. The pathologist's report for Kayla Gavin was in a locked filing cabinet, but the key to the cabinet was contained in a little envelope affixed to its side with a magnet from the local veterinary practice. The place was so small-town that when the clock struck midnight, I heard gunshots instead of fireworks. As the world slid into the new millennium, I discovered that Kayla's body bore marks of molestation dating back weeks. Prior to suffocation, the body had been raped multiple times. It was not until after death that the murderer broke the limbs.

The accompanying report from Detective Harris surmises that the child suffocated to death accidentally. Her assailant placed a plastic bag over her head during the assault. This, Harris notes, is a tactic occasionally employed by pedophiles that wish to dehumanize their victims. Monsters who can't stand to be monstrous; creatures trapped in their bodies by a careless creator. The murderer didn't intend to kill the child, but he also didn't notice when she died.

At least one thing was apparent to me that was not included in Harris's report: Kayla knew her killer. Her mother probably knew him, too. I guessed he was a teacher or a friend of the family. I guessed he was amongst the mourners at the funeral.

At the front of the crowd of bereaved classmates, teachers, and neighbors stood Kayla's mother, Chris, and her boyfriend. He hadn't been included in any news reports or police files, so I didn't yet know his name. He wore a suit that was too small—it must not have belonged to him—under a Carhartt jacket. I could see through the binoculars I stole from a sporting goods store two towns over that he appeared to be overheated. His face was red and he wiped his brow occasionally. He was sweating in the snow.

He was the man I had come here to kill.

It had been one week since Christine shoved Dr. Clink's escape bag into my hands. After Christine gave me the kit and unceremoniously instructed me to flee, I drove east. I felt compelled to put a lot of water between my father and me. Or, maybe between the body of my mother and me. Maybe this is an ancient impulse: Christine once told me ghosts can't cross water.

By the time I was safely on a bridge over the Mississippi, I was breathing normally and my heart rate had returned to its customary rate of forty-five beats per minute. I slowed the car to watch as a dirty floe of ice crackled and separated from the sheet that covered the river. It drifted into the churn of the current and was gone before I crossed into the next state. It was not even lunchtime yet.

The empty coasts of the upper Mississippi are filthy with state parks. Because I was too nervous to pull over and look for an atlas in the trunk, I simply followed highway signs for the park that seemed the most appropriate. By early afternoon, I had pulled the Chrysler off the highway to a country road to a gravel road to a dirt road to a clearing in the center of Starved Rock State Park.

Before getting out of the car, I tucked my hair into my winter hat and wrapped my scarf tightly around my head so that my mouth and nose were well hidden. I completed the look with a pair of Grethe's oversized sunglasses.

In my old life—the one I had fled that morning—I would have

imagined myself as Grace Kelly in that Hitchcock film where she falls in love with a thief. The grand reveal of the film isn't that Cary Grant is the criminal, but that Grace Kelly has a kink for crime and, also, that a teenage girl disguised by nothing but her presumed incompetence is the criminal architect. But I wasn't the starlet, star, or foil. I'm nothing silver at all: I'm anonymous as the black between celestial bodies. It feels just fine, to be the dullness of interstellar space.

I pushed the deep snow up around the Chrysler's license plates to obscure them from the view of passersby. The car was already far off the road, but I broke a few long branches and arranged their leaves to cover its windows.

My subterfuge was a little absurd. The snow around me was pristine, uninterrupted for at least three square miles. As I opened the door to get back in the car, I made eye contact with a skinny red fox at the edge of the clearing. She scratched, casually, and walked away.

Inside, I emptied the contents of Dr. Clink's escape kit onto the back seat. Everything appeared to be in order, except there was a bundle of hundred-dollar bills that had not been there before. When I picked it up to count it, my fingers pressed into a fine grit. Sugar. Christine, I realized, must have known of Grethe's sugar jar stash and put it in the bag for me. Other than the cash, there was an unused first aid kit that contained various bandages, ointments, pills, a cold compress, thermometer, and antiseptic wipes; a ham radio that I didn't know how to use; a Swiss Army knife as well as a six-inch switch blade; bottled water in an unmarked jug; a pack of Diamond Strike Anywhere matches and a flint; an oilcloth tarpaulin; a multivitamin; maps; the directory of encrypted phone numbers; duct tape; a signal mirror; two chocolate bars; and a small gun.

I still didn't know if it was a flare gun or not. I had driven into the woods to find out.

When I picked the pistol up, tiny tendons and muscles in my fore-arms, back, and hands engaged.

There are seventeen muscles in the human hand.

I heard Crystal's voice as if she were speaking directly into my ear.

And you use every one of them when you fire a pistol.

With both hands on the gun, I stepped out of the Chrysler and found a clear spot in the trees.

I aimed at the sky, felt my legs fall into a braced stance, and kept my eyes opened as the gun fired.

Chancellor Lethe told me once that the moon smells like gun-powder: an odor of steak and metal, unstable minerals. As I breathed deeply through my nostrils, I knew three things to be true: the gun was real, I was trained to fire it, and its musk was as familiar to me as the smell of my own breath.

On the phone that morning, Grethe had told me I was no longer a monarch. I did not know what she meant, but as I watched my breath puff into a miniature cloud, I knew she was right. I was alien.

I got the chocolate bars out of the car and chewed them, spat a mixture of waxy cocoa and saliva into my palm, and spread it across the front and back license plates.

Memories I did not know I had lost continued to float back to me. There was, I thought, a watcher inside me.

Years later, I will tell a therapist about this feeling. I'll live through the next vague decade with a sort of Cassandran vibe, bored by terror and temporality. None of it will inspire the watcher inside me to open her eyes until the morning of April 8, 2009. I will see a familiar face on the news. Miss North Dakota, 1997. A picture of her frozen in the mo-ment of her pageant win, her hand held rigid to her heart as she walks onto the stage wearing the spindly crown. The evening news anchor announces that Miss North Dakota has been convicted and sentenced to eight years in an Iranian prison on charges of espionage. For the first time, I'll sink to my knees on the floor of my living room and feel something I don't know how to deal with and so I'll go to the therapist.

She will wear expensive fabrics and have an office with a view of an eastern city. She will be used to talking to anorexics, body dysmorphics, and survivors of assault, so she will assume I am speaking in metaphor when I tell her that until I was nineteen years old, I was hypnotized into believing that my body wasn't my own. Because it would compromise her safety, I will never tell her about the Desert University. I will never tell her that I was trained by operatives of a shadow government to seduce, steal, and murder on command. I will never tell her that when I turned fourteen, they activated me and I sank into a space of no identity. Or that when I was eighteen, they deactivated me and I became a sleeper cell who could not sleep. An operative so rogue, even I did not know what was still inside me. Instead, I will tell her that when I was nineteen years old, I saw some photos of a murdered child. She will like this part of the story very much. She will ask me to repeat it again and again. She will want to know what, exactly, it was about the body of the child that brought back the memories.

Sometimes, I will pity the therapist.

When this happens, I will spend my appointments dwelling on famous mind control experiments. I will tell her that it was the Nazi doctor Josef Mengele who transitioned hypnosis from an occult practice to a science. In detail, I will describe the manner in which Mengele conditioned his subjects to eradicate their sense of self through a mixture of sleep deprivation, torture, and violent images. She won't pick up the hint, and so I will tell her that in the 1950s, the CIA adopted Mengele's theories in order to engineer an elite group of physically and psychologically enhanced agents. I will tell her that some of these agents were women who were recruited from international beauty pageants because they already possessed a strong propensity for obedience, discipline, manipulation, and self-effacement. I will think the therapist might finally be starting to guess the truth, but then she will ask me, randomly, some stock question about my relationship to my mother. Eventually, she will work her way back to the body of the murdered child, and one day it will occur to me that right before I saw the photo, I had been thinking of Veronica. I'll approach the subject parenthetically, as is my sideways habit. Perhaps she has noted the tangentiality of my speech patterns and the fact that the more seemingly irrelevant my response to her questions, the more likely it is I am nearing a topic of significance. Normally, I will interrupt myself to discuss Kevin and Nathaniel when monologuing about Veronica. But that day, I'll disrupt my own flow of speech by bringing up the crime scene photos. For the very first time, the therapist will lean forward in her seat. She will listen raptly, without taking notes, and then I will get a diagnosis. She will tell me I have a depersonalization disorder. The average age of onset for this disorder, she will state, is sixteen years old. Its symptoms include a sense of detachment from other people and one's own actions or body; a belief that life is being watched from far away, as if it is a movie; a basic sense of unreality that the sufferer attempts to remedy by creating complex narratives or origin stories which are often fantastic, supernatural, or paranoid in nature. She will put the cap on her pen as she announces that this disorder is a response to trauma before the age of twelve; one of the many shapes of PTSD. It is not uncommon, she will explain, amongst women of my age and background.

In many ways, her diagnosis is not wrong.

She isn't a good doctor, though. What happens instead is that I start to write this story. I start to wonder if there are any other watchers out there. The urge to find them is overwhelming. Dr. Clink, I expect, would say my compulsion is severe enough to pass an Irresistible Impulse Test.

For now, all you need to know is that that the film of my life has never stopped running in front of me on an invisible screen, but there in the woods that day I was suddenly able to fill in portions of it that had previously been blank; if before I had been a mouth riddled with missing teeth, then I was nearly a full bite.

But we'll discuss my dental records and other identifying information in the next chapter. That day, ancient protections enshrouded me as I left Starved Rock and drove back west to the town where the girl was murdered.

The picture displayed at the child's funeral was already on the cover of the local newspaper, and so it was inside a gas station off I-80 that I learned her name was Kayla Gavin, that she was seven years old, and that she was survived only by her mother in a town an hour south of my own hometown.

"Shame," said a woman working behind the counter. She was in her forties, wore a red vinyl vest, and frequently intuited the grammatical clutter that surrounds nouns can be omitted.

I looked up at her and it occurred to me I had been seen. I'd been standing in front of a gas station camera staring at the photo of Kayla Gavin long enough for the late December light to turn from pulp white to radiant gray.

"Hope whoever did that burns in hell." The woman issued the statement as a command, not a wish.

I nodded and angled my body as though looking intensely at a pack of Trident in order to turn my face away from the store's camera.

"You can have that for free, honey." She gestured toward the newspaper.

I thanked her and got directions to the nearest drugstore, where I bought a Norelco electric razor and a cap and pair of sweats emblazoned with the logo of the state's football team: navy blue, adorned by an orange bear. In another bathroom of another gas station off I-80, I used the scissors from the escape kit to cut the two inches of hair above my neck off at the root and then shaved the underside of my head clean with the Norelco.

In my old life, I would have thought I looked jolie laide, numbpretty as an anemic Chelsea girl, but I knew then I only looked cheap.

With my back to the bathroom mirror, I removed my clothing—thick tights from the Gap, a magenta Aeropostale sweater dress. Oddly, I hesitated before removing my heavily padded Miracle Bra. Sentimental, stupid, I thought and clicked open the three fishhooks that fasten the garment. Without it, I was almost boyish, which, of course, was exactly the point. Quickly, I balled up each article of clothing and shoved them deep underneath the contents of three respective tampon receptacles.

Finally, I crawled into the sweats and pinned my hair tightly to my head so that only the shaved part of my scalp was visible below the hat. Before turning to the mirror, I widened my stance, dropped my solar plexus deep into my stomach, straightened the upcurved line of my mouth into a neutral line, and compressed my voice box so that when I spoke, the air behind my words came from deep in my gut—smashed, anti-ethereal, masculine.

(There is another version of the origin story I told you earlier. In this other version, after Twin kills Queen, she beholds her reflection in the lake and begins to feel a sense of sorrow as deep as the water that carved the waterfalls into the mountains. She blinks the tears from her eyes and envies her dead sister, whose own eyelashes became love: her own image will never be beheld by anyone but herself. To worship the life she takes up within the world Queen created, Twin spits in her hand and concocts a terrestrial rainbow of pastes mixed from ash and dried petals of eyrarrós, bláklukka, and lupine. From these pigments, she paints the image of herself on the face of a basalt column. This is the creation of art. After this, Twin develops a ringing in her ears so loud that it muffles the waves lapping the shores and the rain befalling the beaches. She returns to the clay from which Queen had transformed into the world and weeps that her sister is no longer alive to see her art. She weeps through the cycles of nine moons and in the darkness of a moon as thin as the slit of an eye swollen shut, a long-fingered hand emerges from the tear-softened earth. Twin reaches out to grasp the hand, which could only be her sister's, the hand identical to her own, and drags, instead, a man out of the ground. A brother with eyes to see her art.)

I spun quickly so that I would only see the reflection of myself in the bathroom mirror from the edge of my eye. I knew then what it would be like to be pulled out of the grave of another person: the authority of at least knowing who you are not, the jubilation of the interloper, the triumph of being born without having, first, to die.

"Lee," said the boy in the mirror. "Your name is Lee Andersen."

I nodded.

The boy in the mirror did not nod back.

I practiced this technique with Crystal hundreds of times while developing a personality to suit pageant judges. I had, I realized now, also practiced it other times, for other reasons, alone in bars, hotel rooms, and mansions not marked on any civilian map. For a moment I had an image of myself as the outer doll in a set of matryoshka; inside me were dolls growing smaller and smaller until there was one doll at the center of all the dolls with no seam.

This image of the unbroken center doll reminded me that Christine had told me once that our energy centers sometimes get dirty from the accumulation of all of our past lives.

"That's probably where your nightmares are coming from," she said sagely. Instinctually, I avoided telling Christine that I thought I might be sleepwalking or that I woke up disarranged—dirt under my fingernails or the smell of an unfamiliar perfume on my wrists. But I did tell her about my dreams so that she could look them up in her *Dream Interpretation Dictionary*. I loved to hear her explain that if a spider visited me in my dreams, it meant that there was an overwhelming feminine presence surrounding me. Or, that if I dreamt Grethe had hanged herself from the balcony using the thick old cord of our iron, it only meant she resented housework and the responsibilities of domesticity.

Really, though, my dreams weren't symbolic enough and they eventually began to baffle even Christine. Most of my nightmares were, in fact, extremely lucid: I often woke up in pain, bleeding or stunned as if I had been hit hard on the head. After describing a dream to Christine in which I had woken up in a room with a dirt floor next to a monk dressed in red and brown robes who applied an herbal balm to my chest, she had announced I was probably experiencing nocturnal past-life regressions because my energy field had gotten gross from the accumulation of karma.

"Your energy goes back into time farther than history—I mean, history that's been written down," she explained. "You probably just need to be rebirthed."

She proceeded to explain a series of visualizations I could do to enter a trance state that would allow me to travel backward on the metaphysical sheath and resolve my past traumas. It seemed to be the opposite of the kryokammer: a thawing instead of a freezing. I didn't do it.

As I stared at Lee Andersen in the mirror, I wondered if Christine's theory was simply moving in the wrong direction. It wasn't that I was going back in time in my dreams, it was more that I was moving sideways: into other people's bodies. She was right that energy dispersed itself outside the present form, but maybe the form had more to do with the direction of the energy flow than the present moment.

The contents of the container aren't held in by death, I thought as Lee gathered up the escape kit and walked quickly out of the women's bathroom. He kept his eyes down and jaw tight.

"Wrong john, buddy," a trucker in a flannel shirt remarked as Lee slipped out the door. The trucker had more to say. His eyes were red-rimmed and he was holding a cup of coffee with no lid in one hand and a tube of beef jerky in the other. Lee tucked his chin further down, got into my Chrysler, and had the car in reverse before the coffee cup arced out of the trucker's hand and landed on the closed car door. The hot liquid steamed and sizzled as it slid down the frozen window. Lee didn't hear the trucker mumble the word—*queer*—but I could read his lips as we sped out of the parking lot.

Christine was wrong. The contents of the container aren't held back by death: they're held back by the body.

Watching Lee was a sort of a gift. I spread myself in a layer as thin as a coat of sunscreen and hovered just above his body as he pulled the car back onto the highway without signaling. Simultaneously, he clicked open the Chrysler's center console, dug in to the bottom of a stack of un-jacketed CDs, selected *L.A. Woman*, pushed the disc into the player, and clicked nine times. The sound of recorded thunder filled the car. Lee punched the felt-covered roof of the car three times, rhythmically, as Morrison's cultish voice hissed: *there's a killer on the road / his brain is squirmin' like a toad.*

He set the cruise control for exactly nine miles over the limit and adjusted it as we passed through construction zones and over the state line. Lee didn't pause to look as we crossed the Mississippi. Lee didn't give a shit about scenery.

Soon we were standing in a junkyard surrounded by a chain-link fence. Two bulldogs met the car as we entered, and they escorted us down a dirt road to a small brick house with a sign that said CEDAR VALLEY SALVAGE. The fences and the dogs made me nervous; we were enclosed by trash higher than the roof of a suburban house and the only way out was the narrow way we had come in.

Lee honked the horn and rolled down the window. He was transcendentally rude.

A small man holding a grease-covered rag stepped out of the brick house. His fingernails were black with oil and his teeth were a lovely yellow, the color of the sun beneath a cloud.

"Yep," he said by way of salutation.

Lee hit the side of the Chrysler with his open palm, twice. "How much for a trade-in?"

"Well," the man looked at the expensive Chrysler. It was electric blue: the audacious shade of expensive guitars and tiki drinks. "Don't take trade-ins here. This is a scrap yard." He gestured needlessly to the sign.

"Got anything come in today that hasn't been taken apart yet?"

The man considered his feet. "Yep. Couple old pickups."

"They run?"

The dogs had relaxed and flopped down. They were a little fat, I realized, old and easily winded. So was the man.

"One of 'em," he said finally. "I guess it'll get you where you're going if you're not going too fast."

"That'll work."

"You got papers for that? I can give you more if you've got papers."

"Riders on the Storm" started again and Lee cut the engine. He had the Swiss Army knife opened, I realized. "No papers."

He opened the car door, used the knife to scrape off the seventeen-digit code on the lip of the Chrysler doors, and then flipped the knife to the screwdriver tool and removed the plates.

Lee popped the hood and cut a bundle of wires. "This car's junk," he turned back to the man with the knife still extended. "Got it? When you report this car to the city, you report it as junk. You take the parts you want and crush it."

The man nodded.

Lee gathered the car's papers from the glove box and ejected *L.A. Woman* from the dash.

"Let's see that truck."

Ten minutes later we were driving back down the dirt road in a brown '88 Ford pickup. I kept my eyes on the Chrysler until it was a smudge of electricity on the horizon. I would miss it—it was the car Dr. Clink had taught me Morse code in.

I was sad, but not that sad. Lee acted too quickly to ruminate. It was a relief to see things happen without the superstructure of manners, facial expressions, social nuance. It was, I realized, the inverse of boredom. Power, Chancellor Lethe had once told me, is knowing rules don't exist.

What happened next happened quickly, unconfined by any laws at all.

Lee drove directly to the Mennonite town ten minutes north of the trailer park where Kayla Gavin's body was found and took a local newspaper from a glass stand on the street. He made two calls. The first was in response to a job ad for work at the local hog farm and the second was for a vacancy at the trailer park. Within fifteen minutes, Lee had a job castrating, vaccinating, and notching the ears of pigs and a single wide at Prairie Village Mobile Home Park. Twenty minutes later, he was drinking a Coors from a red-and-silver can at the only bar in town. The bartender, a wrinkled woman in a Def Leppard T-shirt, called Lee *honey*. Within minutes, he had drawn the attention of a girl. She said she was a former Mennonite and had just moved to town last year. I winced at her description of the feed store, bar, churches (one Lutheran, one Catholic, both German), and post office as a "town," but Lee didn't seem to notice. He switched her order from Budweiser to Jack and Diets and the girl was drunk and crying about the murder before the 4:30 p.m. midwestern sunset. She had sat in the same pew as Kayla at church sometimes. She put her hand on Lee's thigh and leaned toward him as if she were about to tell a secret, and instead stated loudly that everyone in town knew Chris Gavin's boyfriend had murdered the little girl.

"He's a scuzz bucket," she said and a few of the farm workers sitting at the bar nodded. "Always peeping and creeping around at the little girls' softball games, sitting there in the bleachers all alone." She took a long drink and then repeated, "little girls."

I guess that was enough evidence for Lee. He offered to drive the drunk girl home and on the way found out that the boyfriend's name was Jeff Crawford and, as Lee had apparently already intuited, he was out of work and lived in the trailers. The girl even pointed to the exact trailer that Jeff lived in. The lights were out, but a television flashed epileptically through the naked window.

Lee listened to everything the girl said neutrally, silently, letting her offer information instead of asking questions.

Drunk girls, I knew from my time at college, remembered only vague impressions, never what they had actually said. As long as Lee left her with a sort of soft ambient sense of attraction, the girl wouldn't remember that anything had happened at all except that she'd met a new guy in town. When they arrived at the room she rented in an old farmhouse on the edge of the town, Lee leaned over the girl to open her car door. When she moved in to kiss him, her breath smelled like beer and corn chips. The ethanol pump at the gas station. He let her lips touch his, counted to two, and then pulled back.

It was long enough not to be insulting and short enough not to be inviting. She got out of the truck without ever asking his name.

For the next six days, Lee wore rubber pants and stood in a pool of mud and filth to inject pigs with antibiotics. By night, he stalked Jeff Crawford, who didn't leave his trailer until the day before the funeral. Lee knew he wouldn't be in town much longer—he knew he wouldn't even be in his current body much longer—so he didn't bother to be covert when he broke into Jeff's trailer and searched it. He found what he was looking for quickly: the child's purple sock, hidden in a baggie deep within a red plastic tub of Folgers ground coffee. A trophy. Lee put the sock back. He knew the police would have a search warrant within the next few days.

I watched Lee stand in the small kitchen, his hand on the pistol he carried with him everywhere but the hog farm. He looked for a moment at a box of generic trash bags, at the cracks in the linoleum floor, and I realized he was thinking of shooting Jeff right here, in the murderer's own home. It's impossible, though, I saw him decide as he looked at the surrounding trailers, spaced mere feet from each other. Too loud, too indiscreet, even for a place as detached as this.

Instead, he rented a room in a house that overlooked the graveyard. He stole some keys to the hog farm. He watched the funeral, he watched Jeff sweat, he followed him to the reception, and he stood by the door of the church basement smoking until Jeff emerged. He offered him a cigarette laced with rat poison. Five drags in, Jeff was curled over from stomach cramps. Lee inserted himself under the now-limp man's shoulder and walked him to the truck. To passersby, it looked like Jeff Crawford was wasted.

Lee drove to the hog farm. It was dark for the weekend and quiet except for the arrhythmic snorts of the animals. Without ceremony, Lee dragged Jeff's body to the kill floor. A metal surface turned rusty from daily blood. He shot once, at the base of the skull, into the bundle of nerves that organize life, and then he dropped the body in the lagoon.

He didn't bother to watch it sink.

CHAPTER TWO

"GROSS TEENAGE BOY DOESN'T LOOK BAD ON YOU, JESSIE."

Before I could even slip the keys into the truck's ignition, I felt a cool metal disc about the size of a dime pressed into the soft space between my jaw and sternal head.

"If I pull this trigger, the bullet will pass through your cerebellum. That might not be too bad on the left side—you probably won't be able to talk or do complex logic problems, but you might live. And you'd still have your memories. The brain is so redundant. People think it's like a factory, each part doing its own job, but that's not really true. Memories get stored again and again, recoding themselves all over your mind. But you knew that already. Your father is the memory studies expert, right? The same expert who erased his own daughter's memory."

"No, that's not correct," I said, scanning the empty hog farm's parking lot. It was a sea of corrugated steel, dirty snow, and barbed wire. My gun was tucked into the back of my jeans, out of reach, and I wasn't going to get far on foot. "My father is a professor of boredom studies. That's a subset of memory."

The gun shifted, digging further into the weak part of my neck until it was pointed at an upward angle. "But if I pulled the trigger here, the bullet would pass through your brain stem and temporal lobe, and then, well—you tell me!" She giggled. "I *told* you I'd kill to be as smart as you, Jessie."

I'd kill to be as smart as you. The accent was like the plaid pattern of a Burberry scarf, unimaginative yet aspirational.

Jane.

The last time I had seen her she had been standing on the steps of Mayflower dorm, wearing a bathrobe, gloves, and winter hat as she waved me goodbye. She stood there watching as Grethe bundled me into the back seat of the Chrysler and she stayed there, rapt, until the car disappeared across the river. *Jane* had been the one to explain what had happened to Grethe, I remembered.

Jane jabbed the gun a bit further into my neck. "Well?" she prompted.

"I guess it depends what kind of gun you're holding," I paused and added pointedly, *"Jane."*

"Figured it out, huh? I wasn't sure you'd recognize my voice since you were never exactly, you know, not a bitch to me."

"What kind of gun is it?"

"Well, it's not a BB gun, Jessie. I can tell you that."

Her voice was pitched a little higher, whinier.

"Because if it's a military-grade weapon with a high-velocity bullet, I would die."

"And a low-velocity?"

"You mean, like a handgun?" I listened to her breathing for a moment. It shallowed slightly and I knew all she had was a pistol, something small. "I'd still die."

"But if you didn't?"

"I suppose you would hit my amygdala and then I really would forget everything. You're right that the brain encodes various parts of the cortex with the same engram so that if one part of the brain is destroyed, it can potentially be reconstructed in another part of the brain at a later time, if neural pathways are stimulated in the exact order necessary. But that's not true if the amygdala is damaged. If that goes, everything goes. Also, that's assuming the bullet passed clean through. And, then, obviously, you took me straight to a trauma center."

"We're about forty-five minutes from the nearest hospital, so I doubt that would do you much good."

Jane was so close to me that the top notes of her perfume— pineapple, lemon, bergamot, the antiseptic asexual odor of CK One— made my eyes water. It also made me realize that I was Jessica again, not an eighteen-year-old boy with the mind and skills of a soldier. Lee never would have noticed a perfume, let alone identified it. Lee would not be exhausted and dying to shower off the smell of pig feces. Lee would not have used the word *feces*.

I was only with myself.

It was around 1:00 a.m. The hog farm would be closed for another two hours, until the first crew arrived to feed the animals. Jane could kill me right here if she wanted to and haul my body into the lagoon. I would decompose next to the murderer.

That's what will happen to you, Jessica, you'll blend with the pedophile until you both evaporate into the cosmic soup.

The thought blunted and vanished. It simply wasn't true: there was no such person as Jessica. There was no *there* there, just an encyclopedic understanding of makeup and dieting tricks.

My only task on earth, as far as I could imagine, had been to avenge the child, and now I had done it. Oddly, though, my lips quivered as I closed my eyes and leaned my head back into the gun.

"Go ahead, Jane. Get it over with. You've only got a couple hours to kill me and get out of here."

I felt the gun tremble and falter against my neck. Jane pulled away from me slightly.

"*What?*" The bratty disgust in her voice reminded me she was just a teenager with a gun. Like I had been, I guess. "Are you *serious?* Oh my god. You have to be kidding. Some girl from your dorm shows up in your *stolen* truck with a *gun* to your head right after *you killed some random guy* and you don't have any questions? You are seriously the *worst*, Jessica. I wish Director Lethe had assigned me to anybody but you. You're such a—" she grappled for the right word—the truest, nastiest word—and came up with "*snob.*"

I swung my head and looked at her for the first time. Now that Jane knew I didn't plan to fight her, she had lost her assassin drag.

"What?" We were facing each other, only about two feet away in the cabin of the truck. Jane looked the same—plain-faced without makeup, her hair cut into a blunt bob. The only difference was that instead of jeans and a Northwestern sweatshirt, she wore a sort of Hillary Clinton-esque business suit. She probably had a lanyard and a headband in her purse.

"Yeah, exactly!"

"Repeat yourself. Who assigned you to me?"

"The Director! Obviously, who else?"

"Director who? Of what?"

"Oh my god." She rolled her eyes so hard I worried her contacts would pop out. "Director Lethe!"

The gun was sitting limply in her lap now. I could easily have taken it from her, but I knew a terrified Jane was a lot less helpful than a confident Jane. It was, I realized, finally time to make friends with her.

"Jane," I let my voice quaver like I might cry, "you have to help me. I'm in so much trouble."

"Well, yeah." Her eyebrows were raised nearly to her hairline. She still didn't pluck. "*Duh.*"

CHAPTER THREE

I let Jane direct me at gunpoint into her white Ford Taurus, which was pulled off on the side of the entrance to the hog farm. Her black loafers were soaked in dirty snow, so I knew she had parked and followed me into the farm on foot.

"You drive. But take your shoes off before you get in." She pulled a plastic grocery sack out of the glove box and handed it to me. "This is a company car."

I almost laughed. Instead, I kept my face straight and respectfully placed my shoes in Jane's Hy-Vee sack.

She handed me a yellow J.Crew sweater, an emerald green Ann Taylor blazer, and a black hooded parka. I recognized the fake fur hood on the parka as the one that hung on the back of our dorm room door.

"Put these on, take your hat off, and put this on." She gave me a black winter hat with a wig of medium brown hair attached to it.

"For real?" I asked, as I pulled Lee's baseball cap off. My hair fell down around my shoulders and Jane gasped like I had done a magic trick.

"Oh! You kept some of your own hair." She squinted at me. "I can't even tell the underneath is gone when it's down. Anyway," she pulled a pack of bobby pins out of her purse, "pin it up for now. We'll dye it later."

No, we won't, I thought, but I accepted the pins and put the idiotic wig hat on my head. I glanced at myself in the rearview mirror. I looked like I was wearing a *Daria* costume from Spirit Halloween.

"This looks really stupid, Jane."

"No, it looks really normal." Jane herself had changed out of her blazer into a North Face fleece and she had her own wig hat with very similar brown hair. "If you're trying to blend in, platinum blonde hair is what looks stupid."

She was right, I realized. We looked like pharmacy reps on a business trip in our economy car. We had achieved average, which was the same as incognito.

"It'll take about seventeen hours to get there," she said, reaching up from the back seat to reset the mileage marker, "so that puts us in New Mexico at about six p.m., accounting for time difference." She glanced at me expectantly, the gun still sitting on her lap. "So . . ." she gestured as if she were waiting for me to put on my lipstick and come to dining hall with her.

"So what?" I responded in the same dull tone I would have responded with back at Mayflower.

"So let's get going! You can take I-80 at this time of night, but stay within five miles of the limit, above or below. Have you done a driving mission before? Probably not, right?"

Instead of answering, I put the car in reverse and let her keep talking as we drove through the unlit countryside and onto the hyper-illuminated highway. She was sitting in the backseat (presumably to keep better track of my movements), which only increased a dynamic that felt more therapist-patient than abductor-hostage.

"I guess they mostly had you doing intelligence? Honestly, they didn't tell me much. Lethe just said to report if you showed any signs of emergent personalities. Which you didn't! You were totally normal! I mean, you were my very first agent. They needed someone who looked eighteen, I guess, and so," she gestured to herself. How old *was* Jane?

She could be at least in her mid-twenties, I decided. "You know, they told me I was getting a job with the CIA—and I ended up in a dorm in the Midwest babysitting a teenager and eating Hot Pockets. They didn't even give me enough orientation to keep from," she paused and glanced at me apologetically, "well, from making sure you didn't lose it. You would think the shadow government would be more organized than the *government*-government, right? But they're *not*." She paused and collected herself. "Anyway, I'm sorry about what happened. I should have stopped you from fragmenting. It's just—I was looking for, you know, a strange accent or *super skills* or something. But you were just an ordinary sad girl who was getting good grades. Now, of course, I know that when one of my MONARCH starts to show symptoms of depression, I have to take her in immediately."

"Wait, what?"

"Like being withdrawn, sleeping a lot—"

"No, I know what depression is. Did you say 'monarch'? Like the butterfly?"

"Sorry—I know we're not supposed to use that term anymore. But, honestly, do we have to be political when we're talking about a program the civilian population *doesn't even know about*? By the way, we're getting close to the hub for I-80, so if you need to pee we'd better stop there. We're only authorized for bathroom breaks in Des Moines, Kansas City, and Amarillo."

A ruffle of déjà vu drifted over me like a curtain blowing in a sealed room, undeniable, impossible, eerie. I had heard that exact statement from Dr. Clink on our way to the Desert University dozens and dozens of times over the years. I had thought it was a dad joke, but in retrospect, we never did stop anywhere else no matter how hard I whined.

Jane reached into her purse and pulled out a bag of Ronny's brand corn chips. "Want some?"

The sound of the aluminum mouth ripping open had a sort of Pavlovian effect on me. Not the kind of Pavlovian effect you learned about in high school psych where the dogs are socially conditioned to respond to external stimulus: a bell rings and the mutt's mouth salivates; a bag of chips tears and I trust Jane.

No, I mean the Pavlovian effect where one spring the basement lab located on the banks of the River Neva floods and the dogs remain trapped in their cages, submerged in freezing water for over two days. They all survive, but obviously, they're totally traumatized. Trauma, of course, is dull, but Pavlov, through the parasitic powers of observation that won him a Nobel Prize in 1904, envisages his final contribution to his field: The Reflex of Purpose. Basically, he says that the dogs (being trapped) had no recourse to a fight-or-flight response, and so, like a woman who has no financial recourse to escape the husband who beats her, the dogs suffered not so much because of the flood, but because they couldn't *do* anything about it. The stuff that happens in the brain—the chemicals that get spilled, the hormones that overproduce—during fighting or fleeing have a strong correlation to recovery. All I'm saying—all Pavlov was saying—is that creatures who find a way to save themselves are more likely to thrive because they believe their actions mean something. They go on to build nests, gather food, find mates.

Caring in general didn't come naturally, but I guess it's what moved me to keep trying a little longer. That bag of Ronny's brand corn chips evoked, in total recall, an image of Veronica. Her mouth salty, smiling. Veronica, my only tie to the world; my reflex of purpose. It occurred to me suddenly that even she had not been real.

"Jane, were you the only handler I had?"

She laughed once, an instantly hushed bark. "Do you have any idea how often I was with you?"

"Well, no. A lot?" I thought of her doing leg lifts in the middle of the floor, of the claustrophobic feeling I always had in our dorm room, the sense Jane was inescapable.

"Yes," she said flatly, "A lot. They made me wear a watch that would send a shock to my wrist if your feet touched the floor at night. They *literally electrocuted* me because they cared so much about making sure nothing happened to you on the way to the bathroom! I had to get out of bed and follow you. I never got a full night's sleep."

"But what about the times when I didn't come back to the dorm room?"

"Oh, you mean when you slept in the dorm's laundry room?" her voice was surprisingly bitter. "When you went in there and didn't come out for the whole weekend, I had to sit in the hot water heater closet and sweat my ass off. I was issued actual adult diapers to wear while I waited for you to come out. Thanks for that."

"I'm sorry," I said. And I actually meant it. Jane was just a girl, like me, doing a job she didn't understand for a man she didn't like.

"So, to answer your question, no. There was no other handler at Mayflower and I didn't receive a dossier on you from a handler before me like I do with the other girls."

"*Other* girls?" The skin between my eyebrows began to pinch and I felt my lower lip quiver, the involuntary tremble that precedes tears. A sudden flash of Veronica turning to me and smiling after she refused to go into the confessional, the look on her face the most sacred thing in the church: a secret between us.

"They acted like you were just so special. The Director's own girl."

Jane seemed oblivious to the fact that I was losing it. "What makes you so different?"

"I don't know. Nothing." Jane scoffed and muttered something through a mouthful of corn chips that sounded like *whatever*. "Really, Jane. I don't even know what 'monarch' is. My mother said it to me the last time I talked to her, but I never got to ask her what she meant."

The car was quiet for a moment while Jane chewed and stared at me. Eventually, I reached into the bag and took a greasy handful.

"I'm not better than you, Jane." I shoved the chips in my mouth and chewed in tandem with her. "I'm a college dropout who lives with her parents. Honestly." I turned my eyes away from the road. Some instinct told me to let her get a good look at me without makeup, my nostrils and eyelids red-rimmed from sleeplessness, my lips cracked from working in the January wind on the hog farm, and my skin zitty from eating exclusively microwavable foods. My breath was still saturated with the porky juice of Lee's last meal, a circular carton of bologna. "I need your help. I have no idea what's happening to me. I need you to tell me who I am." My voice cracked a little at the end, a perfect performance. Except, for once, I wasn't performing.

"Tell me what you know," Jane said finally.

"Eight days ago I developed some photos for my job at University Photography. They were of a dead girl. A child. Something happened to my mind after that. I started to have memories that aren't mine—"

Jane cut me off sharply. "Memories of what?"

"Different places. It's usually really hot. I think it's the Middle East somewhere. There are mosques."

"Do you remember what you're doing or only what you saw?"

"Mostly only what I saw. But in one of the memories there's blood on my hands. I'm holding a knife. I think they're my hands."

She nodded. "Go on. What do you remember doing after you saw the photos?"

"I called Grethe—"

"Stop. Back up. What did you do *directly* after you saw the photos?"

Jane had taken a small flip pad out of her purse that she seemed to be taking notes on. Typical Jane. As if we were going to be tested on a conversation later.

"I panicked. I felt like I was floating."

"Did you?"

"What, float?"

"Did you float above your body and watch yourself walk out of the photography lab?"

"Yeah. I did." And then I remembered what else I had done. "I watched myself reach up and start to choke myself."

"And could you control the body you saw? Like you did with . . . what's the name of your murder boy personality? I think you called yourself Lee Andersen earlier?"

"No." I realized there was a difference. When I'd been at Dead Ringers or watching Lee, I'd been watching myself from above— levitating. In the photo lab, I'd been plummeting. "It wasn't like that."

Jane nodded. "But you stopped. How?"

"I saw myself."

"In a surface, a mirror, what? Was your image distorted in any way?"

"I saw a photo I took of myself. It was distorted; the lens was covered in Vaseline so the edges were blurred."

"Like a ghost?" she asked as if that were important.

"Yeah," I said, "I guess like a ghost."

"So you saw yourself, stopped self-strangulating, and called your mother. Correct?"

"Correct."

"And then?"

"She told me to go back in and finish the photos. I think I was hysterical. I think she said that I was blank and I know she said I'm not a monarch."

Jane reached forward and took my right wrist. "Drop your wrist below your heart. You can steer with your left hand." She placed her fingers on my pulse. "I need to get your heart rate while you tell me this. Jessica Greenglass Clink, tell me what your mother said using her exact words."

It felt like there was a string in my back I had never been aware of until Jane pulled it just then. I opened my mouth and spoke like a ventriloquist's doll. "My name is Jessica Greenglass Clink," I re-repeated, "I was deactivated in 1998. I am clear. I am not MONARCH. My heart is in the air. I am not MONARCH. I feel my feet on the ground."

Jane counted for what seemed like ten seconds and then released my wrist. She made a note in her book.

"Next," she prompted.

"I drove home and when I got there the yard was surrounded by officers. I pulled into the garage and before I could get out of the car—" Jane flipped a page in her notebook and I decided I didn't want Christine's name in it. I also didn't really want Jane to know the exact contents of the bag I had tucked between my feet. "I decided to run. I was worried the officers were there to arrest me for something relating to the photos." Jane was quiet so I kept going. It was impossible to tell if she knew I was omitting information. "It was irrational and I was afraid. I drove east and in a gas station I saw a story in a newspaper about the child that was murdered. Kayla Gavin. It had information about her funeral service, so I started driving to the town where it was being held, and on the way I started to 'float' again, but I wasn't seeing myself from above anymore and I wasn't feeling anything except for sort of—rage? I just watched as a teenage boy entered my body and it started to move and talk and dress like him."

"Describe him."

"I mean . . . there isn't much to say. He's who I was dressed as when you found me."

"Only dressed as?"

I knew without question Lee would have overpowered and killed her. Or, been killed in the process.

"I slipped back into this body at some point. I didn't know it until I smelled your perfume."

"What kind of skills does Lee have?" It struck me that she spoke in the present tense, as if Lee were a bad boyfriend who might come back.

"Combat, I guess. Rapport building. Weapons training. Negotiation?"

"How about pain tolerance? Sleep habits?"

"High. I guess I haven't slept in five days." I blinked. My eyes felt like they had a clear lid over them.

"Okay. What did Lee do after he arrived?"

"He staked out the man who killed Kayla Gavin and shot him. He threw the body in the pit at the hog farm." I was suddenly tired.

"Why did he do that?"

"What do you mean? Why *wouldn't* he do that?"

Jane didn't respond, but she took a very long note. She was so calm. It was infuriating.

"Who are you?" I asked. I was surprised by how even my voice was. It was as if I couldn't be angry even if I tried while I was in my Jessica body.

"My name is Jian Zhao. I was your handler from August twentieth, 1998, until October thirtieth, 1998." I remembered her appearing by my side at the Mayflower orientation table, picking up her nametag, and introducing herself. She had asked me my room number and then shrieked with glee when she realized I was her dorm mate. From there, she had never really left.

"That's why you were always asking me to hang out with you." I felt numb.

"Well, yeah. I went to Yale. I definitely didn't need to be doing flashcards on Gender 101 with you."

"You went to *Yale?* How old are you?"

"Twenty-five."

"But how did you end up doing this? Working for . . . whatever this is?"

"I was signed up to go abroad—I'd gotten an American-Scandinavian Foundation grant to go to Oslo—and this woman I knew from when I was a kid showed up. I was waiting to get my Tdap and MMR shots at the student health center and when I told her I was going to Norway, she got really excited and said what an amazing co-incidence it was because she needed a Norwegian speaker at her com-pany." Jian paused. "Well, I didn't think hard enough about it. I wanted the job to be real and plus, I trusted her. She told me how much it paid and it was more than either of my parents make in five years."

"But the job wasn't real?"

"No, it was," she laughed, "but I only needed to speak Norwegian that one time."

To translate what I said during my blackout. I remembered her repeating my words in a perfect Norwegian accent. At the time, I'd thought she was just a great mimic.

"Wait, what about your government internship? That man you met with every month?"

"He was my contact for you. I reported to him what you had been doing and he reported it—I don't know. To the next person. The right hand never sees what the left hand is doing," she shrugged. "And there are a lot of hands on the way to Lethe."

"What does Chancellor Lethe have to do with it? You said you're CIA earlier."

"No, I said they *told* me I was getting a job with the CIA."

"So who do you work for? Who do *I* work for?"

"Director Lethe, as far as I know. If there's anyone above him, they didn't tell me. We're different wings of MONARCH, no pun intended." She giggled a little. Even then, I could not help but remember that Chancellor Lethe had once told me involuntary wordplay is a strong indicator of mental instability.

Jian, I realized, was just as batshit as Jane.

CHAPTER FOUR

"YOU'RE A SPLITTER." JIAN PRONOUNCED THE WORD "SPLITTER" in a way that made it clear she felt the concept was far away from her— the way I expect she may have said "you're a cutter" or "you're a clown" if she'd walked in on me in the dorm bathroom with a knife or waxy face of red and white paint, respectively. It was the specific tone one uses to respond subtly to horror. "Sorry," she amended, "I mean a Multi-Dimensional Identity Acquisitor."

Over the next hour, she explained that the different "wings" of MONARCH included low-level admin (her) and talent (me). Among other things, I learned she'd been digging my lipstick out of the dorm trash not to wear, but to collect my DNA. While she was willing to discuss the details of her own job at length, Jian seemed generally disinterested in explaining my role. She especially did not want to discuss what being a "splitter" involved, although I got her to explain that I procured intelligence using atypical or otherwise unorthodox means. Additionally, she revealed I had some facility with combat, weapons, covert operations, and atypical approaches to espionage. I knew from Jian's blushing explanation what "atypical" was a euphemism for.

Perhaps because she was relieved that I didn't press her to detail the baser aspects of my "assignments," she finally agreed to elucidate that being a Multi-Dimensional Identity Acquisitor meant I had several different "personas" that I could "transition" into. "Each persona has its own memories, education, talents, languages, gestures, postural and facial muscle memory, voice, yada yada, you get it." Jian explained.

"You mean like different costumes? But inside."

"Sort of. You're supposed to be able to transition at will, but judging from what you've just told me, you were wiped clean in '98. They must have deactivated you instead of just decommissioning you like they do with most girls. See?" she said accusatorily, "You were always getting special treatment. It didn't stop you from being triggered at the dorms for whatever reason, though. After you fractured there, you probably lost your ability to transition at will. Now your body is doing it for you."

"But I never 'transitioned at will.' I was always Jessica." Even before I completed the sentences, I knew they weren't true.

"Well, in a sense . . ." Jian's voice had a weird cadence and pitch to it. *Pity*, I realized. *That's what pity sounds like.* "I'm probably not supposed to tell you this. But your father arranged a deal with the Director. He negotiated a trade so that you would work until you were eighteen and each time you transitioned, he would put you in this tank he had invented that would erase your memory of the transition. Essentially, it would be like it didn't happen because you wouldn't remember it."

The sleepwalking.

The kryokammer.

The memory studies expert who erased his own daughter's memory.

"A trade for what?"

Jian paused. "Shit," she said finally. "I definitely wasn't supposed to tell you that."

"A trade for what, Jian?"

"Well, your mother. The Director agreed to take your mother out of commission in exchange for four years from you. I guess the arrangement might have changed now that—"

Now that she's dead, Jian had been about to say.

"Now that what?" I asked.

In the rearview mirror, I saw her seal her lips in a straight line.

"Director Lethe would like to talk to you about your parents personally."

"Is that why you came to get me?"

"That's what I was told, yes. Take the exit for Kansas City here."

"Wait—you said we could stop to pee."

"We missed the authorized exit. Sorry, my fault." She didn't sound that sorry. She was mad at herself for telling me too much and now she was shutting down. "You can hold it, though, right? A pageant girl can always hold it a little longer."

"Pageant girl?" I echoed dumbly before an image of Jian constantly working out or straightening her spine as if to make sure an imaginary crown was perfectly parallel to the ceiling flashed before me. Tiny traits, the ones a pageant girl never sheds. "Why didn't you tell me at Mayflower?"

"Why didn't *you* tell *me*?"

"Fair."

"Train under duress, conquer every stress," Jian said in a clipped voice. "That's what my pageant coach always said when I wanted to take off a costume to go to the bathroom."

"Mine, too. Crystal—"

"—St. Marie," we finished together.

"Oh my god," Jian shrieked, thrilled. "We had the same coach! Ms. St. Marie was the one who told me about this job, too! That's so crazy!"

I was beginning to doubt the caliber of Yale grads.

"Is it crazy, Jian?"

Her mouth opened as if to speak and then froze.

"Do you really think it's just, like, a crazy coincidence that you and me—two girls who were on the pageant circuit around the *same* time and had the *same* coach are now working for the *same* organization?"

She was shaking her head from side to side. I couldn't tell if she was disagreeing with me or if she was beginning to realize she disagreed with her life as she knew it. The glaze settling over her eyes could be denial or desperation.

"But that would mean . . ." she trailed off, unable, apparently, to think the idea through.

"It would mean we've both been totally clueless," I said bluntly.

"But I quit the pageants when I was just a kid. I hadn't even seen Ms. St. Marie for, I don't know, nine years when she showed up at the health center."

"So you were, what, thirteen when you quit?"

"Yeah."

"Well, me too."

"Why did you quit?"

"I . . ." I didn't know how to explain that I had quit because one day I had woken up and realized the pageants were humiliating without also explaining Christine. "I just burned out."

Jian didn't question this: she had never known me as anything *but* a burnout.

Unsolicited, she explained, "When I started junior high it became apparent that I had other, more exceptional, aptitudes." I could tell this was a speech she had rehearsed with college admissions officers to explain her shameful past as a child beauty queen. "They said I had a true gift for languages and so I quit the pageants to concentrate on my studies and focus on getting into an Ivy." I could almost see the montage passing across Jian's eyes as she recalled trading her taps for a foreign language dictionary, of transposing the joy of a pageant sash to a certificate signed by the Dean declaring her *cum laude*, of the feel of her ass as the muscles atrophied from sitting in a library.

"And who suggested you had an aptitude, Jian?"

She was quiet for a moment. "Ms. St. Marie," she said finally. "But—"

"So they had lessons in Norwegian at your junior high," I cut in quickly.

"Well, no—"

"Then how?" I asked, already knowing the answer, "How did some girl from a shithole town in Illinois—"

"Aurora," she interrupted compulsively. "It's a suburb of Chicago."

I respected her for managing to remain classist even at what was probably the most critical juncture of her life. "Fine. How did a girl from Aurora get lessons in a language less than, what, point four percent of people in Illinois speak?"

She shook her head helplessly. "My best friend's mom gave lessons."

"Best friend from where?"

In a small voice, at length, "The pageants."

I let that sink in as we crossed over the Missouri River, its brown water spewing chunks of ice. "Don't you want to know how you got here?" I asked, gesturing to the desolate river. "Don't you want to know how much of your life was real? If any of it was?"

Maybe I decided to tell her because it was obvious to me that we were enslaved by the same circumstance, yoked together by childhood beauty and adult incompetence. I sensed that, like dogs in a kill shelter, Jian and I were now trauma bonded; we did not especially like each other, but we were each other.

Maybe I told her because I thought she was the only other person who would ever understand.

Or, maybe I told her because I had no other choice.

Anyway, I told Jian about Veronica. In the end, it was so much simpler to tell than I had convinced myself it would be. When I finished the story, Jian used a saying so ordinary, so cliché—so, well, John Hughes—that I had never even considered such a simple idea applied to me.

"She was the love of your life," Jian said succinctly.

Maybe I cried a little, maybe I remained stoic.

"I need to find out what happened to her," I said. "I need to know if she was MONARCH."

"Where is she now?"

"I don't know," I said dully. "They said she disappeared."

We made eye contact in the rearview mirror, Jian's mouth a black O. The orange glow of the sun began to crack the horizon behind her, the atmosphere momentarily burnt red.

We fell quiet and didn't speak again until we had passed through Texas.

After we gassed the car in Amarillo, Jian had silently taken the driver's seat and replaced her gun in the holster concealed under the flap of her blazer.

She took a familiar exit for Acme, one I had noticed the sign for hundreds of times on my way to the Desert University with Grethe and Dr. Clink. It was written in a font that looked like ash on a background of egg yolk yellow. Underneath the name of the town were the words CITY OF DUST in a haunted house font.

"It's a ghost town," Dr. Clink had told me once when I had asked if we could stop and see it. "There's nothing there."

"How did everyone die?" I was eleven years old. It would be a few more years until I realized he didn't mean actual ghosts.

"There was an accident in a factory. An event."

As Jian guided the car further off the highway, handmade signs written in white spray paint on plywood began to appear. PELIGRO was written on one. NO DIGGING ALLOWED on another. The last was simply a circle with three misshapen squares surrounding it: the symbol for radiation. Jian pulled onto what must have once been a main street. Acme was the skeleton of a small town, white and whittled down to its essential structure.

Oddly, I had always pictured the accident Dr. Clink had mentioned occurring in a candy factory. Sticky streams of red and white oozing out the windows, rivulets of peppermint running down the city's street, chasing women in flat shoes and gray factory uniforms. Obviously, that was incorrect. Jian stopped the car in front of a heap of stones. Where a glass window must have once been, there were now boards painted over with a red plume. No, the spore of a mushroom cloud.

"Come on," she said. It was the first thing she'd said for a few hundred miles. Her voice was flattened, emptied of affect. "Take your knife and leave everything else."

Actual tumbleweeds blew by us as we walked deeper into the town. In the distance, I heard a dog or a coyote laugh and I realized how silent it really was out here.

Jian led me down a series of paths to a graveyard that was about the size of my parents' living room. There were only a few family names across the couple dozen graves—BELVIN, COOPER, HITE. We stopped in front of one with a small pile of stones atop it. BABY HALCOMBE, no dates.

Jian regarded the grave for a moment and then turned to me, her face very still. "We have to disappear," she said.

I had expected this. Before today, Jian had thought she was making choices. She didn't need to tell me that she had gotten out of the pageants when junior high ended and decided to spend her time on excelling in debate club and Model UN instead. She didn't need to tell me she had worked hard and gotten good grades and gone to an Ivy League school on a fellowship and then gotten a job working for the U.S. government that her mother and father were proud to tell their family in another country about. She didn't need to tell me that in the background of her life an emergency alarm cried nonstop or that from the corner of her eye she sometimes saw the flashing lights of disaster. She didn't need to tell me that she had escaped the catastrophe of her birth because she was too goddamn *smart* to be tricked into wanting what the pageants told her to want. And she definitely didn't need to tell me that until right now, right here in a cemetery populated by graves whose bodies bore no relations left to grieve them, she would have hurt anyone to stay safe. And now she knew she never had been.

The only difference between us, really, was that Jian now had to mourn the life she thought she had lived and I couldn't even remember most of mine. Jian knew what there was to lose. She had a past and so could see the future.

Instead of the future, though, I could only think of Grethe, frozen in her gorgeous sleep. Vaguely, I wondered how different her life was now that she was dead. I felt a sharp prick of anxiety at the thought that the mortician wouldn't do her makeup right. *She wants to be buried in the blue silk sewn through with seed pearls and edged in white gold filigree*. The impulse to make sure it happened was otherworldly and urgent. It arose from some desire deeper than memory.

"I can't," I finally answered. I still had too much to do to disappear. "My family—"

Jian cut me off bluntly. "Your mother is dead, Jessica. I was taking you to Director Lethe so he could have your memory of her erased." She let out an odd, bitter laugh. "Why else would I have told you so much about who you are? The Director is worried that there's a glitch in your strain of MONARCH. He thinks it started with her, but from what you've said it started with *you*."

"What about my father? Is he still alive?"

"Presumably. But he's literally the last person you should be looking for. How do you think your mother died?"

I shook my head. I had dreamt so often of Grethe's death, so specifically of her hanging from the banister that crested the upstairs hallway. Her throat wrapped tight in the thick cord of the iron she used every morning, her bare toes hovering half an inch above the grand piano.

"I thought she killed herself," I mumbled. "I used to dream that she had done it all the time."

Jian's face softened momentarily. "They do that to you girls. They implant narratives in your dreams so that you don't ask questions in life. Mostly they do it to the honeypots—they implant these vivid dreams of fucking strangers so that the girls don't wonder what compels them to seduce the assets. They think it was their own idea."

"But why would he kill her?"

"I don't know." Jian shrugged. "I'm guessing it's because she told you to develop those photos, though. She didn't have the authority to clear you, but she did it and then she told you to preserve evidence of a murder. She committed a profound breach of protocol."

"You're saying that you think my father killed my mother because she told me to develop photos of a dead child?"

"I'm not saying I think your father killed your mother. I *know* he did. Everyone does. The proof-of-death photos were faxed to all of us. And if he finds out that you know about your personality implants and that you've figured out how to activate them on your own, he'll have to kill you, too."

Jian plucked the Swiss Army knife from my fingers and began using it to cut a small patch of hair off at the nape of her neck.

"But why?" Again, I thought of Grethe's body. Had they left her rings on? Only thirteen days ago, for Christmas, Dr. Clink had knelt beside the sofa and placed a violet diamond ring on her finger. It was so enormous that when my mother lifted her hand to sweep a stray hair off her brow, it looked, momentarily, as if she had a third eye. A trinity of smoke-purple chasms. "My father loved my mother."

"Jessica, he made a deal a long time before they ever gave your mother to him. He took an oath. If he didn't kill her, they would have." She was hacking at her hair with the blunt knife-edge now. "Then they would have killed him, too. You would have walked into that fancy house in the suburbs to find your parents stuffed into two body bags and a third unzipped and waiting for you."

"But what do the photos have to do with it? Why do they care?"

Jian had managed to shave off about a square inch of hair. Her skin bled a bit.

Instead of answering my question, she handed me the knife again. "Listen, we need to dry clean. You have to cut my tracker out. We're in a dead zone. They dumped a few thousand pounds of lead out here to try to contain the radiation, so right now our signals are muffled. We would have to go to Nagasaki to find somewhere else in the world this safe. They'll see us come in, but if we cut the tracker out inside the zone, they won't see us leave. We can vanish." She lifted the curtain of her hair. "Go ahead."

The sight of Jian's raw flesh made my face hot and my hands numb. "I can't." I looked away. "I'll be sick."

"Jesus Christ, Jessica! You just killed a guy and dumped him in a pool of pig shit!"

I shook my head. "You know that wasn't me."

Her hand twitched, as if she were controlling the urge to slap me. Instead, she asked, "Do you know how they take proof-of-death photos at the Institute?"

She knew I didn't. This was rhetorical.

"They sever the head from the body, like a . . . digital war trophy. So everyone knows the MONARCH is really dead." I remained still, the knife hanging limply at my side, so Jian sighed and added, "And anyway, if you don't help me then I won't tell you why they care about those photos of that dead girl."

As soon as I touched the blade to Jian's skin, my hand steadied and my fingers grew a bit longer. Another energy slipped into my body. Instead of floating above and watching the presence remove the tracker from Jian's neck, though, I stopped and looked at it. Just as quickly, it disappeared and the tremor returned.

"I'm sorry, Jian. I don't think I can do it. I'm not . . . I'm not programmed to hurt anyone when I'm—when Jessica—is in my body."

Jian nodded and furrowed her brow. The desert surrounding us was so still I could hear the second hand of her gold Casio like the ticking of a fashionable bomb, a metronome counting us down to our certain disaster.

"Do you have a mirror?" she eventually asked.

CHAPTER FIVE

OF COURSE I HAD A MIRROR.

As I located the small signal mirror in the escape kit, I thought of the glorious oval surrounded by bright, naked bulbs that hung above my vanity back home. Its lights would be off now, of course, its reflective surface occulted.

I handed Jian the tiny heliograph, expecting her to use it to look at the back of her own neck so she could remove the tracker herself, but instead she held it to the side. "Watch your hands in the mirror while you cut. I think the layer of remove will override your system and allow you to access your original bioarchitecture."

She was right. It could control the disembodied hand in the mirror as effortlessly as I had emptied out my personality in the vanity back home. I had no idea how to remove the tracker, though, and it took several minutes of digging into Jian's neck muscle before I hit the same tiny chip that I had found in my own neck last year. Jian bit down on the leather strap of her Coach bag and didn't cry, even when the blood seeped under her shirt collar and along the ridge of her spine. When I was finally done, her knees buckled and she sat down abruptly in the dirt.

"They probably wanted the photos destroyed because the child was MONARCH." Jian's voice was drained. "I don't know very much about what MONARCH do, but sometimes when they fracture they say things. Well, like you did. That night on the roof you kept saying 'We didn't jump.' That was creepy as hell, by the way. I thought maybe you really were possessed. But then it happened with the other MONARCH, too. I was assigned to three girls after you. They all fractured, occasionally, and said things like that—'It wasn't an overdose,' 'She didn't run away,' 'They burned off her fingerprints'—weird things. But it's a weird job." She shook her head as if surprised by something, by herself. "I didn't overthink it, honestly."

Jian flinched at my single harsh bark of laughter.

"Are you kidding me?" An image of Kayla appeared before me. A shot of her face close-up, a tooth jarred out of the mouth and embedded in a chapped lip.

Jian's shame converted to resentment almost instantly. "You have no idea what it's like to have nothing and no one to help you."

I raised an eyebrow and this time it was she who laughed bitterly at me.

"You think you've had it so bad because someone wanted to protect you from the awful things that happened to you? Because you grew up in a big fancy house with everything you wanted but you don't have, what, 'a sense of self'? Who gives a shit, Jessica. Most people never even have *time* to begin thinking about what you take for granted every single day."

"Like you're an expert?" I asked sarcastically. "I'm sure you had it really hard at Yale."

That was, apparently, exactly the wrong thing to say.

"You don't have any idea what you're talking about." Her eyes narrowed and she took a step toward me, her voice dropped an octave. "I worked my ass off to get into that school and when I got there, nobody wanted me. Everybody else knew somebody, or somebody's father or their fucking *grand*father, and I was this loser from Nowhere, Asia. I was a nobody from nowhere."

An acrylic nail chilled up my spine. I had heard those words before.

Dr. Clink's yearbook. His signature under the words, *a guy nobody else in the group had heard of, ever . . .*

The memory sucked me out of Jian's hysteric orbit, but I was pulled abruptly back in at the words "Blowjobs, for Adderall. And then, I had to graduate a semester early because I couldn't afford the med bills that were adding up for the Valacyclovir. Those Ivy League rich boys are filthy, did you know that?"

I thought of Jeffrey. I nodded.

"I knew they wouldn't give me my diploma if I racked up any more bills I couldn't pay. You've probably never even heard of such a thing, have you, Jessie? Can you believe that? *Universities keep the piece of paper that can get you a job to make money if you don't have the money to pay the University.*"

She paused briefly between every word of the last sentence, as though the point were too complicated for me to grasp unless she said it slowly and aggressively. She sounded like my father, animated by the same undying, low-level rage he had held toward his own university, toward the unknown university that had expelled the Chancellor decades ago. I'd been hearing rants like this one my entire life.

"So I got my diploma and you know what it was apparently worth?"

"Nothing?" I ventured. I had heard Dr. Clink say as much many times.

"Nothing," she spat as if I hadn't spoken. Most grievances come in the form of a monologue. "So I spent six months looking for a job and systematically got turned down for not having enough experience," she laughed bitterly, "but too much education. I failed a personality

assessment at a goddamn Sam Goody because they said they had problems in the past with people who scored too high on 'original thought.'
When I found out I got the grant to go to Oslo, my rent was two
months overdue. I was hanging on to the shitty studio in New Haven
just to keep the mailbox that the decision letter would arrive at. So,
yeah, I didn't overthink it when I got the job with the Institute and I
didn't want to think about it when the girls started to say weird things.
You wouldn't either, if you were in the position I was in."

She paused and considered me. She had the same glint in her eye
as a judge trying to determine if a girl had edged over the weight limit.

"But you will," she said finally. "One way or the other, you're going
to be out in the cold when this is over."

"So are you," I reminded her.

She shrugged. "I know. But I'm trained to survive at the bottom. I
know how to get from here to Tijuana with twenty dollars in quarters
stolen from a Kotex machine. I know how to walk into a crowd and
never walk back out. I know how to find a safe spot to sleep. I know
how to starve. *That's* the part that's going to be hard for you. I'm guessing the worst hunger you've ever experienced is the pang between your
lunch SlimFast shake and your dinner Zone bar."

"If it's going to be so bad, why are you doing this? You could have
taken me to the Desert University and kept on collecting checks."

She removed the compress she had been holding to her neck and
considered the rich blot of blood on the white gauze. Her face looked
really old, her eyes unfocused. In that moment, it was hard to believe I
had ever thought we were the same age.

"Because of the girls. After I messed up with you, the Institute
only assigned me kids. Little girls."

"Pageant girls?"

Impossibly, her face paled another shade and she kept her eyes fixed on her own blood. "Yeah. Pageant girls. The younger they were, the more they said when they fractured. I didn't want to believe it. They were just little girls . . . they sounded like they were describing something they saw on television. Something that had happened to someone else. They used words . . ."

She trailed off. "Two of them believed they were dolls. They were programmed to think they looked like a Barbie, to think their bodies were made of plastic. One thought she was an angel sent to earth to lay with the sons of God. But not one of them even had all her adult teeth yet.

"I took them in for maintenance and they would come back with their little nails painted and their hair freshly dyed. They would also be a lot quieter. They moved their eyes less." She paused and replaced the soaked-through gauze on her neck with a fresh bandage. "The last two didn't come back at all."

Just like Veronica.

"But how can that happen?" I asked. "How can girls just disappear without anyone asking any questions? Without their schools or friends wondering where they are?"

"All kinds of ways, I suppose. They're pageant girls so usually they just say the kid got a part on a TV show and is on location indefinitely. Sometimes they say there was a sudden transfer to some other school. An arts academy or a religious school."

Josephinum Academy of the Sacred Heart. I had never forgotten the name of the school they had sent Veronica to.

"What happens to the girls, Jian?" Extra spit began to pump from my salivary glands, a churning nausea. "Are they killed?"

Jian shook her head. "No." She held up the bloody chip. "They're sold. The chip isn't just a tracker. It's a currency. If a MONARCH is purchased, the chip is reprogrammed to assign them to their new owner. It's a crime to kill a MONARCH. But, yeah, I think it happens sometimes. Just like sometimes money and flags are burnt. It's illegal, but it's only the violation of a symbol."

"So you think Kayla Gavin was MONARCH? And something went wrong?"

Jian shrugged and pulled herself to her feet. The bleeding was slowing, but she looked too pale to be moving.

"I have no way of knowing, but I don't see any other reason why the Director would care if those photos were developed or not. He's not going to allow some shitty PD out in the sticks to take down the Institute, and if your mom was trying to make that kind of blowback happen—" she cut herself off before explaining further. "Listen, we need to get going. Our arrival at the Institute is in ten minutes. As soon as they notice we disappeared into a dead zone, they'll come looking. You can use your mother's passport to go to India or Australia—or wherever you want—and just disappear."

Jian had seen Grethe's passport when I removed the mirror and bandages from my bag. It had flipped open and for a moment it had been like I was looking at a ghost of myself. In the photo, she wore the single silk scarf she had brought with her to America in 1972. She kept it in her bedside drawer, folded into a small square and preserved in a velvet pouch beside her little locked diary. Among the many epiphanies I had out there in the desert with Jian, the one I felt dumbest about was my realization that those foreign numbers in Grethe's book hadn't had anything to do with an affair nor had she hired Christine because she wanted to "help an old friend." One day, I would dial one of the international numbers and, in a voice identical to my babysitter's—but older and inflected with an accent like my mother's—a woman whose name I instantly recognized from my mother's stories about her days on the Scandinavian pageant circuit would answer. No, Grethe hadn't been helping an old friend. An old friend had been helping *her*. She'd been building us an escape route—saving her sugar jar money and creating contacts on the outside. Resources concealed from Dr. Clink.

"I can't. I have to find my father."

I could tell from Jian's slow nod that she knew I meant I had to kill him.

"And . . ." I couldn't get myself to even say the other reason I couldn't go with her. I didn't have to, though. Jian was happy to say the worst possible thing for me.

"You have to find out if that girl was one of us," she said matter-of-factly. Then, as if we were in a John Hughes movie instead of the world's most fucked James Bond reboot, "You've got to find out if your true love was . . . you know, true."

"Veronica," I said. "She told me her name was Veronica."

We were quiet as I drove her to the bus station. I suppose we were both scrutinizing every moment of significance in our lives. Every crush who liked us back, every teacher who told us we could be something, every moment of connection that made us think we were real people. Before she got on the Greyhound headed for El Paso, Jian turned to me, her eyes shining with the kind of wrath usually reserved for depictions of fallen gods, deposed queens; figures who have lost their worlds.

"Burn the whole thing down. Don't stop with just your own father." She pressed her chip into my palm. "Use me if you need to. And remember to look in the mirror."

CHAPTER SIX

THE CAMPUS OF THE DESERT UNIVERSITY WAS ODDLY STILL.

Usually men in tweed jackets walked from stone building to stone building in preppy, sweaty factions. Today there was nothing but the sound of a secretary's heels clicking across the cobblestones, an amplified metronome.

The checkpoint had been abandoned, the gated entrance I drove through with Dr. Clink and Grethe so many times before—Grethe leaning across my father to relay the entrance code to a blank-faced guard—was simply open. The lever broken down the middle, as if a car had gone straight through it.

Normally, a valet would have materialized and taken the Chrysler to a garage. Grethe and I would hold our purses over our heads to protect our makeup from the heat on the walk to the Chancellor's quarters. Today, I drove straight through campus and parked the Taurus right on Chancellor Lethe's lawn. In the rearview mirror, I could see the car tracks in the thick Bermuda grass. This grass, I knew, was imported from a sod farm in Northern California whose only other clients were golf courses. This was general knowledge, distributed as a component of the yearly Desert University Colloquium's Welcome Dinner, right before guests were asked to conserve shower water and refrain from flushing toilet paper.

"The campus runs on its own energy grid," Dr. Clink explained every year. "It's part of the Chancellor's environmental initiative." In accordance with this policy, the University disallowed high-energy items such as hair dryers because they might blow out the generators. They also required us to dig a hole in the backyard to dispose of our compostable waste. City sanitation services were not allowed past the gates.

Yet the Chancellor's lawn is a vibrant emerald, an actual oasis in the desert. Walking on the green patch was forbidden, and traps were placed at the perimeters to catch the tassel-eared squirrels and desert cottontails that sought refuge from the hot stones. I felt a tightening in my throat as I dug the tires into the grass. *Satisfaction*, I realized.

Inside the Chancellor's mansion, it was equally silent. There was a lip of light burning beneath the door to the Chancellor's quarters, but the room itself was empty. I passed through to the Chancellor's office and paused momentarily before twisting the door's glass knob. I knew only the Chancellor and his secretary had copies of the old-fashioned brass key that unlocked it, which they each wore on golden chains they pinned to the inside of their clothing, pocketwatch-style. The door opened easily though, almost as if a phantom hand had twisted the knob right before me.

The moon was bright, insolent, in the desert's darkness. Lunar beams shone through the Chancellor's stained-glass window, illuminating the office in a red glow.

I felt like I was inside of the thurible the priest at Veronica's church swung in a reckless loop as he walked down the aisle: smoked ruby, the color of a new burn.

Some of the Chancellor's drawers extruded from his desk like tongues. They were all empty, but the top of the desk itself was smothered in papers. I was so habituated to the croon of the grandfather

clock that I actually turned and regarded its silence as it was supposed
to strike 7:00 p.m. Its arms were paralyzed at 9:37.

(Bear with me here. I have another intrusive memory from Grethe's
book of folk tales.

It is a drawing of a clock, just like the Chancellor's, stuck at 9:37.

The drawing accompanied a story about a flat kingdom called Utslette, which was surrounded by stone walls so high no one could see
over them. Because the world ended at the edge of the wall—it simply
dropped off into an interminable cosmos—it was forbidden to plant
trees that could be climbed or to even bring a ladder within one hundred feet of the kingdom's perimeter. Only the queen's men were allowed to walk the top of the wall, from which vantage point they were
able to peer out into the dark matter of the universe and protect the
kingdom from celestial intruders. Only the Thirteen Faeries of the
Realm were granted access in and out of Utslette, and only in exchange
for gifts bestowed on holidays and celebrations. One of these special
occasions was the sixteenth birthday of Princess, the first daughter of
Utslette. The faeries planned to bestow Princess with a gift of grace
or beauty suited to their own magic. The gold faerie was expected to
bestow moral excellence; the pink faerie was expected to bestow beauty
of the blood; the white faerie was expected to bestow the gift of silence,
and so on. But Queen feared the gift of the red faerie, whose magic
originated from the passage of time. Her fingertips drained the mountain lichen of its greenness and the cheeks of women of their mois-
ture. She was responsible for age, decay, and death. She was also very
ugly. Queen did not want her seated at the head table with the high
court, where her beastly visage would be memorialized by the royal
portraitist. So a missive was sent into the cosmos stating that one of
the thirteen dishes used to serve the faeries had been broken and, thus,

one faerie would not be able to attend Princess's birthday. Because the red faerie was the last in the order of nature to arrive at any banquet, she would be disallowed from crossing the kingdom's threshold. Furious, the red faerie gathered the skin of the bubbles which brewed at the base of each waterfall in the kingdom, the petals of a mountain flower known to induce drowsiness, and the shed skins of one hundred black snakes. Although she had never revealed it to anyone, not even her twelve sisters, the red faerie knew she did not really control the passage of time. Rather, she manipulated perception of it through tricks of memory, amnesia, insomnia, and hypersomnia. After the twelfth gift was bestowed, the red faerie used her bubbles and snakeskins to create a potion which paused every clock in Utslette at 9:37. She blew a sleeping draught made from the petals of the mountain flower into the nostril of every courtier, lady-in-waiting, clockmaker, farrier, farmer, governess, cook, huntsman, chambermaid, shoemaker, and royal in the kingdom. As a final punishment, she left awake only Queen, who would be bound to suffer the living death of her kingdom for what would seem like eternity. In her grief, Queen carried the body of her daughter to the deep wood, where a portal to the unlawful magic of the cosmos was rumored to enter. She lay Princess on a velvet cloth in her birthday gown, asked the invisible elements to awaken her daughter, and returned to her throne to await her own death. A long time passed. Queen remained frozen in her youth, yet miserable. Her melancholy deepened like the earth beneath a ribbon of lava and eventually she stopped visiting the body of her daughter. After fifty years of stillness, the dark energy Queen had called forth emerged from a portal concealed by a waterfall and entered Princess's body, who blinked her eyes open and beheld the black branches of trees tucked most deeply in the dark forest. She had seen tattoos of the trees on the arms of huntsmen, but she had never seen them in real life. Princess sat up with a rigid spine and began to walk, one foot in front of the other, to her mother's throne. The Siberian jays, snowy owls, and bramblings alike took flight at the mechanical steps of Princess. Even the arctic fox, who had been known to trick and steal from the most dangerous of Queen's soldiers, ran far and fast at the approach of Princess. It was not until she came upon a human body, asleep at the narrow entrance to the dark wood, that Princess met another living being. She peered down at him from her unnatural height and saw he was covered in black scrawls: trees. He was her mother's own Huntsman, who had fallen asleep in his tracks under the spell of the red faerie. Princess, of course, was present in body alone. It was the dark energy long expelled to the cosmos which worked through her and undressed Huntsman, revealing the crest of antlers all of Queen's huntsmen carved into the flesh of their own chests at the age of eighteen. Princess forced a violent coupling with the somnambulant Huntsman. She named Huntsman's resultant twins Sun and Moon and sent them out to her home, the cosmos, where they shone so brightly they awoke the kingdom and from then on fought each other daily to show the people of Utslette that there was a world beyond their paltry walls. The clocks of the kingdom began again to tick and the body of Princess continued on her course to the throne of Queen, who had been weeping for nearly one hundred years. With the Queen's own Huntsman's blade, she cut the throat to the mouth that gave orders to the kingdom and took her place in Queen's throne. Princess was now sole ruler of the cosmos. At the side of the zombie Princess sat the red faerie, who gilded every baby born in Utslette with the imperfection that made them Real. Babies born too beautiful were believed to be the undead offspring of Princess's wild energy, and were burned.)

"Are you here to play the yes-yes board?"

Some buried memory stuck its fingers out of the grave at the sound of those words. They were too familiar, as was the woman-shaped shadow who stood silhouetted in the doorway, a pair of pumps hooked over two fingers. The Chancellor's Secretary had slid barefoot, silent across the outer chamber. I didn't know how long she had been watching me stare at the clock and think over the old folk tale. I didn't know her name or, I realized, even know what her face looked like. I had only ever seen her black figure controlling the projector slides from the back of the office.

I stepped into a beam of light, which shone brightly through a star in the stained glass, so that she could see my face.

She sucked in her breath and then released a tiny laugh, the noise like air escaping the punctured tire of a bicycle.

"Oh my, I thought you were your mother for a moment. That gave me a *fright*. I've dealt with quite a few problems from you girls, but not one of you has bothered to haunt me." She emitted the laugh once again and I felt cold. "Not yet!"

"I'm here for my father. For Dr. Clink." The gun was tucked into the back of my waistband, but I didn't want to remove it unless I had to. I didn't think there was much chance I could use it. It would be harder to shoot a woman, I realized.

"Oh, darling." The secretary sighed and placed her heels on the floor. "Your father isn't here." She stepped into the shoes and her shadow loomed another foot across the oaken floor. "None of them are. I'm afraid they've left me and the other secretaries to keep watch."

She reached into the air and pulled a metal cord attached to the overhead lamp. In the light, she was less frightening. Pretty, even, with medium brown hair and a rosebud mouth too young for her face. Her dress was plaid and stopped just below the knee. On her lapel was a golden pin shaped like a poodle. In the poodle's hair was a tiny-jeweled bow.

"Do you know where he is?"

"Yes, certainly."

She moved behind the Chancellor's desk and sorted through a ring of keys attached to her waistband.

"It's just awful, but your father has fled the country. Director—I'm sorry, I know you call him Chancellor—Chancellor Lethe suspects he's in Vatican City, avoiding extradition for the incident with your mother. The Institute could have protected him, of course, if he hadn't lost his head and refused to perform the proof-of-death protocol. Oh goodness." She pressed two fingertips to her lips as if to suppress a giggle. "No pun intended. You do know your mother is dead, yes?"

I nodded. "Jian told me."

The secretary shook her head. "That girl. She's not especially couth, is she? I always suspected she would lose the plot, so to speak. Her loyalty scores were consistently very low, but the Chancellor believed her ambition index compensated for it. Well, we see who was right about *that*, don't we? He never read my blueprints well enough. I certainly told him you weren't as special as he thought and look what you've done—gone all to pot and killed a man! I *told* him your bioarchitecture was too deeply ingrained. That's what happens when you girls are raised by your mothers. The practice was abolished after the Second World War, but your mother, well. The Chancellor has—had!—a soft spot for her."

She finally found the key she was looking for and used it to unlock a drawer in the desk, from which she pulled a box shaped like a game of Monopoly or Life.

"Who are you? I thought you were just . . . the secretary."

"You would think that, dear. But I'll tell you this for nothing—behind every great man is the woman who did his paperwork. Behind every evil man, too, I suppose! But I'm also the architect. When a MONARCH is born, I assess every aspect of her—her personality, her physicality, her psyche, her ethical framework, her chemical composition—and I determine which personalities she'll best adapt to. Some girls, like Jian, are best suited for gathering intelligence. She's brilliant and disciplined, but not morally flexible enough to really be of much use. That's common, in the less privileged girls. They have an irksome bent toward . . . democracy. You, though! I could tell when you were only four years old that you had a high capacity for deception, for trickery and lies—you have the brain of a cephalopod and very little activity in the amygdala. You were such a darling baby. It's a pity and a shame they kept erasing you, trying to freeze you in the moment before your inception. I told them it wouldn't result in happiness. I told them you would still remember the . . . impression . . . of the events. And that's so much worse, isn't it? That would have driven anyone insane, so don't feel too terribly, dear."

She spread the contents of the box out on the table, but I was too far away to see much more than a large, flat piece of cardboard. She walked to the Chancellor's bar cart and picked up a crystal shot glass.

"What events? Who did you program me to be?"

"Oh darling, it's over and done with. If you were going to be put in the field again, I might see the sense in telling you, but as it is there's no need for you to know what you've done. You've been an excellent asset and you won't be punished for murdering that man, if that's what you're worried about."

"What? No—that man killed a child. He had to die."

She raised her eyebrows. "Did he now?"

"Do you know they're using little girls like that?"

"Who's using little girls, dear?"

"The Chancellor! Jian said some of the MONARCH are just children."

"Ah." She frowned. "Jian perhaps knew a titch more than she could be trusted with. It's unfortunate she divulged that information to you."

"So you knew?"

I felt my hands begin to shake and a lightness begin to rise to my head. My face filled with helium, stretchy and high.

"Well, yes, I drew up their blueprints, darling. The Chancellor needed a rare currency."

I put one hand on the back of the Chancellor's leather couch and the other on my gun.

"But the Chancellor would never have done that sort of thing to you. At least not until you were an adult, regardless. You're a Daughter of the Institute. Why, quite literally, in fact! The very last mothered MONARCH. We protect legacy, above all else."

"An adult?" I repeated faintly. "I was fourteen."

The Secretary's face remained impassive, her tone even, as she responded, "Exactly. An adult. Frankly, dear, that's a full year older than I was, when I joined up. You honeypot splitters are the lucky ones, really. At least you get to stop working when you turn eighteen."

In the wide pane of black surface that comprised the stained-glass stone upon which sat the stained-glass tower, I caught my reflection and pulled the gun out. My hand was steady and my legs had fallen into a natural base.

"Tell me where to find the Chancellor." I aimed the gun directly at the Secretary's brown, blunt bangs.

She began to laugh. Mirthfully this time, her lungs filled with air. She held her hands up at her sides, a parody of a criminal caught in the act.

"Dear, you really don't understand. I couldn't tell you if I wanted to."

She turned her head and lifted up a flap of hair to reveal an inch of hardened white skin, a small scar. "This is how it was in the old days, before they started to do so much with lasers. You girls are so lucky now—you don't even know when they put the chip in."

I lowered the gun an inch. "You're MONARCH, too?"

"Of course. I was the *first* MONARCH. The Chancellor rescued me from the basement of a bar at the end of the Battle of the Somme. I was just a girl—I'd never met a man with such a beautiful accent in my life—born in Norway, raised in Britain, and educated at the finest colleges in the States! Oh, but you don't want to hear all that."

Unbidden, a few calculations flew through my mind before I decided she was right, I didn't give a shit about her *or* Lethe's unnaturally long history. I stepped forward, the gun again pointed at her head, until only the Chancellor's desk separated us.

"I'm serious. I will kill you if you don't tell me how to find the Chancellor."

"I'm quite serious as well. I'm programmed to keep the Chancellor's secrets. The only person who knows is, well, perhaps your father." She moved something with one of her hands, but I couldn't break eye contact with her, I couldn't lose my own reflection in the lenses of her glasses. "But you needn't fret. We'll play the yes-yes game and you'll feel much better, you won't need to think about any of this any longer."

The yes-yes game. I still couldn't place the words, couldn't locate which direction of my memory they were emerging from.

"Jessica Greenglass Clink, look down and place your hand on the planchette."

Against my will, I glanced down. She had placed a Ouija board on the desk, the shot glass she had taken from the bar cart positioned on the *yes*.

Just as I had that day on the roof of the dorm, I felt myself begin to slither out of my body.

Oui. French for yes. *Ja*. German for yes.

And then I remembered where I had seen the yes-yes board before. It had been in the dream. The one where the Chancellor's Secretary had shown me the prices for Christine and Jian and Veronica.

The prices, I realized, weren't a dream at all.

The board, I realized, had been there when I was born. Or, rather, programmed.

An image of my own hand, small, perhaps four years old and holding a shot glass that flew across the board—spelling, spelling—flashed across my eyes.

These people had taken everything, this woman the architect of my nightmares. Of what I thought were nightmares, anyway. Something about the movement of her arm, the long line of dark energy between her heart and the shot glass, graceful as an executioner's arc, made me remember a dream I had once had about Veronica.

"Ask me to play the yes-yes game," she says playfully, holding a shot glass of her father's. A tiny clear glass cup with the words BRANSON, MISSOURI emblazoned in red, white, and blue on its side.

I walk toward her and take the cup. A bottle has materialized in my left hand. It is blue-black and heavy. My right hand slips over Veronica's to hold her hand to the cup and I pour. The bottle isn't black, I realize; the fluid inside it is. I lift the liquid to Veronica's lips and she drinks it with one knock of the skull back, leaving her lips and mouth obsidian. Slowly, she smiles and I see the liquid has stained her teeth oddly with strange symbols. I lean forward to look more closely and the symbols turn into figures, into numbers.

Veronica kisses me, her mouth medicinal and sweet.

"Was I worth it?" she whispers.

The figures on her teeth are her price, I realize. She then begins to evaporate, hair then skin then bone, until she is a floating heart before me.

"What about Veronica?" I asked, uncocking the trigger. "Did you make her? Is she in your books?"

"Who, dear?"

"Veronica Marshall! From the pageants. Was she MONARCH?"

The Chancellor's Secretary furrowed her brow. "We had more than one Veronica, of course."

"She would be twenty-two now. Black hair, tall. My best friend."

"Ah, *her.*" The secretary's eyes cleared with understanding. "The dyke."

The shot fired before I knew I had pulled the trigger.

The Chancellor's Secretary's knees buckled. With her last surge of energy, she sat backward, collapsing firmly into the Chancellor's desk chair, allowed to sit in the Director's Seat in death alone.

CHAPTER SEVEN

ON THE FLIGHT TO ROME, I BEGAN FOR THE FIRST TIME TO think about Dr. Clink's octopus, alone in the wild.

It was the closest creature I had ever had to a pet, although after Dr. Clink stopped allowing me to play with her, our interactions were limited to tapping at the glass. Privately, I had named the octopus Edith, and I was proud when she learned to slide the lid off her own tank and steal small objects from my father's desk. At first, Edith took just a penlight or a book of matches and returned to her tank with them. Dr. Clink wrote a paper about her that theorized she was trying to steal objects she found the most novel, the most capable of amusing her. He never considered the situation from Edith's perspective, though. He never put his head in her briny tank and looked out at his office from her viewpoint. I had done this once, as a small child, and I had learned that all the light in her world was magnified by the glass corners of her aquarium. At the wrong angle, it was blinding; impossible to see anything but the structure of her own prison, the rest of her universe eclipsed.

Even humans will do uncharacteristic things when forced to stare directly into the sun, so it should have occurred to Dr. Clink that Edith was simply stealing his light sources.

It wasn't until Edith began to repeatedly spray the overhead lamp with a jet of water that Dr. Clink became suspicious of her. He thought she had some sort of malicious intent—who knows what—and so one afternoon, he fumbled through his dark office and removed Edith from her tank.

"He put her in the mopping bucket," Grethe said, "and drove out to the University's boathouse and threw her in the river. I think you can see the boathouse from your dorm, can't you?"

I could. Mostly, I looked out the window of Mayflower and assumed Edith was dead. Sometimes, though, I imagined she was thriving, growing monstrous and mythic at the bottom of the lake. It was possible that she had learned to eat new foods, to adapt to freshwater, to follow tributaries and float across flooded marshes until she arrived at the river's mouth, far away in the Gulf of Mexico. Maybe, I thought as I crossed the Atlantic, Edith is under me right now.

Mostly, this has been a story about being in the middle of the middle and not even knowing it. A story about the fetishization of mediocrity, of etymology, of gates, of monocultures, of corporate letterhead, of the middle class, of grade inflation, of blonde hair. Finally, though, this is becoming the story of the spiral that I promised you it would be. Now that we have obliterated the origin, this is the story of the curl that becomes more deadly with each rotation away from its root.

It follows, then, that Rome is a city of circles which radiate from the seven hills upon which its first citizens lived. In its centermost circle—*Vaticanus Collis*—sits Vatican City, and within that ring, my own father.

A broad main street led straight from Rome into the heart of the country. I walked right in on foot. No one asked for my passport or, to be honest, even looked at me. It was 5:00 a.m. I knew I could walk the entirety of the country in less than fifteen minutes, yet I had no idea how to find my father. The city went deep underground—the Vatican

Necropolis was twelve meters beneath the earth—and the uppermost bell of St. Peter's was nearly ten times higher than that.

I assumed my father was curled away in some dark corner, tucked by an indebted priest in a concealed panel. I figured it would take weeks, if not months, to locate him.

The only bright spots in the city were the happy metal boxes painted sunshine yellow and emblazoned with the words POSTE VATICANE that surrounded the country's single post office. For now, I had no plan except to linger around the mailboxes and hope that my father would, eventually, need to communicate with the outside world.

There was nowhere to sit in Vatican City—not a bench or a fountain ridge in all of St. Peter's Square—and I was aware that my posture was changing, my breath slowing, my stomach toughening, and my eyes sharpening. I could smell the soap of the nuns as they passed and the coffee on the breath of the priests. It occurred to me that I was tapping into some sort of programming that would help me track my father. A calmer, more alert version of myself. Jian would have explained I was "going gray," blending in. It was a comfortable place, so to be honest, when I saw the NASA logo materialize out of a crowd of black-shirted priests, I was a little bit disappointed. I had been preparing to be at peace in Vatican City for a while and the actual last person on the planet I wanted to deal with was Jeffrey LaPlant, my father's TA.

I watched him weave into the crowd with his head down, his jawline tucked into his coat collar like a spy, and I wondered what he was really. Maybe he was programmed, too. A collection of nuns passed me, each rubbing their thumbs over beads on their respective rosaries and whispering in unison, and it occurred to me maybe everyone on earth was programmed and always had been.

The epiphany made me think of Christine. I knew *no shit* would be her likeliest blasé retort if I ever got a chance to tell her about any of this.

Jeffrey dropped a few letters in the post and disappeared into a service entrance for the janitors that kept the Vatican museums clean. It was no trouble for me to pick the lock. My hands gravitated toward a small wire device with different corkscrew shapes on either end of it and a magnet. I hadn't even known those things were in my escape kit until I found them in my hands, clicking open a door to the most sacred museums in the Western world. On the other side was a concrete service hallway lined with mops and buckets, push brooms, and those squeegees on long sticks window cleaners use. Above the scent of ammonia, though, I could smell Jeffrey's hair cream. The stench of aluminum zirconium and castor oil. Piney and cloying. Christine had once told me she thought Jeffrey smelled like a horny Christmas tree.

She was right. Graduating from MIT and having an astronaut for a father hadn't made Jeffrey any less of an asshole. He spent his days talking to my father about the neural basis of semantic and autobiographical memory, but he had once told me he was into the "neo club scene" and "chill wave" and other of "the more derivative forms of post-punk." He listened to A-ha and used the word "money" as an adjective.

I followed the stench of his hair through the underground tunnels of the Basilica of St. Peter, down the Via delle Fondamenta, past the Square of the Furnace and onto the Rampa dell'Archeologia and finally to the stoop of a stucco and brick house covered with a tin roof. An ornate blue-and-white-tiled fountain sat next to the house, which would have been a million-dollar home in the Midwest, but here it was Casina del Giardiniere. The Gardener's Lodge.

The door was wooden, curved at the top like an elf's house in a movie for nerds, and the windows were all shuttered. Jeffrey stepped back out of the Lodge, his NASA jacket replaced by a navy hound-stooth blazer that he probably bought from the Halloween section of Hot Topic and convinced himself could pass as Euro-trashy. (I had learned that term from Kevin, who used it so fluidly I couldn't tell if it was good or bad, but I knew it often applied to men who didn't use all the buttons on their dress shirts or women who lied about the origin of their handbags.)

Jeffrey had his usual gray Patagonia backpack slung over his shoulder and, with the exception of the jacket, looked pretty much like he was rushing from class to class back home.

"Hey" was all I had to say to make him freeze, one hand on the lock to the house and the other holding the strap of his bag. I knew he had recognized me by voice alone because he didn't turn. Instead he simply went still, like an animal at the bottom of the food chain—a possum, a toad.

"Drop your bag and turn around."

I had expected him to look afraid, but instead he looked annoyed. Jeffrey was the only person I knew who could look like he was doing you a favor when he was the one at gunpoint. At his core, he was a NASA brat: the smart kid of a bona fide genius. Grethe once told me he was born on third base and acted like he hit the homerun himself. It was one of the most colloquial comments she had ever uttered, a little bit hilarious when smothered by her thick Norwegian accent.

He rolled his eyes. "What are you going to do? Shoot me in Vatican City?"

"It's not off the table."

"You know, it's a waste. Your mother dead and your father gone, just to protect you. An off-the-res AI."

He pronounced "res" with a Z. I wondered if he knew the etymology of the phrase and decided he probably didn't.

"I'm not artificial intelligence."

"Yeah, big diff between a robot or a brainwashed beauty queen." One of the things I despised most about Jeffrey was his insistence on abbreviation. "Look, I'm running late. What do you want? Your dad is AWOL and the Institute has gone dark. No one has talked to me since I got here."

"Did you come here with my father? What are you doing here?"

"Lethe made me come after your dad refused to—" *cut off my mom's head after he killed her.* I guess even Jeffrey had some sense of decency, because he recomposed his statement to "comply. Clink was all hot to attend a symposium at the Pontifical Academy. Something about exorcisms or necromancy. Some spooky occult shit—"

"Mediumicity?" I asked, "Like, talking with a Ouija board?"

"Bingo." He made a gun with his finger and shot it at me in confirmation. "Also, most countries with anti-extradition laws are shitholes and you know your dad's gotta have cloth napkins."

"So where is he now?"

"Fuck if I know. He said he was going to study some papers in the archive here and he never came back. He took his luggage with him. Maybe after all these years, he's going to try to outrun the Institute."

"But why?"

"I don't know. I guess sometimes a guy has a change of heart after his wife goes ballistic and tries to kill him?"

"Grethe tried to kill him? Jian said—"

Jeffrey snorted, "Jian's hot but not exactly top brass. I doubt they showed her the security footage."

"From my house?"

"Look, you're not really authorized to know, either. Actually, Clink left a letter for you. Who knows how far gone he is. Maybe he goes on full villain-about-to-die monologue and explains it all."

Jeffrey opened his backpack and pulled a navy blue envelope out of an inner pocket. It was closed with my father's signature seal, CWC palimpsested over an infinity symbol.

"So?" Jeffrey prompted.

"So what? Give me the letter and I'll let you go."

The sun was almost fully risen, but its bottommost curve was still concealed on the other side of the earth. The duomo-spotted skyline of the city was like a body in a fun house mirror: bulbous and disorienting. Increasing numbers of people were filling the streets now, speaking in metallic Italian or corroded Latin. Jeffrey raised a hand and his face took on the ingratiating glow I was used to seeing when he spoke to my father. He was waving to a large group of priests headed toward the Pontifical Academy.

"Let me go? Look around, Jessica. There are witnesses everywhere. Did you know the Pope has his own army? They don't have an official jail here, but, between you and me, they have an *un*official one. You'd have better luck walking into the White House and assassinating the president than you would killing me and walking out of here." He stepped further into the square so that he was surrounded by two huge topiairied bushes. They were so square that he looked like he was standing in a picture frame. "There are cameras on either side of me right now, concealed in the trees. It's a little freaky if you think about it too much, you know? How we're on camera right now, but we won't even see the pictures. Well, you were a model, right?"

"Beauty queen."

"Same. Did you ever think about how much of your image is

actually yours if you never see yourself? Like, I can only see from my eyes but I'm looked at from all sides?"

"Totally. God is the concept of the Other taken to its ultimate limit. I get it. You're basically, like, Jean-Paul Sartre."

"Acting like a bitch isn't going to get you your letter, Jessica."

I looked around for a surface to see myself reflected in. I was hoping that if I caught my own image I'd be able to think the situation though. He was right that I couldn't kill—or even touch—him here and make it out. The city's surfaces were flat, unreflective as the cover of an old black Bible. I was out of moves.

"Okay. What do you want?'

He raised his eyebrows and his mouth went slack. His eyes dropped across my body like handful of soil into an open grave. A dirty, ancient ritual.

Unfathomably, I felt my back arch and my head tilt. My tongue licked my lips. I had read hundreds of articles in teen magazines about "body language" and "how to tell if a guy likes you." I knew they were talking about preening behaviors and that some programming was deploying itself in me like a stink bomb, foul and allegedly harmless. Deep within Jian's puffy coat, I was appalled to feel my nipples harden. My body was making it easy for me to use it.

Use me if you need to, Jian had said.

"I have a chip," I said. "Jian's device."

Jeffrey's eyes widened. "No you don't. How?"

I got the metal disc out of the escape kit—I had stowed it in a waterproof bottle of aspirin protected by the metal first aid kit—and held it out flat on my palm for him to see. "I cut it out of her myself. Her coding information is on it, her price."

"It's not worth anything if the Institute has shut down. Like I said, it's been dark for a week now. Without your father, I'm completely in the cold," he whined.

"I guess you'll have to take the chance that the shutdown is temporary."

I was also taking a chance, obviously. The Institute had gone dark because I killed its operator, but once Chancellor Lethe realized his secretary was dead, the system would right itself and resume. If I didn't kill my father before that and Jeffrey managed to find Jian and reprogram her—well, I couldn't think that thought through.

Jeffrey considered it for a moment and agreed. His eyes were glassy and overexcited as we traded our items. It was pretty gross. I watched him as he disappeared into the city and then sat down on the step of his cottage to read the letter from my father. JESSICA GREEN-GLASS CLINK was written in silver pen on the front of the envelope in Dr. Clink's spidery penmanship.

Jessica,

You are a strange girl. Likely, you believe I have not noticed, or even possessed the critical awareness necessary to appreciate or deduce, the exceptional eccentricity of your composition. Indeed, you were born with a caul covering your entire face. The nurses in attendance told your mother and me that this inflicted no undue trauma upon you as you had not yet seen the world and therefore were not aware of your own blindness. Nor, in turn, were you astonished to gain sight. Your mother, however, had often told me of your dreams *in utero*. I had felt you move with my own hand, your skin and spirit already articulate, distinct long before the hour of your birth—what had you seen, already, in your dreams? What is there for an unborn child to imagine? And what, with the caul affixed to your face, could you have seen to dream about? Your mother has explained to me that in the logic of the otherworld, what is seen in dreams sees us in return. Your first word, after all, was *eye*. The abysmal pedagogues at your Children's School insisted you had said, instead, "I." This was far more common, they told us, in terms of cognition: that a child would exhibit self-reflexive vocabulary before displaying knowledge of a concept as abstract as gazing. I would like to ask you now that you are an adult which it was. *I* or *eye*? And I wonder, Do you think it matters? Or rather, Do you think they are different?

This wretched desire to be seen seems to be the characteristic of our epoch. Perhaps this is the reason I tried not to look at you. Inherent in the redundant phrase *newborn* is the idealization of progression over progress, of novelty. When you were born, it was obvious to me that you were old already. You were rich with the aura of prehistory. It was apparent that, metaphysically, you were mid-journey. I felt that to overly witness you would be to place you too firmly in this world, pin you as a butterfly upon velvet. It was too little, of course. Jessica, I write to you in the spirit of apology, but not of regret. Not by way of excuse, but merely explanation, please know that I wholeheartedly believed you would be born blank. You were one of the first babies born into the Institute and the only raised by her own mother. There was a great deal of research, state and private funding, that convinced me you would not be burdened by personality, by a cumbersome sapience. I told myself you would be a bundle of bones, flesh, and nerves. It was quite apparent from the first moment I held you that you were much more than that. You were heavy with spirit. I was dismayed at the trade I had already made. As you likely know by now, I agreed to allow the Institute to train you from birth and employ you as an agent in a covert program from the ages of fourteen to eighteen. Although she herself did not entirely agree with this pact, it was made in exchange for your mother's freedom. In an effort at preserving what we could of your essential nature, I tried to erase all memory of your activities associated with the Institute. If it is of any comfort to you, please know I rerouted my life's work—my scholarship—to the study of memory and its malfunctions after I came to understand your true nature. The Greenglass Method was not just named after you, but developed for you. You are, of course, painfully aware that my Method was not only ineffective, but ultimately disruptive. I now concede, fully, that nothing—no memory, impression, emotion, or idea—*is ever lost*. The psychic economy is more resilient, more invulnerable to bankruptcy, than I had ever hypothesized. Truly, the world has no end. Because I have seen you seeing this as well, I regret nothing.

Admittedly, fatherhood has often proved stylistically problematic for me as I am neither inclined towards natural displays of emotion nor did I have the benefit of a parent upon whom I could model my own paternal pedagogy. As your mother has told you, I was raised in a home for abandoned children. Grandfather and Grandmother Clink were amongst the first Parisians murdered in the Second World War. At the age of twelve, I received a scholarship to study at a boys' preparatory academy. My life unfolded from there, ventriloquized by the once invisible hand of Chancellor Lethe and the Chancellors before him. Lest you mistake me, please be assured this is not a toadying bid for sympathy. My life has been the same as anyone's: I was born into a system and I never saw it from the outside. My fixation on insanity was, perhaps, a pitiable attempt to see my way out. But I now believe it's you who knows how to locate the portal.

Jessica, you were born without a face and you created one with your own hands. I've seen in you the ability to remember the face you had before either your mother or I were ever born.

In the lining of the escape kit given to you by Christine, you will find your mother's chip and papers, which grant her entrance to the secret city of Utslette, located within the mountains of Bergen, Norway. You will find Director Lethe in hiding there. Your mother intended to live, unnaturally, forever. This perhaps makes her dying wish all the more poignant: Grethe requests you allow her to inhabit your body for the purposes of exacting revenge on Director Lethe and the Institute at large. Once you have done so, seek the help of Christine. She can bring you back.

Please forgive me my awkward prose; as you know, despite my prolific scholarship, I have rarely had the opportunity to write in "the first person," as some say.

CWC

P.S.
.. / .-.. --- ..-. / .-- --- .-

CHAPTER EIGHT

I BECAME A BIT OF A NYMPHO FOR EDGES AFTER THAT.

Things surrounded me: trees, furniture, curtains, the general miscellanea of life, but I could only grope at them. I sensed an entire wall had gone missing and that if I could only get on the other side of it, I could control the camera. But it was impossible to know where the set ended, where reality began.

There was no reason for me to believe my father's letter was anything but artifice, another prop in the stage set of my life. Already, though, I'd begun to want to believe that when Jeffrey mentioned my father's refusal to "comply," he had actually indicated, in his own absurdly euphemistic manner, that Dr. Clink had not only declined to perform the proof-of-death protocol, but also to murder Grethe. That the real reason my father fled the country and abandoned the Institute was because he loved us more than he was loyal to Lethe. But Jeffrey's primary function as my father's TA was to be the silent author of the article—to do the tedious work of proofreading, of cutting out the redundancy. Which, in this case, was me. It would come naturally to Jeffrey to implant a hysterical sentimentality in me that would override my intuition, my hidden drive to live. He was that kind of guy: the sort who could get you to erase yourself.

And yet, the letter had aroused some dormant sensation—a feeling I had only experienced with Christine and Veronica. I thought of it as an amber glow, a hidden light deep inside me that flickered on when Veronica winked from the audience or when Christine slipped a mixtape under my pillow for me to find later and play all on my own. The glow was, I realized, the totally irrational sensation other people called trust. No—not trust, with its insistence on patterns built and maintained over time, its scientific adherence to consistency. The feeling wasn't trust; it was worse. It was faith.

Maybe it was the Morse code that did it. I remembered the lights of the Chrysler beaming into my bedroom every time my father left for a trip, the dots and dashes the only language he ever told me he loved me in. Dr. Clink was a genius and a liar, but I simply could not believe he possessed the creativity to add the flourish of the postscript. He lacked the imagination required for such an emotional manipulation.

Or maybe I followed the glow because at the edge of reality, there was no other guide. The world had not ended, and now we all had to endure.

As I waited for my flight to Norway in a terminal of the Leonardo da Vinci International Airport, I watched as traveler after traveler stopped to laugh at an advertisement for Millennium Bug. The ad was a picture of an hourglass, nearly empty on the bottom and filled with roaches on the top. It read in orange letters: DON'T RISK IT. MAKE SURE. In a smaller font, there was a phone number and the words ONLY 1 MONTH LEFT.

It was Monday, January 10, 2000. We were now living in the after. As I boarded the flight to Bergen, it occurred to me that after the camera, there was a door, and after the door, there was the world, but no one seemed to want to look.

Perhaps because the before of my life had never really been real, I had no interest in maintaining its contours, no sense of nostalgia for an existence that had mostly not been mine. I knew it was idiotic—suicidal, even—to head straight into the hidden heart of the Institute at the directive of the man who traded me for a woman he may have murdered. But in the after, there was nothing left for me but the buried places, the crypts and crevices of the earth.

There was only me. I was the one who, in the after, had to look. I had to do it so that, one day, I could tell you the story of what it was I saw.

CHAPTER NINE

THE PASSENGER SEATED BESIDE ME ON THE FLIGHT WAS A cloud of petrochemicals, coal tar, and animal secretions. Inside the cloud was a teenage girl with yellow hair. Her perfume sat on the desks of most of the girls at my old dorm. The stuff was called Bombshell and studies had been issued that declared it was a more effective insect repellent than DEET.

The girl's skin was orange, a fake tan. American, obviously. From her black foam earphones, I recognized the voice of another American teenager who had gotten famous for a song about a genie in a bottle.

Genies are slaves, I thought dully. They aren't even symbols for slaves. They just *are*. Of course it was Christine who had prepared me to make such a critical observation. She'd once told me that an opressively popular song about Barbie put out by a Danish-Norweigan pop group was actually social criticism, a critique of the children's toy inspired by a nearly identical German doll. "But Bild-Lilli," Christine explained, "was straight up porn."

Lee's memory of the last time I'd seen the doll stained my brain, and so, in some effort to cleanse myself, I waited until the girl fell asleep, lifted one black pad from her ear, and leaned in to whisper, "Everything you've ever been taught to love was decided for you by some rich man." I felt a little lightening after saying this—the levity of extending Christine's influence—so I continued, "The whole world was invented by one person who gets rich off of convincing you that you want stuff that hurts you." As an afterthought, I added, "And when I say *man*, I don't mean God." Then I removed the disc from her Walkman and replaced it with the one I had just bought myself in the airport mall.

I listened to the album ooze out of the girl's headphones: *I could have been wild and I could have been free, but nature played this trick on me.*

Inception worked both ways, I figured. I watched the words go into the girl's subconscious and then I fell asleep as the voice from Manchester intoned that pretty girls make graves.

When I woke up, I was seated in a glass trolley car with a dozen other people. The trolley was moving slowly upward. To my left were thick snow-covered trees and to my right was a devastating view of what I gathered to be a shoreline of the North Sea. It was dotted with houses that looked like the tips of crayons in a deluxe box of Crayola: saturated coral and cerulean and raw umber. The people around me spoke in voices rich with *tiks* and *taks* and *uhhfs*; every sentence included a melodious upsweep. Norwegians, I realized. They were talking about the view from the top of the mountain, the fish market, the cold.

I could apparently understand Norwegian.

A sign at the front of the trolley said FLØIBANEN FUNICULAR. I didn't know how I got there, but I was ascending into the Fløyen mountain outside Bergen, just as Dr. Clink had told me to in his letter. My right hand was wrapped around the handle of my escape kit and my left hand was wrapped around my ticket to the funicular. I could feel a heavy coat of makeup on my face. I touched my fingertip to my lips and it came away covered in bright red wax, Dior 999; Grethe's shade. Had

I actually gone to one of those makeup counters they had in the airport and gotten a makeover? I hoped not. Grethe said they never cleaned the samples. She called them *herpes traps*.

The funicular came to a halt and I exited onto a freezing patio with an astonishing view of the mountainside and ocean. The other riders immediately took out cameras and fumbled with the buttons, their fingers freezing in the frigid air. I was freezing, too. I had no gloves or hat, just the fur-hooded parka Jian had given me back at the hog farm.

Involuntarily, my teeth began to chatter. My fingertips were already turning blue. Once again, I had no idea what I was going to do next. I looked around for an entrance to a café or gift shop—anywhere to get warm and think things over—when I saw the door from Grethe's book of folk tales sitting right there on the side of the mountain. It was red, circular, and had a small house shape carved into it: the entrance to the Yggdrasil, the Nordic Tree of Life. The last time I had seen the Tree hadn't been in Grethe's book, though. It had been projected onto the wall of Chancellor Lethe's office during his catechism on sacrifice.

The tape reel in my mind rewound, the way I now know it was trained to, to remember the lesson verbatim:

"What you touch and feel and call the world is only a threshold. You accept this. You accept that sacrifice is not a removal from this world, but an addition to another. In this way, you dwell in bounty. Jessica, how do you make $2+2=5$?"

"I believe in the proof."

Had I ever really known what that meant? It was the most inscrutable of Chancellor Lethe's many unfathomable riddles. I had never considered them any further than I had considered the puzzle on the back of a box of Cinnamon Toast Crunch: it was enough to know the answer.

But knowing the solution without knowing the theory that justified it was actually antithetical to the concept of proof itself, I realized.

The story that accompanies the illustration of the Yggdrasil is about the chthonic Goddess of Faith, Fidelitoria, who has a perilous obsession with the Upperworld. She becomes infatuated with ionized air and the sound of birds and the feel of her skin under the sun. Eventually, her bone-white complexion begins to golden and glimmer until it irritates the eyes of the other gods and goddesses of the Underworld, and so it is decided by the rulers of the threshold that in exchange for each passage through the house that separates the worlds, Fidelitoria must trade one letter of her name. This is a trick: the rulers of the threshold know that the name of a thing and the thing itself are inseparable in the Underworld. No goddess would suffer more greatly from this sacrifice than the Goddess of Faith herself. But the deal is struck and to the dismay of her brothers and sisters, husbands and wives, and creators, Fidelitoria trades the last letter of her name. A small shift occurs in the Underworld after this. It becomes more difficult for the citizens to see one another from a distance, to hear the footsteps of the Upperworld. Alas, Fidelitori falls in love with an earthly pool of Water. Her journeys to stare into the eyes of the golden goddess who lives under the pool's surface become longer and longer. She trades more letters of her name; the other gods and goddesses begin to forget each other. They walk the Underworld repeating their own names to one another, increasingly aware they have been forgotten. In the end, Fidelitori trades her *d*, *l*, *t*, *o*, and second and third *i*. In exchange for the faithlessness of the other gods and goddesses, Fidelitoria's name is distilled to Fire in the Underworld. In the Upperworld, she becomes the lover of Water. The Underworld's sacrifice is the Upperworld's gain.

I ran my fingers around the edges of the door and over the edges of the house engraved upon it. The door had no handle and no hinges, just delicate carvings of the windows of the house. I leaned forward and peered in, as though I were trying to look through a peephole. I saw the other side, fish-eyed and rounded, too blurry to know that I was seeing anything but light and movement.

Proof.

I tried to imagine what I would say if Chancellor Lethe asked me to synthesize the lesson of Fidelitoria's verbicide. I suppose I might quote Picasso, tell him "Every act of creation is first of all an act of destruction." He would like that answer, but it didn't help me right now. I might tell him that the story of Fidelitoria was a sort of demented version of *The Little Mermaid*; Fidelitoria a vengeful Ariel. A total refusal of the notion that worlds must be separated in favor of an insistence on tolerance. Indeed, intolerance was punished, cleansed by fire. The very name *Ariel*, I would tell him, was supposed by some Shakespearian scholars to mean "a place of burning; in the modern world, a holocaust."

And that was it, I realized. The answer was the name itself: Fire. I took out the pack of waterproof matches from the escape kit and held one to the miniature window of the house. At first, nothing happened, and then the whole house lit aflame, just as it had in the slide Chancellor Lethe once projected onto the wall of his office. The entire door crackled, turned hot blue as if drenched in gasoline, and then burst into a low red flame—the coolest kind. Without thinking or looking back at the tourists behind me, I wrapped myself in the escape kit's fire-retardant blanket and ran through the door of fire.

CHAPTER TEN

On the other side, there was a secretary.

At this point, I wasn't surprised that the threshold to the inner-most sanctum of what was apparently the shadow world was guarded, first, by a woman in a headset and matte mauve lipstick. She didn't look up from her desk. Instead, she held one finger in my direction and continued to write with the other hand while murmuring into the microphone hovering in front of her lips.

Her desk sat in the middle of a massive marble-and-gold room, like an information center in an American museum built by a Rockefeller or a Carnegie at the turn of the century: opulent, undeniably rich, and functional in spite of its apparent leisure. The room had the expensive smell of nothing, of ions before a snowstorm. At first it seemed silent except for the secretary's intermittent mutterings, but then I realized there was the soft girding of a harp played in *tempo rubato* beneath a layer of white noise. The edges of the room were lit by candles burning in five-armed candelabras, and behind the secretary's desk sat a pit of fire, its smoke funneled upward by a natural stone chimney.

Four massive white marbled pillars upheld the room. They were carved into the mountain's side so that the ceiling was simply jagged, natural rock with glimmers of quartz strewn throughout. I thought of Christine and her crystals and I knew she would say this was a magic place. She believed mountains were conduits for extra energy because they were the collision of actual energy, of tectonic movement. She would have put her hand on the floor and closed her eyes.

I stepped further into the room and realized that beside each pillar stood a sentry armed with a rifle. None of them looked at me. Instead, their eyes seemed fascinated by some point in the distance. They stared so intently that I actually looked over my shoulder to see if they were looking at something—a television screen, a window, anything—and then there she was.

Grethe.

She stood glowing in front of a mammoth piece of quartz, radiant and sublime as an iceberg. Her gown, as ever, was a luminescent silk, the milky color of the cosmos caught mid-shimmer. The flickering light of the candelabras made her appear as if she were undulating. Her hair and skin bioluminescent, the only point of color natural to the terrestrial world the red slash of her lips. Dior 999. I lifted my hand toward her and she lifted hers as well. I stepped forward and she stepped forward. I was, I realized, very, very calm. Also, very, very cold. As I reached out to touch Grethe's fingertips, I felt as solid and impossible as if I were made of ice.

No, not ice.

The euphoria on Grethe's face dissolved. She looked down to her dress and I looked down as well. I was wearing a white silk gown. I had hurled Jian's flame-soaked jacket off in the door of fire.

A mirror.

I had pulled the vardøger trick on myself. Grethe was as dead as ever, her body lent to me only to avenge her. I was my own mother now.

On the secretary's desk sat a guest ledger just like the one in Chancellor Lethe's quarters. I signed it with a heavy fountain pen: Grethe Greenglass Clink. The secretary had not yet looked up from her spreadsheet, so I reached across the desk and depressed the phone's switch hook with one red fingernail. When she finally looked up at me, the blood in her cheeks rushed to her feet, leaving her skin gray beneath a layer of vanilla foundation.

A true Nordic, she nodded and replaced the phone in the cradle, her eyes wide. The soldiers did nothing. I suppose they had no protocol in place for ghosts.

I smiled like Grethe, pleasant and remote. "Please take me to Chancellor Lethe immediately," I spoke in Norwegian, my cadence rich with my mother's actress voice, dulcet and overly elocuted. "It's urgent."

The secretary's voice shook. "I'll need to scan your chip, please." She held up a device that looked like a department store scanner. Bureaucracy ever the dark twin of monstrosity. Power, I remembered the Chancellor telling me, is simply believing rules don't exist.

"I'm afraid my chip has been removed," I said simply and then I pressed it into her hot hand, holding my freezing fingertips on her flesh for several seconds too long. She looked sick, like I had spat a bloody tooth into her palm.

She recovered quickly though, professionally, and placed the chip in a small machine that looked something like the Nikon stainless steel tank we used to agitate film at University Photography. The little metal device made a noise like a bird chirping in reverse. It sounded wrong—both mechanical and occult, the post-sentient noise of a car about to combust. In the reflection of her glasses, which were affixed to her computer screen, I saw columns of numbers whirring on and on. A long algorithm that would tell her if I was Grethe or not, I suppose. Eventually, the numbers settled and the screen blinked black, twice, and was replaced by a brilliant image of an anatomical heart overlaid by an entomological illustration of *Danaus plexippus*. A monarch butterfly.

The secretary nodded and silently stood to press the numbers into a keypad that opened a door that led further into the mountain. Her breath was rapid, but she kept her coiffed head held high as she escorted me through the candlelit labyrinth. Our heels clicked contentiously on the hexagonal tiles so that we sounded like a drunken horse dragging her hooves through the streets of a medieval city. I noticed that we were only taking left turns. The walls turned inward at subtle thirty-degree angles every twelve feet or so. It wasn't just the floor which was hexagonal, I realized, it was the building built within the mountain as well. A spiralic city; a wasp's nest. Occasionally, we passed a door with another city's name above it: OSLO, LILLEHAMMER, and my mother's hometown, TROMSØ. More often, we passed doors that simply listed the names of civil institutions: BANK, POSTKONTOR, FENGSEL. *Bank, post office, jail,* I translated in my head. One door was secured with a golden bank vault lock. Above it, written in navy blue, the words UTSLETTE KRYOKAMMATORIA.

We walked for nearly thirty minutes, occasionally passing men in black suits who wore lanyards just like the one my father had worn within the borders of the Desert University. Eventually, we arrived at a white door. Above it, written in golden letters, was the word FAREN. *The Father.*

The secretary entered another, longer, code and pressed her thumb to a pad. The door unclicked politely and we walked into a hexagonal room. It was mostly empty except for a chandelier, several navy blue velvet couches, and a flag emblazoned with an image of a crown circling the earth. In small block letters on the flag were the words CITY OF UTSLETTE.

I had seen the symbol on the flag before, of course. It was the same as the one on the ring Dr. Clink and Chancellor Lethe and other professors at the Desert University wore. The symbol for the secret city of Utslette, apparently. If I hadn't been in Grethe's body, I would have rolled my eyes at the pretension of it all: as if a crown is anything but a useless hat.

The secretary regarded me one more time and then she stepped toward the door beneath the flag and pressed a button below a small speaker.

"Director, Mrs. Grethe Clink is here to see you," she said into the intercom.

The speaker emitted several seconds of static. Finally, Chancellor Lethe's own voice filled the room.

"I sincerely doubt that, Ingrid."

Ingrid flushed. "I've confirmed her identity. Her chip has been processed and approved."

Another silence, then, "Has she been checked by security?"

"N-no," Ingrid stuttered. "Her credentials did not flag a security check."

Lethe sighed heavily into the intercom. The room was filled with a sound like an alley in a windstorm. As Ingrid cringed, I withdrew the pistol from the escape kit I had carried with me throughout the tunnels of Utslette as if it were a Chanel handbag and not a burlap haversack.

"Check her yourself, then, Ingrid."

Before Ingrid could fully turn her head to me, the pistol tip was pressed into her temple. Up close, I realized the whites of her eyes were blue tinged. Her breath stank of the sweet smell of antifreeze. She was exhausted, just as my mother had been, from overexposure to the kryokammer. Silently, I lifted one finger to my lips and pushed the escape kit toward her with the toe of my stiletto-ed foot. Slowly, I lifted the hem of my gown and placed the gun inside the waist of my silk pantyhose. The metal was cold against the bottommost vertebra of my spine and I felt a thrill of gooseflesh erupt on my arms.

The pupils of Ingrid's eyes were huge, dilated by terror, and in their black aperture I could see my own reflection, identical to that of Grethe in the dream about the hanging beauty queens. I did what I had always wanted to do in the dream: I leaned forward and wrapped my arms around the person in front of me. My lips close to Ingrid's ear, I whispered, "What's your full name?"

"Ingrid Blackstone Mason," she said in a quivering voice.

I pulled back and placed two fingertips to her sternum and began to slowly tap the sheath of bone above her heart. "Ingrid Blackstone Mason, your feet are on the ground. Your heart is in the air."

She stared, now more confused than terrified, so in the same impressive tone Grethe had used to clear me, I added, "Repeat it. My name is Ingrid Blackstone Mason. My heart is in the air. My feet are on the ground."

Ingrid, hesitant at first, repeated the words after me until her voice grew steady and her pupils slowly returned to normal.

"You are clear.

"You are clear.

"You are clear."

As she echoed me, I listened to the girlish lilt of her speech mature and I watched myself grow smaller in the tunnel to her brain. When Ingrid's voice had finally reached the alto more appropriate to her age and I was returned to my original size in the blacks of her eyes, I said firmly, "You are no longer MONARCH."

She blinked and nodded.

"Push the button to the intercom and tell the Director you've checked me. Tell him I'm clean."

She did. As she lifted her finger off the intercom to hear Chancellor Lethe's reply, I pushed the escape kit into her hands. "Now run."

Ingrid didn't hesitate.

Neither had I, I realized, when Christine first handed me the bag.

I could hear her heels click, then pause as she stopped to remove them. The last noise I heard before the door to the Chancellor's office swung open was the sound of her nylons swishing across the tiled floor.

✦

It probably won't surprise you to hear that the Chancellor didn't look great. He had stripped down to his shirtsleeves, as Grethe would say, meaning that he had taken off his jacket and bowtie and his forearms were exposed, pale and un-sunned as milk in the udder. The pits of his white dress shirt were yellowed with sweat and his top button had popped off from being tugged once too often. His beard had begun to grow in unevenly. He dyed his hair black, I noticed for the first time, and now its roots were exposed and graying. I had never thought the Chancellor was young, but it wasn't until right then that I realized he was old. Bottles of prescription medications and viscous pink liquid littered his desk. There was a paper plate with a grease stain on it in his trashcan.

The office smelled rank. A top note of old pizza—oregano and mold and foul oil—and under that, something worse. Something I had never smelled before. It made me think of a cat litter box in the basement of the alcoholic woman in my suburb. But the smell was heavier than that, colder. Less acidic and more earthly, like shit and rotten fish mixed together. Innately, I knew the odor was cadaverine; there was a dead body somewhere in the office with us.

On his desk were piles and piles of paper. The right side of his palm was stained with ink, and I could see that he had been signing his own signature over hundreds of forms.

It was unsettling, the smell of death and ink.

I began to reach behind me for the pistol when, in a bored tone, the Chancellor said, "I suppose you're here to find your original face. The one you had before your parents were born."

Nearly word for word, he echoed Dr. Clink's letter.

He picked up a remote control and clicked a button to dim the lights. Absurdly, a screen fell from the ceiling and he walked to a transparency projector. I flashed back to the college classroom at the Midwestern University, to the soft-spoken Religious Studies professor who had projected the image of the tiny figure sitting within the center of four progressively larger outlines of his own body. Not outlines—sheaths. And, also, not a body—the soul.

What Chancellor Lethe had to show me was the inverse.

His projector displayed not my eternal self, but a photo of a blonde girl sitting on the lap of a handsome man wearing a white thawb covered by a beautiful jacket in a rare shade of sorrel. I recognized him from the news as a dignitary in a country we were at war with. The girl's face was obscured by the curtain of her hair.

Another image. First I just saw the girl's back, nude, an unbroken canvas of pale skin from the nape of her neck to the top of her thighs. Tanline-less. Her ass was mostly covered by the hands of the dignitary, whose face was square to the camera.

Next was just a close-up photo of bloody hands, the oval fingernails a flamingo pink.

Finally, a grainier image of the blonde girl standing over the slumped body of the dignitary. Her eyes were too bright, her hands now clean and her dress replaced, but backward, so the zipper teeth were visibly straining against her chest. She was smiling, one finger raised to her lips. *Shh*, she was saying to what I knew to be a hidden camera.

She was, of course, me.

"Stop," I said as he reached for another slide. "Stop it. I don't want to know this. *I'm not supposed to know this.*"

Before he could project another image, I held my cupped hands over my eyes, a gesture equivalent to that made by a child watching a scary film.

"Isn't that why you're here?" he asked. "To find out what you are?"

I shook my head behind my hands.

I couldn't determine the exact point when I stopped caring what I had done while I was sleepwalking, where the bruises and the filthy taste in my mouth originated.

(For a hovering moment, I slung myself out of my body and saw the earth from far away. A sort of metaphysical handspring. Even from a great distance, I could see a glowing point back in the Midwest, a bright star in a clotted constellation, and I knew it was the photo studio of University Photography. As if part of my energy were still hovering above the photography lab, suspended in the moment I saw Kayla Gavin's dead body, I watched Kevin walk through the red light of the darkroom and observe the photographs I kept hidden from him. They all still hung from the clothespins I had been drying them on when I fled. I watched his face as he looked at the images I had taken of myself, made doubly real by overexposure. In the most recent pictures—astonishingly, taken only a couple weeks ago—I had overlaid film so that in one photo, an image of myself sat beside another image of myself, an extra arm extending like a wing from between my shoulder blades to caress my own cheek. I had made myself a twin, a creature to keep me company.

Apropos of nothing, Kevin had once read me these words from a book by a dead man:

IN FOLK SYMBOLISM, DISTANCE IN SPACE CAN TAKE THE PLACE OF DISTANCE IN TIME; THAT IS WHY A SHOOTING STAR, WHICH PLUNGES INTO THE INFINITE DISTANCE OF SPACE, HAS BECOME THE SYMBOL OF A FULFILLED WISH.

I knew he would not need to think very long about what I had been trying to accomplish with those pictures. From behind my hands in a mountain in Norway, I traversed space and time once again to watch Kevin open the door to the studio. When he saw my photos, I would have been crossing the Mississippi—putting space between my old life and me. Now, it would be that same moment that would bring me back, that would allow me to envision Kevin as he picked up the phone and called Christine. That would allow me to come back to my body.)

"No, I already know who I am," I said evenly. "I invented myself."

The Chancellor laughed and clicked off the projector. The room brightened with halogen light, de-luminating the planes of his face so that his flesh looked like uncooked pie dough. He sat back down behind his desk and gestured for me to sit as well. He picked up his pen and set to work again, rotely signing his name on dotted line after dotted line.

"Well, then, why *are* you here, Jessica? As you can see, I'm quite occupied at the moment."

Much later, I knew I hesitated to kill him because I thought I would feel some sort of relief if I heard his confession first, if he looked me in the eye and told me he had had the child killed and Veronica disappeared. Naïve as I was, I had, at some point, developed the Romantic's sense of justice. Christine's canonized celebrities planted the seed, perhaps. Her candle of Lorena Bobbitt, burning in tribute to vengeance itself.

I just wanted an apology, for all of us.

Even as he flipped pages, refilled his stapler, and otherwise ignored me, I believed he could produce the words that could make me feel better. This is how it is, though, when your language is invented by someone else. That's why etymology matters so much. Those who don't invent words must especially know their worth.

"Kayla Gavin," I said finally.

He looked up briefly and shook his head, frowned a bit and shrugged. "I don't know who that is."

"She was MONARCH."

"No. I know every MONARCH. I remember each and every one of you, even the frozen." He gestured at his papers. "You're all right here."

I saw that each sheet he signed had a small photo of a beautiful girl in the upper right-hand corner, a fingerprint, and a list.

"She was in the photos I developed." I heard an over-oxygenated tinge of uncertainty beginning to strangle my voice, but I continued. "The crime scene photos. Of the child murdered in the trailer park. Grethe told me to develop the photos."

"Did she? Well, that explains that mystery, I suppose."

He was now inserting the forms into manila envelopes.

"I'm sorry," I heard myself say in a petulant voice. It was the voice, in my old life, that I used when the pretzel stand was out of queso or Grethe wouldn't let me drive her car. It was shameful to hear it now, as if my only recourse were brattiness. "But I don't know what mystery you're talking about."

"Calm down."

Perhaps I would have shot him then if I hadn't been so disoriented.

"I know you killed that girl!" I screeched, "Admit it!"

Chancellor Lethe held his hands up as if the sound of an irritated girl's voice gave him a wretched migraine. "Admit what? I have no idea who that child was. I've never even heard her name before. Do you think I'm the force behind every little girl who goes missing or murdered? Behind every rape, molestation, and petty bit of pedophilia on earth? Truly, Jessica, why would I care about some American trailer trash? Do you think I spend my time plotting trivial little evil deeds for my own enjoyment?"

I opened my mouth to speak and closed it again.

"No, you don't have any idea what you think. That child was killed by some rube, some ordinary monster, some mundane pervert with atypical chemicals floating in what only a very charitable being would refer to as a brain."

"Then why . . ." I blinked stupidly, "Why did you care if the pictures were preserved or not?"

"I'm beginning to find you disappointing, Jessica." He looked me up and down with distaste. "I didn't give a goddamn about those pictures."

"Then why did you have my mother killed?"

"I didn't," he said flatly. "After your mother cleared you, she planned to take you and flee. She called that degenerate babysitter of yours to help her. Your father came upon them as she was packing a bag and she attacked him. It's unfortunate, but the programming can fracture sometimes. Once every five years or so, a MONARCH with too much outside influence will turn on her Master and kill him. Statistically, it's very difficult to completely quarantine the, shall we say, psychic immune system. Your father should have never let a contaminant into his home, that girl. What was her name?"

"Christine."

"Yes, something like that." He pushed the button for his intercom. "At any rate, the footage shows that your mother and father struggled while he attempted to disarm her—she had quite a long knife, held very professionally, of course—and she lost her footing. Went straight over the railing. It's a profound loss. Your mother was a brilliant asset. We're hoping to make another one just like her, now that you've proven inadequate.

"Of course, that all depends on reinstating our infrastructure." He buzzed his intercom again and this time barked "Ingrid!" into the speaker. "Currently, I can't even get a cup of tea."

"What do you mean you're going to make another one?"

He raised his eyebrows. "Well, you're all copies of copies at this point. Look at you, a walking cliché."

Then, he leaned backward and pulled open the door of one of the dozens of filing cabinets behind his desk. A small cloud of air came out, dank as a freezer opened in August. "We keep the originals, of course. You wouldn't believe the trouble your father's assistant—Jeffrey?—had retrieving your mother's body." The reek of decay that had been hanging over the room thickened and I felt myself gag before I comprehended what was within the refrigerated drawer.

A silver object, round and mystic as a crystal ball, smudged by one red wax thumbprint. Grethe's frozen head, mid-thaw.

Beneath my mother's makeup, my face numbed. I had been trained to go still when terrified; I bent my head and found my reflection in the glass surface of the Chancellor's desk. I kept breathing.

"Your mother was an original." The Chancellor continued, "You, you're just a copy. Can you tell? I've always wondered if the reprints feel it somehow. If they have the sense that they're merely the . . . stain of another's energy." He pushed his intercom button once again, and, for a moment, he unhinged completely and screamed, "Ingrid, immediately!"

"No," I said softly. "I can't feel it."

"Interesting. It is quite unusual for a copy to develop original thoughts—even unconsciously—but you seem to have done it. That stunt you pulled at Mayflower, for one, that was really extraordinary. I wanted to have you frozen right then, but your mother swore she would take you in hand and your father threatened to withhold significant research. Really, it took me aback to see them care so much for you, a doll."

I thought of Dr. Clink's frenzy to complete his issue of *Boredom Studies* in time for the new millennium, of the somnambulistic slur of Grethe's voice when I returned home from Mayflower last November. It had, of course, never occurred to me any of it had anything to do with me.

"The stunt I pulled at Mayflower? The seizure?"

"I suppose there may have been some sort of electromagnetic storm in your brain, but I wouldn't classify that as a seizure."

"What was it?"

He stared at me for a moment. "Again, I don't know. Your father told me he would find out. He promised to run a battery of tests, but I suppose he never did, did he?"

"Tests for what?"

"Oh, mostly nonsense. Psychic capacity, mediumicity, a seventh sense. All we really needed to know was whether you had figured out how to reprogram yourself, if you had some evolutionary instinct, some reaction to inherited, oh, let's call it *trauma*."

"But . . . all I said was they 'didn't jump.' I was just talking about that stupid urban legend, about these girls who committed suicide at my dorm in the '70s."

"Hmm. Is that your understanding? I thought some rumors would have reached you, at the very least. Didn't you have any friends at Mayflower at all?"

Obviously, Jian had not reported back to the Institute that I spent most of my time sleeping in the dorm's basement, not attending slumber parties.

"I don't know anything. I saw the Ouija board and when I woke up everyone was afraid of me."

"I suppose you never realized what Mayflower is."

"No."

"You're really terrifically self-centered, Jessica. Mayflower is an incubator for MONARCH. Didn't you ever notice it was substantially— nicer—than the other dorms? Or wonder why it was so far from campus? Or why your flat mates were all so well turned out?"

I had not.

"Those three girls who jumped from the roof . . ."

"Brigit Swallowtail Adams, Mary Waxwing Axel, and Imogen Hartsgrove Brand," he recited.

"Veronica Dearbháil Marshall," I added flatly.

"True desire," he replied absently.

"So you did know."

"Gaelic? Of course."

"No." I rolled my eyes and was appalled that my response was so mundane, so teenage. "You knew I would fall in love with her. You knew she would be my . . ." I was weirdly embarrassed to say it all of a sudden, such an arcane phrase, "true desire."

"Again, you baffle me, Jessica. Dearbháil is a Gaelic name. It *means* 'true desire,'" he frowned. "We should have drilled our etymologies more, I suppose. It seems you still can't identify the source."

"You're the source, though, aren't you? Of everything that's ever happened to me, aside from Christine. You planted Crystal St. Marie and you made me believe I wasn't anything but a body and you planted Jian and you made me believe I had a friend and you planted Veronica and made me believe someone could love me. Then you made me sacrifice her."

His frown deepened and he walked to one of the burgundy oak filing cabinets that circled the office. From his vest pocket he pulled a small key attached to a thin gold chain and opened a drawer.

Muttering to himself, he flipped quickly through a leather-bound folder and began to shake his head.

Hope, I realized, hurt. Revenge wasn't so much an emotion as it was a dogma; self-imposed and straight at the edges. Killing the Chancellor in retribution for Grethe and for Kayla made me feel nothing. But the sudden hope I felt as I watched the Chancellor shake his head and it began to seem possible that Veronica had been real was visceral and overwhelming. It made me feel alive again, I guess.

"No," he said at last. "I have files here of every MONARCH that has ever been created." He riffled through the pages of a volume the size of a small town's phonebook. "Ninety-three originals and all their copies. There is no Dearbháil."

"But—" there was a weird feeling in my chest now, a twisting rose quartz blush. "Your secretary knew who I was talking about." His expression remained blank, so I added, "Veronica was my girlfriend."

Now the Chancellor's face melted into an impassive mask, lineless and emptied of emotion. I had seen him smug, satisfied, contemptuous, impressed, and bored. I always thought of him as patrician and professorial, but he was just one of those old-world liars. Probably from a bloodline that assisted in the poisoning of kings and the assassinations of dukes; an espiocrat with megalomaniacal aspirations. The type of man who wiped off his identity easily, but hadn't had to do so for a very long time. I had never before seen him surprised.

"You didn't know?" I asked.

He cleared his throat. "I wasn't told. I don't have time to track the exploits of every MONARCH on my roster." Agitated, he shook his dossier of MONARCH so the pages fluttered. "There are nearly a thousand of you currently deployed. Your trainer—who was she again?"

"Crystal St. Marie."

"She did not report that information."

"But why? Why would she tell me to get rid of Veronica?"

"I expect she thought she was protecting you." He was flipping through the thick leather-bound folder again, the fountain pen he kept in his front pocket poised over the pages. A bit closer up, I saw that gold letters deeply engraved into the leather spelled out my full name.

"Protect me from what?"

He glanced up at me, an eyebrow raised. His face had settled back into its usual expression: appraisal freaked through with malice. "The incinerator," he said, as if that needed no explanation. And I guess, really, it didn't. "You aren't designed to develop sexual or emotional attachments to others. You simply don't have the chemical components to achieve a limerent state."

"What if it wasn't limerence?"

"Then it was love." His odd accent held the vowel of the final word for a long time, flat as a needle dropping on a record. He was writing something in my file so quickly that his fountain pen burped ink. As he leaned forward to blot it on a roll of bibulous paper, I saw that he was writing a note under the heading PSYCHOSOCIAL BEHAVIORS.

"What are you writing?"

"I'm noting that your deviant sexual impulses likely made you vulnerable to the debased nanny's influence." He shook his head sadly. "I doubt it would have ever occurred to you to act on a sapphic impulse if she hadn't already corrupted your shame receptors. MONARCH simply don't have the tools to dismantle their own architecture. Your conditioning is too powerful."

He wasn't right, but he wasn't wrong, either. What I had done had been neither entirely social nor entirely biological, but it had required imagination to envision who I was. Christine, Veronica, the photos floating in a darkroom in the Midwest. They were links on a chain I used to tether myself to the invention of myself.

"But what about the other girls?" I asked suddenly. The rose quartz feeling was blooming. I felt like my heart was pumping sparkling wine through my veins: pink, effervescent, alcoholic as a crate of cava. "Brigit Swallowtail Adams, Mary Waxwing Axel, and Imogen Hartsgrove Brand. Were they like me? Is that why they jumped?"

"No, no." He paused and reconsidered, "Well, perhaps. But you were right, they didn't jump. They were using a Ouija board to try to reprogram themselves and, sadly, they made some surprising advances. Campus security was forced to cleanse the dorms. The question is, how did you know that they didn't jump, Jessica? The eradication of the aberrant models in the first generation of MONARCH is classified. So much so, in fact, that it exists only here," he pointed with one finger to his own head, "and, for safe-keeping, in the memory of my secretary. Which means, as far as archives are concerned, it never happened at all. But then you brought it up." He shuffled through his dossier until he arrived at a photo of me, thirteen years old and smiling. He considered my image for a moment. "To be honest, I had planned to send you to the incinerator with the other redundancies and defects. But perhaps you'd be better placed in the Kryokammatoria. With what's left of your mother. When the Institute is up and running again, we can thaw you and determine where your architecture has gone askew. You know, if we did find a remnant of those girls lingering behind and causing you undue—ah, *affects*—we could potentially erase it and relieve you of your deviant impulses."

He finally looked up. Our eyes met. I saw myself reflected, a girl wearing the costume of her mother. An idea of an idea.

"Yes," I said finally. "I would like that."

✦

Would you like a scene of terrific vengeance relayed to you?

Here's a list of words for you to create it with: viscera, nipple, hood, teacup, arsenic, static, slice, eyes, iris, fog, organ, hair, air, aura, eye, iris, exposure, over-exposure, eyelet, ice cube, tongue, taste, arsenic, bile, cream, tongue, nipple, viscera, ash, hood.

Great violence can never really be explained, can it?

I'm kidding. It can: the Chancellor opened the door to the Kryokammatoria and inside of it was a vault, a stainless steel catacomb of kryokammer atop kryokammer, women frozen and stacked like layers of an iceberg. No, more like frozen dinners in a grocery store locker. It was enormous and anonymous, mundane in its order. Each chamber alphabetized and labeled in a standard font.

Inherent to its order was the fingerprint of some secretary, somewhere, filing.

In the foot of every steel box, I saw my reflection. For each frozen MONARCH, there was me, alive, looking back. I put my hands to my chest and I didn't fracture. There was something about knowing that the world doesn't end in fire or ice. At the end, there is no chaos. At the end of the world, there is only order.

In the end, all I had to do was point the gun and close the door.

In my last image of him, the Chancellor stands in the center of his own structure, freezing.

It's a comfort to me, to know he is suspended in endless unapology.

It's a comfort to me, to know he is pinned to the mortal plane in which there is no end, no edge, no closure.

It's a comfort to me to know he will never get to die.

Our narrator is now ready to admit that this was no story at all.

Stories get told by people with one tongue. A monster cannot tell a story, an exile cannot tell a story, a creature who crafted a second body that floats outside their first body and keeps it safe cannot tell a story. Our narrator is too smart to speak in unison with herself, our narrator is now the polyphonous beam of light that shoots from the mouth of the survivor: the source never ends, the origin is impossible, the existence never knows its own opening or closure.

Our narrator is now ready to admit that this was no story at all, in the sense it never stops. No, the child beauty queen never forgets how to stand up straight.

✦

Of course, it was Christine who lifted the veil that revealed the next body.

She arrived at Terminal 5 of O'Hare International with a Ouija board in one hand and a box of strawberry Pop-Tarts in the other. Sugar, an offering to the spirits.

The board was a grocery sack, gutted, and spread open on the backseat of the babysitter's Nissan. It was an American exorcism;

self-reliant, electric, manifestdestinal as tape played backward, the backmasked message of history spoken in reverse. Intelligible only when rewound. No one thought of inviting a priest: they harnessed the entitlement of the oppressed. Christine and Jessica wrote the alphabet in black liquid eyeliner for lack of a pen and used the aluminum cap of a bottle of Boone's Farm Strawberry Hill as a planchette.

They held hands and asked to contact the spirit of Jessica Greenglass Clink.

The silver lid shivered once. The beauty queen placed her fingertips atop it and spelled her own name, as if there were any other.

YOU'RE IN

SIDE

YOUR

S   E
L

        F

YOU

S

E

E

Y

O

U

SHE SAW MORE AND SHE MADE MORE TO SHOW, AFTER THAT.

With the help of the babysitter and an account number in the little black diary that she had never forgotten, she could more than afford to move her mother's body back to the States, where it was buried beneath a headstone unadorned with dates. For the first few years of grief, she tried to assemble the pieces of her self that would constitute a body. She had an idea to construct herself part by part until she was a whole person and then to find a soul to crawl into. She had the sense that she was a snail born without a shell, a severed tongue, a fingerprint from no finger.

Sometimes she performed her acts of transmographication in art galleries, in underground spaces and darkrooms. She became very famous for an exhibition of bodies, levitating. Some critics said they were ghosts, others said they were angels. They unclenched from their skin and it drifted off like ash, or snow. They froze and thawed. Underneath the layers were more layers. Everyone agreed it was amazing how the faces never ended.

Her name became a name certain people knew; specific girls in particular art schools all over the world purloined postcards emblazoned with images of her work from the front desks of art galleries. They pinned them to the walls of their studio apartments or the mirrors of their dorms and stared at them religiously when they felt the world was too much.

The world, mostly, bit by bit, ceased to be too much for Jessica herself and became instead almost the right size. Eventually, she began to accept invitations issued by galleries in Tokyo and Paris, Berlin and Beijing. At a U-Bahn stop in Alexanderplatz, she exited the station in one of those breezes created entirely out of the weather system of the metro itself, and she felt a bone she had never felt before. At the edge of Montmartre, a street she believed would be a dead-end exploded into an artery of light, a beating heart of beams, and a muscle throbbed in her left thigh.

Déjà vécu, the Chancellor had once told her, was the sense of having already "lived through." Through *what*, exactly, he did not illuminate. Instead he made her write her name until it covered his entire chalkboard, and then he made her erase it and begin again. She got to stop when she no longer believed her name existed. An image of a bullfrog, verdant and osmoregulatory, was beamed onto the projector. It sat in a simmering Le Creuset. "Semantic satiation," he explained, "is a highly effective means of moral re-conditioning."

But what was happening to her had nothing to do with ultra-exposure.

Nor was it, as Christine would have suggested, past lives gurgling through the metaphysical throat of history.

It was worse than either of her mentors' theories: it was actual memory, the crooked gift of identity delivered in an anonymous package. City by city, she began to metabolize her life and eventually she felt she could process what had passed. The sugars of existence entered her bloodstream, and eventually it occurred to her that now that she was beginning to know the coordinates of her soul, she might use it to find the woman who had given her a body. She had forced herself to push Veronica from her mind in almost the same moment the Chancellor told her that she had not been MONARCH. Any survivor knows you don't scream until you're in some quiet ER or locked car. In the same way that she had been trained not to be overwhelmed by terror, she had learned not to be overwhelmed by joy. Jessica stopped her heart mid-pump and just tried to glow, to hold the bloom of rose in her heart. She knew better than to look back, but as she grew older she couldn't help but remember.

Not every memory that came back was miserable.

Beneath the boom of the Westminster Abbey bell, she felt the soft pads of her knees come into existence and she remembered a cool hand resting there, five strawberry lacquered nails swirling figure eights on her skin until the flesh rose and goosed, each hair an antenna. Their thighs pressed together beneath the kitchen table, their heads bowed over some Sunday school homework.

"This part," Veronica had said, pointing to a passage underlined in bed the night before, the jagged ink betraying a book pressed to the reader's thighs, written in right before sleep. "This part is so crazy."

The book was *The Confessions of St. Augustine* and, as Veronica explained, it was written directly to God. The passage she had underlined was about Augustine going to some sort of pool or spa or something with his father.

"Wait—what does *inquieta adulescentia* mean?" Jessica had asked.

"A hard-on," Veronica whispered.

Jessica turned the page to a passage which was both underlined and highlighted, "In his glee he told my mother—it was the sort of tipsy glee in which this sorry world had forgotten you, its creator, and fallen in love instead with something you've created."

Next to this passage, Veronica had written, in block letters, THE INVENTION OF SEX.

"What's it mean?"

"I think it means you can invent yourself."

Really, this scene came back as more of an idea than a memory. She had never really known what Veronica had meant that day, nor had she truly connected the revelation with the events that occurred after: the same strawberry-tipped fingers slipped hesitantly beneath, and below, the inner edge of her black cotton Hanes Her Ways. How Veronica's fingers had curved and beckoned into her dark center as if they knew all she needed was an invitation out. As if they knew, with certainty, that the corridor to her core would slicken and shudder if only acknowledged.

Oh, the teen queen had thought, *this is where I am.*

The idea was that if everything about her had been someone else's idea, then that feeling with Veronica could only be her own. It was the one thing no one had ever told her to want; an impulse both irresistible and undeniable.

In retrospect, the clearest thing about her life was that the Institute had made her put an end to it that night she exposed Veronica. She had been too close to finding herself.

By the time she finally boarded the flight to Medford, Oregon, she was thirty years old. It had not been hard to keep track of Veronica over the last decade. She was one of those compulsive chroniclers, an archive addict who posted the minutiae of her life to public social networks. It took none of the old spycraft at all to discover that Veronica and her father had reconciled and, by way of apology, he had paid her tuition to a college in Portland that looked like it was from a storybook for children. Jessica was not surprised at all that after that, she became one of those actresses with a voice like a cello who performs Shakespeare or Shaw or Ibsen in some idyllic park. Not many days had gone by that Jessica had not thought of young Veronica standing on a stage, engulfed in tulle, practicing her iambic pentameter.

From her seat in the very back row of the darkened theater, Jessica watched the girl she had known walk the stage as a woman. She was full and present, thirty-two years old and abundant with a self-possession that was a sort of antidote to haunting.

After the show ended, Jessica stood and clapped and she thought, perhaps, Veronica stared right at her. She felt, for an instant, seen.

It was the jolt of this moment, the sense that all the stars in the constellation of her body had lit and there were still vast empty patches—missing bones—that told her to turn and go. Even with the institute that had invented her abolished, her father missing, her mother dead, and her creator rendered powerless, she could not yet imagine a place for herself on Veronica's stage.

Some criminals mark the bodies of their victims with tattoos, burns, elaborate scars. Jessica knew this was unnecessary. Visible or invisible, the imprint of the awful doesn't slide off like lipstick under baby oil. Really, that's the most awful thing about it: the worst is always just to come.

She turned one time to watch Veronica take a bow. She memorized the swoop of her spine, the tail of her hair as it touched the floorboards, and knew it would be enough. This memory, now, was hers. And hers alone.

She walked through the world, aged, lost touch with her first life, forgot nothing. Sometimes, she visited the grave of her mother and knew, under the earth, she was buried in the silk sewn through with seed pearls and edged in gold filigree. An ancient beauty queen buried in the middle of America, a silk scarf from an old world around her neck.

ACKNOWLEDGMENTS

Thank you to everyone at Soft Skull Press who helped bring this book into the world. Kiele Raymond, thank you for hearing Jessica's voice and for getting it. Sarah Lyn Rogers, thank you for bringing your enormously generous vision to *MONARCH*. Your incredible understanding of this novel was near clairvoyant, which is to say you saw it more than I did at times—I'm pretty sure Christine would say we knew each other in our past lives.

Thank you to my teachers Rebecca Rovit (an *actual* memory studies expert); Joseph Harrington; and University of Kansas' Alice F. Holmes Summer Institute professors Cary Wolfe (whose "scandal of the cephalopod" captured my imagination) and Cathy Caruth (whose scholarship changed the way I think). And especially thank you to the poet (and my high school English teacher) Mary Szybist—your encouragement twenty years ago changed the course of my life.

Thank you to the University of Kansas Chancellor's Doctoral Fellowship, the Foundation for Contemporary Arts, the Authors League, and Artist Relief for support that allowed me to complete this novel. Thank you to the librarians at KU's Watson Library, where I wrote much of this book in a study carrel overlooking the prairie.

Thank you to my Iowa friends Meredith Blankinship, Rachel Milligan, and Sean Zhuraw. And especially thank you to Patrick Reed, my oldest friend—you've reminded me what it means to be an artist for a couple decades now.

Thank you to Deborah and Randy Wuehle, Patricia Wuehle Rollins and David Rollins, and the rest of my family.

Lastly and above all: to Andrew Morgan, who supported this book throughout every phase of its long journey to here. At the most crucial stage of the process, you reminded me who I am and what I came here to do. Thank you, forever.

CANDICE WUEHLE is the author
of the poetry collections *Fidelitoria: Fixed or
Fluxed, BOUND,* and *Death Industrial Complex,* short-listed for the Believer Book Award.
A graduate of the Iowa Writers' Workshop,
she holds a PhD in literary studies and creative
writing from the University of Kansas.